DEDICATION

To the descendants of Squire David Graham

AMBITION

Legends of Graham Mansion
Book Two

Rosa Lee Jude

Mary Lin Brewer

The Keys to Our Success

Writing a novel is like bringing a child into the world. It begins with passion and the seed of an idea. There are months of planning, dreaming dreams, and nurturing. As it starts to develop and later when it takes form, there are long hours of making sure every aspect comes out just right. During the final weeks, it keeps you up at night, and the actual birth is rather painful. But how you love it, once it is here, it is your pride and joy.

There are many people who have played key roles in assisting to make this, our second book, possible. While this list is not all-encompassing, we hope it will show our heartfelt gratitude to those who have been extra special in the process.

To Our Readers – there is no question that there is a Book Two, because you loved Book One. We have been overwhelmmed by your many messages, excitement, and encouragement. It warms our heart that you love our characters as much as we do and that you want to learn more about them. We will try our best not to disappoint you, but we may take your heart on some twists and turns as Grae makes her way through this and the next three journeys.

To Our Editor, Donna Stroupe – Once again, you have saved us from ourselves. You taught Rosa Lee the true meaning of commas and made Mary Lin check and recheck her historical facts. Your enthusiasm about this book makes us happy, and we consider you a friend and a very valuable part of our team.

To Our Ex-Officio Editors – Pam Newberry and Marcella Taylor – There's nothing like a set of loving, but careful, eyes on a story. Each of you possess knowledge and wisdom in different ways and read these words from different perspectives. Your support throughout the process and beyond is humbling.

To Our Graphic Designer, Julie Newberry – Patience is a virtue, my dear, and you are developing that by working with us. Thank you for hanging in there and learning new things. It has provided us with a look and brand for our special product.

To Our Vendors – Thank you to our local and regional brick and mortar stores! We are grateful for your showcasing our series and nurturing it as if it were your own baby—a lost art, and we thank you.

And finally, and most importantly,

To Our Significant Others & Families – It's wonderful to have two patient and understanding men behind us, who have humored us with our dream. We apologize for the late nights, limited homecooking, and for the boxes that are everywhere. You are a part of our journey. You are a part of our success.

Our utmost thanks to all of the above and to all the others who have inspired and empowered us. And, most of all, our gratitude goes to all those who will read these pages and travel with us to another time.

The Story Behind The Story

Planned to be a five-volume collection, the *Legends of Graham Mansion* series is set in the beautiful Blue Ridge Mountains of Southwest Virginia on the historic Major Graham Mansion property and surrounding area. Rosa Lee Jude, writer, and Mary Lin Brewer, researcher and historian, teamed up to create Mary Lin's dream of a Graham Mansion book series that would take historical information about the people and events of the Graham Mansion's two hundred plus year history and weave a story to help solve some of the property's most interesting mysteries.

Redemption was the first installment and focused on the 1786 murder of Joseph Joel Baker. Central heroine, Grae White, travelled back in time to meet the property's first family and discover the unwritten story behind Baker's grizzly murder.

In this second book, *Ambition*, Grae travels back to 1830 and meets David Graham. Later known as Squire David, he is the original builder of the Graham Mansion and an ambitiously driven man. In this story, Grae will discover the secret behind the tragedy that changed this man forever.

This is a work of historical fiction. History has been used

in the creation of this story, but the majority of what will be found within these pages is pure fiction, a speculative look at what might have occurred. The authors have endeavored to be true to the time period and respectful to those real persons who are fictionally portrayed. The story also has the twist of time travel and a glimmer of paranormal. The latter aspects are due, in part, to some of the accounts that the many ghost hunters, clairvoyants, and paranormal experts have relayed to Mary Lin in recent years.

Major Graham Mansion is a very real place. It is located in Wythe County, just a few miles from the historic Great Wagon Road and the New River, as well as, modern-day interstates I-77 and I-81. The property has been owned, renovated, and maintained for over twenty years by Virginia native, Josiah Cephas Weaver. The Mansion is often open seasonally for a variety of special events, haunted history tours, paranormal investigations, and the wildly popular fall event, Haunted Graham Mansion™.

PRESENT DAY

ONE

Snap, snap, snap, Grae broke the long half-runner green beans in a rhythmic motion as she watched her mother, Kat, washing Mason jars at the old sink in the Mansion's kitchen. The beans made a pinging sound as they hit the worn aluminum dish pan on the stool in front of her. It was a hot humid mid-July day in Southwest Virginia, so hot that the air seemed to be standing still. Grae longed to see the white lace curtains at the window just move even slightly, but instead they stood in still attention like guards in front of a palace.

"You know, Mom, we are going to have to talk about it eventually."

Kat's large, wide-set ocean blue eyes cut toward the strangely, grown up voice behind her as she set the last scalding hot jar on the sink's sideboard. It seemed as if she and Grae had been canning beans for weeks. Her father's garden had produced bountiful proportions that summer. Canning them was a two-fold project for Grae and Kat. Half of the over two hundred jars would be kept in their cellar for the family to eat during the upcoming winter, and the rest would be sold at local farmer's markets and the mountaintop country store where Grae had recently started working part-time. Travelers from the North liked the idea of buying homegrown, home-preserved produce. It would help pay for Grae's college textbooks, her car payments, and other expenses.

"Yes, I know, it's inevitable." Kat ran a dishcloth over her red hands; they looked as if they had been in hot water for hours, which they had. "I just keep thinking that if we don't talk about it, maybe it didn't happen. Mothers are allowed to minimize pain by avoiding the discussion of it. It's in the Parent Handbook."

Grae shook her head, and set the beans on the table. She didn't blame her mother for wanting to pretend it hadn't happened. Facing the fact that Grae had spent a month in 1786 the previous spring was hard to swallow, even for Grae herself. Still, two to three months later, Grae would wake up to the sound of that ax in her dreams. The ax had come down on the skull of Joseph Baker; it wasn't something anyone could soon forget.

"Yes, Mom, I am sure that avoiding painful discussions is in the Parent Handbook, but the particular subject of time travel is not."

Kat's blue eyes shined with laughter at her daughter's sarcasm.

Just a few weeks shy of her eighteenth birthday, Graham Belle "Grae" White discovered that she possessed the ability to travel through time. Grae had travelled over two hundred years in reverse through a portal in the hall closet of Graham Mansion, the massive house that she, her brother, Perry, and her mother, Kat, lived in with Grae's grandfather, Mack. She had learned firsthand about the labors of the eighteenth century and the inequities among the people who lived in this New World of America during its earliest years. She had made friends and a few enemies, but her innocent life as an indentured servant somehow lead her into the middle of a scheme for freedom and forced her to become a pawn in a game of jealousy and revenge. In the end, two men had died and two others had paid with their lives for the murder of Joseph Baker.

Just then an image of red flashed before Grae's eyes, and she rubbed them to try and make it vanish. She thought the flashes would diminish, but, like a nagging headache, they reappeared with a vengeance. She'd noticed that the color was getting darker and sometimes now almost had a hue of….

"Graham! Are you there?"

Grae's thoughts were interrupted as her mother tried to recapture her attention. She must have been lost in thought for several minutes as her mother was now sitting at the kitchen table with a glass of lemonade tea in front of her. It was her mother's favorite, half iced tea, half lemonade. A matching glass sat in front of Grae where she had been breaking beans.

"These 'lost in thought' moments are happening more frequently," Kat announced. "It's worrying your brother. He came to me the other day and said he talked to you for almost five minutes before you acknowledged him." Kat paused, twirling the straw in her glass. "We don't want him to start asking questions."

"And why would that be? Don't you think he should be warned about what might happen to him? I mean, a little warning would have been great."

"No. No, it's not necessary, it will not happen to him. It's only the women in our family who have this ability."

"So, there's no way that Perry could find himself shackled

in a prison cell in 1786?"

"No, not unless...."

"Unless what?"

Kat became silent as Grandpa Mack stomped into the room. "I hate to tell you all this, but I think there is at least another two bushels of beans on the vines even after I picked this bushel." With a thump, he placed a weathered wooden basket in the middle of the floor; it was heaping with long green beans, a deep dark color almost like what Grae saw when....

"Grae Belle! Answer me, child." Grandpa Mack passed his calloused hand in front of Grae's face, bringing her back from where her mind had taken her.

"I'm sorry, Grandpa, I was a million miles away, I guess." Grae tried to laugh it off, but a quick glance at her mother showed a concern that left many unanswered questions in Grae's mind.

"I don't even like green beans!" Perry shouted as he walked into the kitchen late that evening. After turning sixteen in early June, Gav had helped Perry get a job at the grocery store across from the high school. Gav being Grae's boyfriend had its benefits. Perry had also made friends with several of Gav's teammates, and, if he kept practicing, he might find himself on the varsity basketball team in the winter. Perry had the height, if he could just get rid of the clumsy.

"We promise that you don't have to eat all of them yourself, dear," Kat smiled at her son. "Some of these jars will help finance Grae's car payments."

"People will actually buy them up at Big Walker?" Perry shook his head as he read the label on one of the jars he had taken out of a box on the floor. "Graham's Green Beans, sounds really formal, using her full name."

"The Graham really stands for the land here, the Graham family," Kat replied. "It is Graham ground that these green beans are grown in."

"Don't try to say that three times real fast, Mom," Grae laughed. When Grae began working at the country store at the top of Big Walker Mountain, she quickly learned that the store carried a variety of jams, jellies and honeys that were produced by vendors throughout the state. As the summer garden bounty began to emerge, Grae asked her mother what she thought about them canning as much as they could and offering it at the local farmer's markets and the country store. Kat loved the idea, and began doing all of the research necessary for their home kitchen to pass the health standards needed to sell the canned goods.

After the beans were done, they planned to can peaches, make spaghetti sauce, and some jams and jellies. There was also an herb garden, a personal favorite of Kat's. Grae might learn its healing powers or maybe make some sweet smelling sachets. It would be a lot of work, but they would have that time together, and the profit would help with college expenses and extra things that Perry might need also. They were a working family now; their privileged life in Charlotte was behind them.

TWO

Despite everything that she had experienced in 1786, Grae's desire to learn more about the history of the Mansion and what had occurred on the property had only increased. She found herself poring over her grandmother's research. And, then, one day, an opportunity came that gave her a reason to keep researching.

"Grae," Kat said, one evening after work. "Missus Crockett called me today. She said the historical society wondered if we might be interested in developing an early fall tour of the Mansion. They would like to offer the tour a couple of Sunday afternoons in September. They've already asked J.C., and he told them it was fine with him as long as I would organize it. It will take a lot of research, and I don't want to ruin your summer, but would you…"

"Yes!" Grae turned from the stove where she was preparing a spaghetti dinner.

"Wow! That was a fast answer. I didn't even get the question out."

"I know, but I am really interested in this place. It was something that Granny Belle wanted done, and, well, my trip has kind of changed my feeling about history."

"Now, Grae, please do not misunderstand me. I don't want to use this as an excuse to try to travel again. Please promise me that you will not..."

"Mom, I don't think I can make such a promise. You know as well as I do that it really is beyond my control."

"I know, I know, but..."

"What timeframe do they want the tour to cover?" Grae interrupted, needing to get her mother off of the time travel topic.

"They would like the tour to cover when the Mansion was first being built, the early Squire David Graham era."

"Do we have very much information about that time period?"

"I recall that your grandmother had researched Squire David quite a bit. If I remember correctly, he was quite a driven man and accounts concerning him in later life do not depict a very nice person." Kat paused as she pulled the garlic bread out of the oven. "She also said he was the strongest ghost presence in this house."

"What?!" Grae dropped the spoon she was using to stir the spaghetti sauce. A trail of red could be seen on the floor causing Grae to flashback. For a moment, she was in Joseph Baker's barn and could smell the powder from the gunshot.

"Grae! Honey, are you okay?' Kat was shaking her daughter. Grae had started to fight back right before her eyes cleared.

"I'm okay."

"What just happened to you? You left me, you weren't here at all." Kat's worried look scared Grae. She herself didn't understand what was happening. It was more than a flashback; it was like she was transported there again.

"It's okay. My mind just wanders." Grae began to clean the sauce up off the floor. "What are you talking about?" Grae's hands were trembling. A strange feeling came over her. "What do you mean that Squire David is the strongest ghost presence? How many do we have here? I thought Clara was the only one."

Kat sat down at the table. "Oh, Grae, it's hard to say. This house is almost two hundred years old. There have been a lot of people who have passed through here. There have been many tragedies in this house." Kat looked at her daughter. "Grandpa says that Squire has a hold on this house because he built it. For a very long time, this was his kingdom and he was king. As long as you don't ruffle his dominion, he stays peaceful. But if you disrupt something, he makes his presence known."

"Disrupt something? Sounds like a good excuse not to clean." Grae laughed as she set the table, but an eerie feeling crossed over her.

"Dad says that when J.C. first purchased the Mansion, he was still touring with his band. One night, he and some of his buddies were having a jam session in the front parlor. One of the guys was playing the piano, and the lid that covers the keys kept coming down on his fingers. It even broke one. Things also kept falling off the mantel that night. The guys were recording the session, and later on, in the background, they could hear someone shouting 'I DON'T LIKE THAT SONG! GET OUT!'"

"And they thought it was Squire David who caused this?"

"It wasn't the first time something had happened like that."

"Why are you telling me this?"

"Well, I just want you to be prepared. If we create a tour about Squire David and those early years when the Mansion was being built, we may disrupt some things. We may show or tell things that Squire doesn't want told, and he may make that known to us."

"Mom, somehow I don't think it can be any worse than what I saw in 1786."

"That may be true, but from what you have told me, you saw events as they were taking place, which is quite different from the wrath of a two-hundred-year-old tyrant who wants you out of his house." Kat paused. "We will need to be careful not to get caught up in his time. We don't need to be making any unnecessary trips there."

Her mother's stern look took Grae's thoughts to the chain around her neck that held the key and the small knife. It amazed her that her mother seemingly still hadn't noticed them.

"I still want to hear about your journey. You've never told me what the item was that helped you with your passage and return." Kat stopped talking as Perry came flying into the kitchen.

"Hello, Ladies! I am one hungry farm hand. What's for dinner?"

Grae started laughing. She had been saved by the Scarecrow from a question she didn't want to answer. Perry looked as if he had fought a bale of straw and lost. There was straw in his hair, on his shirt, coming out of the pockets of his jeans, and even attached to the mud on his shoes. Her mother's radar had honed in on the latter.

"What have I told you about taking your shoes off at the door? I bet there is mud and straw, and who knows what else, all through the hallway."

"Sorry, sorry, I blame the hunger." Perry's big grin made Kat smile as she shook her head.

"Get yourself a snack and go take a shower. It looks like Grae has about got dinner ready." Kat watched as Perry took the remainder of a gallon of milk and a handful of cookies and turned to leave the room.

"He's starting to consume more food than me, you and Grandpa, all three combined," Grae said shaking her head as she went back to chopping up a salad.

"We'll just have to can more beans," Kat said and they broke into laughter.

Life on the Mansion property had grown on Grae. When her schedule allowed, she enjoyed long walks and explorations of the many acres of land. She'd often take a book and her iPod and sit in a shady spot for hours. Her experience back in time had changed her, but she had tried to keep it in perspective.

The land seemed to have layers of lives. There were old buildings made of weathered wood and rusting metal. There were little cabins built for secluded retreats and time with nature. Miles of trees that stood tall and study, blankets of wildflowers that delighted bees and butterflies. Old vines and new crops, ancient dirt paths and new slabs of concrete; it was a place of extremes, but they all seemed to fit together somehow. Grae began a journal of these times of seclusion that she allowed herself. She not only included her thoughts and feelings about her life, but also what she was seeing, hearing, and smelling around her.

Her days and weeks were full of many activities, but Grae really missed having close friends. Gav stayed busy; Carrie had been away a lot. When she had first moved to Virginia, she had wanted to be invisible, now she wished that she had made more effort to get to know a few other girls in her class. It would be nice to have a buddy in the same century who she could confide in, go shopping with, or just hang out. She hoped that college would offer her the opportunity to make some friends.

Between her part-time job and canning all those green beans, Grae didn't have much time to devote to research; but she managed to find a few minutes late at night to begin digging through her grandmother's papers in search of Squire David Graham and the Mansion's early beginnings.

"You know, Mom, I think it would be good to include some information on the tour about Squire David's life before he built the Mansion," Grae said one morning at the breakfast table. "I've been reading some of Granny's research. He was a really ambitious man, even when he was young."

"The first David Graham became a very wealthy and powerful man at a young age," Grandpa Mack said, between bites of eggs and bacon. Kat noticed that her father's left hand now shook occasionally; she made a mental note to mention this to his doctor at his next check-up. "All the stories I've heard say he seemed like he was out to prove something and that he was also a real hard man to live with."

"What do you mean by the 'first David Graham'?" It was the first time Perry had gotten into the conversation that morning. He seemed to be concentrating more on eating his second plate of biscuits and gravy.

"The first David Graham was the one they called Squire. The second one was his son, who was called Major David Graham."

"There's that word 'Squire' again. Didn't you tell me something about that earlier this year?" Perry asked Grae.

"Yeah, I thought you were going to research that for me and find out what it meant," Grae replied as she rolled her eyes.

"I must have got distracted."

"By a video game, no doubt!" Kat teased, tousling her son's hair as she placed a plate of eggs and bacon in front of him. Every week, it seemed that the grocery bill became higher. In her past life of comfort, she had never realized how hard being a single parent would be. There was always something to worry about. "I think I may need to get a second job just to pay for your appetite."

"Grae, you may be right about including information about Squire before he built this place. I seem to remember your grandmother talking about how he must have practically worked night and day to be able to earn enough money to pay this land off so quickly." Grandpa drank the last of his coffee and stood up from the table. "Just be careful what you include because he won't take criticism too well, I imagine."

"What are you talking about, Grandpa? How would he know what Grae put in the tour?" Perry drained a half glass of orange juice in one gulp before rising to follow his grandfather.

"Oh, son, you just don't understand. Squire David Graham may have died some two hundred years ago, but he never did leave this house."

THREE

It was the last Monday in July and Grae didn't have to work. All the beans were finally taken care of, and it would be a few more weeks before she and her mother would be working on any other vegetables or fruits. So Grae decided that it was time to delve deeper into the life of the early Graham family and start writing some of the information for the tour that she and her mother would give in September.

"If I am going to learn about David Graham, I better first learn a little about his family," Grae said to herself as she opened one of her grandmother's files labeled "Robert Graham."

Since she was alone that morning, she sat in the floor of her room and spread her grandmother's files around her. Out of the corner of her left eye, she could see a jack rock ball slowly moving across the floor near the fireplace. It was her latest gift to Clara, the young orphan girl who had died over one hundred and fifty years earlier in that very room. Grae had become her unwilling roommate, but she felt sorry that someone so young and gentle was forever trapped there.

"Good morning, Clara. Would you like me to read aloud about Robert Graham? He was Squire David's father. I realize that Squire wasn't very nice to you, but maybe his father was a nice man." The little ball stopped moving. "I'm going to take that as a yes."

Grae began to read. "Robert Graham was twenty years old when he arrived in Pennsylvania in 1774. This was his first stop in the New World after making his way from County Down, Ireland, with his first wife, Mary Craig, and a brother and sister. Later, they travelled through Southwest Virginia on the Great Wagon Road on their way to Mecklenburg County, North Carolina. They lived there several years, before establishing a homestead in Montgomery County, Virginia, in 1782." Grae paused. "His home place was on the Great Wagon Road, not more than ten miles from here. That was four years before Joseph Baker died. I wonder if I saw Robert Graham, maybe at the wedding party. I don't remember him."

Grae turned toward the fireplace. "You see, Clara, before this area was Wythe County, it was all part of Montgomery County. That's now where the Hokie Bird lives," Grae giggled. "But I don't suppose that means anything to you." In the far left corner of the room, a lightweight ball, a gift from Perry, started moving. It was maroon and orange with the Virginia Tech mascot emblazed on the side.

Grae laughed loudly. "Why, Clara, you pay more attention to us than I thought." Grae leafed through a few more papers. "So it says that Robert Graham bought ninety-three acres on Reed Creek called the Boiling Spring Tract and that he lived on the Old Baltimore Road, often referred to as the Wilderness Road, at a place now called Locust Hill. That area is about ten miles north of the Mansion. He later added more tracts for a total area of four hundred acres. He had been a captain and a lieutenant in the Revolutionary War and was known to be a gimlet maker, wagoner, and farmer, and had worked in the iron business in North Carolina."

Grae stopped and stood up, walking toward the window. "I wonder what a gimlet is. I'll have to do some research about that." Through the window, Grae could see someone walking up the road in front of the Mansion. With the angle of the morning sun, she could not tell who it was, but it looked like a man. She heard a pecking noise and looked down to see a bird hitting its beak against the window. In her mind, an image of the Hitchcock movie *The Birds* immediately came into view, and she backed away from the window stepping on the jack rocks.

"Oops!" Grae said, as she then stepped on the Hokie ball causing it to flatten. "Sorry, Clara, maybe Perry can fix it." She looked out the window again and saw that the man was gone. "Perhaps I should take a break." Grae left her room and walked downstairs. She went outside and sat on the front porch. Looking around her, she noticed the massive, cast iron columns. From her reading, she knew that these had been made at the original Perry Mount Furnace on the property. It was evidence of Squire David's handiwork.

Grae looked up and down the road and wondered who the man was that she had just seen walking. She didn't recognize him, and now that she thought about it, the figure looked a little strange. He appeared to be dressed in very raggedy clothes and seemed to be carrying something. She would have to ask Grandpa if he had seen anyone unusual recently. She hoped it wasn't some homeless person who had found their way over from the interstate.

Grae stepped off the porch and walked around to the left of the Mansion. She saw that Lucy, the owner's crazy cousin, was sitting on her own porch in the former caretaker's house. Lucy was reading a newspaper with the radio going full blast through an open window.

In early May, when Grae had returned from 1786, Lucy had helped Grae fix her chopped hair. Joseph Baker's slave, Aggie, had cut off Grae's long hair. Something unusual had happened to her hair on Grae's journey back in time, and when Lucy trimmed the ends, the tips turned an eerie silver tone. It was a pretty unusual look for the prom, but Gav didn't seem to mind. He thought Grae was beautiful no matter what.

"Hey, Lucy!" Grae shouted, as she walked up the hill.

"Hey, yourself, what have you been up to these days? Haven't seen you around much," Lucy didn't look up, just kept staring at the newspaper. This week, Lucy's hair was jet black, in a bouffant style high up on her head. There were tendrils of hair that curled at her temples. Lucy was a beautician who loved to experiment...on herself.

"I've been working a lot up on the mountain. It's been really busy, lots of travelers from all over the place. Mom and I have also been canning those beans that Perry and Grandpa raised. It's been a lot of work."

"I know what you mean. Mack brought me a bushel. I froze most of them, but I have a few drying out in the sunroom on the back."

"Making leather britches, did you know that you could do that with sweet potatoes?" Grae said, sitting down on the edge of the porch.

Lucy looked out from behind the newspaper. "How do you know that? That's from way back there. You are a city girl." Lucy looked straight at Grae as if she was trying to read her thoughts.

Grae froze. She had learned about "sewing sweet potatoes" in 1786 from Sal. She paused and thought about her friend from long ago. She had missed Sal a great deal during those first few weeks back in her real life. Sal was one person who Grae would always carry with her.

"Maybe I learned about it from Granny." Grae stared back at Lucy. Maybe she could stare her down.

"Well, I don't remember Belle ever making any, but I do know that Great Granny Weaver used to make them every year. She'd only use the earliest sweet potatoes of the season. They made the best pies in the fall. She learned to make them from an old slave's daughter that she knew over on Baker Island." Lucy went back to her paper.

"Baker Island? Where's that?" Grae wondered if there could possibly be a connection.

"It's over near Foster Falls, on the New River."

"Do you know why it is called Baker Island?"

"Hmmm," Lucy looked away from her paper momentarily. "I think it was because Joseph Baker's family went to live there after he was murdered." Lucy folded up one section and began looking at the advertising flyers. "I guess you would want to live on an island after you had seen your husband murdered."

Grae gave Lucy a shocked look. "Missus Baker saw the murder? I don't remember reading that in any of Granny's papers."

Lucy tilted her head to the side and looked at Grae in deep thought. Grae could now see that she had on long silver earrings with rhinestones. "Well, you know, I'm not sure where I heard that. I'll have to think about how I know that." Lucy folded up her papers and stood up. "I better get at it; there's a bunch of laundry downstairs with my name on it. Got to get the place spruced up a little, my niece is coming to spend two weeks with me before school starts."

"Oh, that's nice. How old is she?"

"Pepper is twelve and a little spitfire."

"Pepper?"

"That's her nickname. Her real name is Sydney. She's a ball of fire, just like me. Lord, help her Daddy, my brother. He's got his hands full." Lucy headed to the front door. "I'll see you later, Grae. Let me know when you want another trim. We'll see what other color those ends will turn."

"Thanks, Lucy. I will probably need one before college starts. I'm just trying to let it grow back out some now." Grae turned to leave, but thought of something. "Hey, Lucy, I've got to ask. What's with the bouffant hair?"

"You like it? I just thought I would channel a little Priscilla Presley today. I watched an Elvis movie marathon yesterday afternoon. May he rest in peace."

"I love movie marathons!" Grae said. "A few weeks ago, Mom and I watched all these Fred Astaire movies. My favorite is *Singing in the Rain*."

"Ah, no offense to Mister Astaire, he was a great performer, but it was Gene Kelly who was in *Singing in the Rain*."

"I always do that! Mom has corrected me before. I've got a mental block on those two."

"That's why I stick to Elvis, darling, there's no confusing The King."

"Uh, okay," Grae said, walking away. "I'll see you later." Grae chuckled to herself as she walked. "Maybe I could take Lucy back to the 1960s sometime."

"Who are you talking to now?" Perry asked as he came up behind her. He was always doing that and it irritated her.

"Perry, one of these days, I'm gonna…"

"Careful, Sis, remember Mom's rules."

"I'm not breaking them. Because I am not going to

threaten you, I'm really going to do it one day."

"Ah, lighten up," Perry draped his arm around Grae's shoulders as they walked toward the house. "I'm starving. Grandpa sent me ahead to ask you to fix us some lunch."

"Well, I guess I can do that for Grandpa. I think we have ingredients for sloppy joes."

"Yeah, I could eat about four of them." Perry took the front steps in two jumps and opened the door for Grae.

"You must be hungry; you are now being nice to me."

"Just practicing holding the door for a lady; you are the closest thing around."

Grae rolled her eyes, but it amazed her at how much Perry had changed in the last few months. After taking Carrie, Gav's sister and Grae's friend, to the prom, Perry had all of a sudden seemed older. Since he had started working at the grocery store, he had gotten a cell phone and texted Carrie quite often. Carrie and her mother had spent most of the summer caring for Carrie's grandfather in another state, but Grae could tell that there would be some dates upon her return. Carrie's and Perry's night at the prom was the beginning of a budding romance.

FOUR

Perry and Grandpa Mack consumed most of the lunch Grae prepared. She served them on paper plates to avoid most of the cleanup, and now found herself back in Granny Belle's research. As she continued to read about Robert Graham, she learned that his two marriages had produced fourteen children and that he had died when Squire David was almost eleven years old.

"That must have really made an impact on him, losing his father so young." An open window in her room fell suddenly, closing with a boom. The incident sent chills down Grae's spine, but she continued her reading. "So, he lost his father as a young boy, and his mother died when he was nineteen. I wonder who the significant people in his life were during his teenage years." Grae continued going through the files and came across several letters written by Robert Graham. She began reading aloud one with the date of 1788.

Robert Graham
Baltimore Stagecoach Road
Montgomery County
Virginia

13 May, 1788

Excellency Major Joseph Graham, Esq.
Rural Hill Plantation
Mecklenburg County
North Carolina

His Honourable Major Graham,

It is with great esteem and reverence that I write to you this day. As we have corresponded these many years since the War for Freedom, I continue to be blessed, indeed, by a growing family of now six young ones and prospering business enterprises. Since my letter last I may report a substantial increase in volume of industrious persons traveling west in hopes of settling there. Thus my humble homestead, farm fields, store, distillery, and waggoning services have expanded and benefitted directly and for that blessing I am very much pleased. Did I mention earlier that I reside not ten miles from Lead Mines where the Fincastle Resolutions were writ? It is with great pride to be associated now with some of these fine men and with Yourself and Major John Davidson as well, for you are both distinguished signers of a most similar, esteemed document, the Mecklenburg Declaration of Independence! God be praised!

As I consider my present circumstances, Sir, I must state that I am forever in your debt for your generous counsel these past eight years since I proudly rode in your Cavalry fighting the noble War for Liberty. It indeed fortifies my being to hold with respect your fine character and boundless talents as we are a kindred lot, both having descended from the sturdy Graham stock of County Down Ireland,

Sir, I take great pleasure to read of your most splendid tidings! You have my warmest regards upon your marriage to the lovely Miss Isabella Davidson. I vividly recall our encampment at Cowan's Ford on the fine plantation Miss Isabella's father, Major John Davidson, beside the banks of the Catawba. As we made ready the evening before battle, Miss Isabella did serve us a welcome and unexpected hot meal, to which surely fortified our bellies and spirits. Indeed at day break our meager yet determined forces succeeded in slowing the menace of the Tory Advance. Amen! Sadly, I too am reminded of the horse Major Davidson loaned his revered cousin, General William Lee Davidson. I saw the lone steed without rider as it made its way back to the plantation the morning of our charge, the General being shot dead from his mount. The years do not diminish my memories of these horrors yet when I recall the unyielding spirit and faith of our fellow Militia under the supreme leadership such as yours, Sir, I am filled with Grace and hope for the Future.

Though the ghosts of our mutual past will follow us the rest of our days, it is the present state of affairs to which I write. I find that on the fifteenth day of July next, just before the crops are laid, I will journey to

Charlotte to sell the balance of my properties on Sugar Creek. I shall be accompanied by sons Samuel now fourteen years and James, a tall lad of twelve years. Upon completion of our land transactions it would be my privilege to call upon your fine hospitality and visit your Excellency. Due to the proximity of my business there I will take Samuel and James to visit the revered cross roads site at Mecklenburg Courthouse, or shall I say the "Hornets' Nest" to quote our inglorious adversary General Cornwallis. With your kind permission I wish to tell my sons of our fateful battle and my blessed good fortune in having been directed as if with God's Providence to your slumped and bloodied body that solemn evening. I feared you were dead Sir. May I be so bold as to confess such a thing now? I will tell the lads the story of your gallantry and even-tempered persistence while leading our small force against a multitude of Red Coats! I will show them the half-piece of your tarnished silver stock buckle, split into two pieces, as if a shield guarding your neck as you were struck down repeatedly by a Tory sword. You honor me with this great symbol of God's enduring Hold on our Fates. We shall walk then, to dear Mrs. Susannah Alexander's home, the humble sanctuary where your nine saber and bullet wounds were bound and tended by her hand. Our sons must learn of such things as it is our duty under God.

It is with sentiments of high respect and deep appreciation that my sons may know of your illustrious life through the privilege of our valued acquaintance.

Your Excellency's most obedient and humble servant,
  Robert Graham

"Well, that was interesting. I'll have to read some more of those. It's getting awfully hot in here." Grae remembered about the window closing then. As she walked over to open it again, she noticed that under the window frame, there seemed to be a panel that was now loose.

"I wonder if the force of that window closing jarred this panel." She tried prying it out with her hands, but she realized that she needed something to leverage it. She knew that her grandfather kept a toolbox in the closet downstairs and quickly went to get it.

Walking past the front door, Grae glanced toward the road. Once again, she saw a man walking down the road away from the Mansion. She tried to get a better look at him, but a truck went past in the opposite direction. It looked as if it might have hit him.

Grae opened the front door and ran down the steps and down the hill to the road. Looking in both directions, she searched for some evidence of the man, but found none. She didn't realize that she was herself standing in the middle of the road until the horn of a car startled her.

"Grae, what are you doing in the middle of the road?" It was Mister Fisher, the mail carrier. He was a slightly eccentric man who was friends with Grandpa Mack.

"Hi, Mister Fisher. I thought I saw someone in the road, and it looked like a truck hit him. Did you pass anyone walking?" Grae was in the middle of the road and looking all around for the man. He couldn't have gotten away that quickly.

"Now, Grae, don't you be like the rest of them believing all that ghost stuff. It's all a bunch of foolishness. Here's your mail. Get out of the road, child." Mister Fisher waited for Grae to walk to the side of the road before he pulled off, waving and shaking his head.

As she climbed the hill, she thought about what Mister Fisher said. Surely that was a real man who she saw, it couldn't have been…. Her thoughts were interrupted by the glimpse of a familiar cat jumping off the front porch and scampering to the back of the house.

"General! Come back! I need to talk to you." While Perry and Grandpa had mentioned several times about seeing The General during the past two months, this was the first time Grae had seen him herself. Turning the corner around the back of the house, he was nowhere to be seen. She knew he said he could not communicate with her in this time, but she had still harbored hopes that it wasn't true.

As she walked back through the front door, she remembered why she had come downstairs in the first place. With everything that had transpired in the last few minutes, she couldn't help but feel some butterflies in her stomach as she got closer to the closet. It had been her portal to another time, and she was now very leery of opening the door. As her hand touched the doorknob, the phone rang, making her jump and catch her breath.

"Hello," she said, answering it on the second ring.

"Hey, baby. How's my best girl doing?" Gav asked cheerfully on the other end.

"Best girl? How many girls do you have?" Grae chuckled. It was so good to hear his voice. Gav had been in Tennessee seeing one of his cousins who would be heading off to boot camp. They had texted several times each day, but they hadn't verbally spoken while he was gone.

"Oh, you know, I've got them everywhere. But none of them are as high on the list as you."

Grae knew he was joking with her, but she also knew that there was some truth to what he said. He could have about any girl within an hour's radius—he was that popular. But, for some reason, he had chosen the weird girl that lived in the haunted mansion whose father was in prison. Probably many girls had wondered why, but Grae knew they had a connection that transcended time.

"I just got home, and I don't have to work until tomorrow. I was thinking that maybe we could go out to eat and to a movie tonight. Since I was gone over the weekend, I'm sure I will have to pull some hard shifts the rest of the week. Our schedules don't seem to allow us many nights to go out these days. What'cha think?"

She wouldn't tell him what she thought; it would boost his ego too much. But the truth was that meeting Gav's ancestor, Patrick, in 1786 had only made her fall in love with Gav more. She was dreading him going off to Virginia Tech in the fall. Even though it wasn't very far away, Grae knew that between both of their class schedules, working, and the sports he would play, there wouldn't be much time left for them to spend together. Gav had asked her to consider going to Tech too, but she knew that it would be a hardship on her family right now, even with loans. Maybe, after a year at the community college, she could transfer.

"That sounds great! What time should I be ready?" Grae looked at the clock on the wall. She was amazed to see that it was almost a quarter to four. Where had the time gone?

"How about around seven? We can have dinner, and then catch the late movie. Do you have to work tomorrow?"

"Yes, but I work twelve to eight."

"Great! I don't go in until two. We can stay out a little late." Gav paused as if he was distracted by something. "Ah, I've got to go. You go get extra beautiful. That should take you about five minutes."

"Oh, Gav! You're a mess! I've missed you!" That slipped out quick, but there would be no hiding her feelings when they were face to face. "See you in a little bit. Bye."

Grae hung up the phone and walked back to the closet. Preoccupied with thoughts of her date with Gav, she opened the door, kneeled and reached for her grandfather's toolbox. She began feeling a little dizzy and looked to see that her foot was over the closet's threshold.

"I have got to be more careful. I don't want to spend the rest of my summer stuck in another century." Grae laughed, but she knew it wouldn't be a fun experience. She had almost ended up imprisoned in 1786; she needed to be more careful. Retrieving a small crowbar from the toolbox, Grae went back upstairs to try and open the panel below the window. It took several attempts and all the strength she could muster, but finally the panel popped out. Thankfully, it was all in one piece and seemed unharmed. She didn't want to have to explain why she had messed up the wall.

"It looks like it's a secret compartment," Grae said out loud as she got her flashlight from the nightstand and shined the light into the wall. "Oh, I think I see a box in there." Despite the fact that she knew the area must be full of cobwebs and spiders, Grae reached into the wall. Her arm was just small enough and long enough to grasp the handle on the box. Struggling to lift the box up, she gradually maneuvered it to the hole. It seemed to be just the right size to fit through where the panel had been.

"That's convenient," Grae said, laughing. "But I guess it was made to be." True to her imagination, the box was covered in cobwebs. A spider that had come along for the journey quickly trotted away. "You can live on this side of the wall for a while."

She tried to open it, but it was obviously locked. A tiny keyhole was visible in the middle of one of the sides. "Oh great, another key to find; bet this one will not be so obvious and easy." Imagining that the key to the box was like its owner, long gone, she began to think about how she could get it opened. Absentmindedly fingering the chain around her neck, she remembered the small knife that was now on the chain with the key. She had found it in the dress she had been wearing when she returned from 1786. It had been hidden by Mary, the daughter-in-law of Joseph Baker, in a secret pocket near the hem of the dress. Grae suspected that Mary had also travelled in time.

Taking the chain off, she fingered the old, ancient brass key that had helped transport her to 1786 and back. Had it not been for it unlocking her shackles, she would have surely been doomed to stay in Joseph Baker's time. The small knife had a dark green handle and the initials J.J.B. engraved on it. She wasn't sure why Mary had thought that Joseph's knife would be useful to her, but if she could use it to open this box, perhaps she would find out the answer.

Grae opened the knife which revealed the small blade. She tilted the box and slid the sharp edge into the keyhole. She then noticed that there was a small button next to the hole. Pushing it in and turning the knife, Grae heard a snap. At first, she was afraid that she might have broken the tip of the old knife; but, soon, she realized that the button and knife had worked their magic and the box was now unlocked.

"Thanks, Mary!" Grae said and smiled.

"Who's Mary?" This time it was her mother that came up behind her. Grae spied the rag she had used to clean off the box and quickly pulled it over the knife, key, and chain to conceal it from her mother.

"Oh, it's just an expression!" Grae's mind raced quickly. "You know, my friend, Catherine, in Charlotte used to say it. It was like a Catholic thing…like a 'Hail Mary.' Thanks, Mary! I picked it up from her." Grae knew that it sounded totally ridiculous, but perhaps her mother would chalk it up to a teenage thing.

"Well, that's different." Kat looked over Grae's shoulder at the box and the hole in the wall. "Oh, my, what have you been doing here?"

"Well, it's funny you asked," Grae said, standing up. "I was over there on the bed looking through some of Granny's files about the Graham family, and all of a sudden the bottom half of the window dropped and shut. It scared the life out of me." Grae looked at her mother and saw the worry lines in her forehead appear.

"It didn't break the window or anything; it was just strange. A little later, I started getting hot, and I came over here to open the window back up. It looked as if the force of the window closing had jarred a panel loose under it. So I pried it off and found this metal box down in the wall. It's like it was a secret compartment."

"What's in the box?" Kat was not really looking at the box but seemed to be looking all around the room for something.

"Well, I had just gotten it open when you came up behind me." Grae picked up the box and set it on her desk near the door. It still took a little effort to get the old hinges to work, but after a little prying it began to open.

"You know, it sort of reminds me of an old safety deposit box," Kat said.

"Hmmm, I don't guess I have ever seen one of those." Grae began to look at the box's contents. On top, there was a very old document folded several times. Grae carefully lifted it out and handed it to her mother.

As Kat began to unfold the paper, Grae continued to look in the box. She saw that there were several old coins in a corner. Underneath the other documents, she thought she saw the edge of a pocket watch. She picked up a long worn leather notebook. It had been doubled and had an old leather cord tied around it. She was about to try to untie the cord when her mother began to speak.

"Grae, come here and look." Kat had unfolded the document and it was now lying on Grae's bed. "I think this might be one of the original plans of the Mansion. It shows the first section that Squire David built, and then the second section. The only thing that is missing is the additions that Major David made."

"Well, I guess that would make it over one hundred and fifty years old. It has held up well." Before Kat could reply, the phone started ringing.

"I'll go get that and start dinner. Please fold that back up and bring the box downstairs. I want your grandfather to see it." Kat ran down the stairs before Grae had a chance to tell her that she was going out with Gav.

"It won't matter. Perry will easily eat my share." Grae folded the document and returned it and the leather notebook back to the box. "I need to start getting ready for my date." Looking in the mirror above her bureau, she realized how dirty she had gotten. "I will definitely need more than five minutes.

FIVE

"Casey looks like he has lost at least ten pounds and he was in pretty good shape before he enlisted." Since they had ordered their dinner, Gav had constantly talked about his cousin's boot camp experience. Despite her interest in anything he had to say, Grae had found her mind wandering.

"It's got me to thinking that maybe I should have considered joining one of the armed services. See the world, serve my country; it would be a great life."

"But you've worked so hard on athletics, how could you give all that up?" Grae got a scary feeling in her stomach thinking about Gav joining the military. It was one thing for him to be an hour down the road; it was another for him to be halfway around the world.

"I know, but it still is an interesting opportunity. Don't get all blue on me, baby. It's just a passing thought. I'd hate to have to cut all this gorgeous hair." Gav laughed as he ran his fingers through his blond locks. That movie star smile melted away her worry.

"You're the one with the radical haircuts. You never did tell me what that was all about. It was cute, but I'm glad you are letting it grow back out." Gav's long arm reached across the table and flipped her hair up. "That silver stuff is gone, but what's this green stuff you've been putting on it? It looks like you have been rolling in money."

"What?" Grae ran her fingers through her hair. "What are you talking about?"

"I noticed it before I left, but I didn't say anything. Now it's getting darker. Have you been back to that crazy woman behind the Mansion?"

Grae excused herself and went to the restroom. She stared into the mirror and gasped as she realized that he was right, her hair did have a green tone to it. "What in the world is happening to me? What did they do to me?"

In the reflection of the mirror, Grae saw a woman slowly come out of the stall behind her. She hoped that she hadn't paid attention to what she had said.

"Are you okay, dear? Did someone do something...oh, my stars, what has happened to your hair?" The woman was short, but looked rather intimidating in her blue pantsuit.

Grae fingered her hair. "Ah, it is a bad color job. The beautician was new." Grae smiled and ducked into a stall. She hoped that the woman would just leave, but Grae didn't hear any movement for a moment. Then she heard the water run, and then stop.

"You get help if you need it, dear. There are people who would help you."

Grae finally heard the door open and close. Leaving the stall, she looked at her hair again. She would have to go see Lucy.

32

Grae and Gav sat in the dark movie theater. Being a Monday night, they almost had the whole place to themselves. That seemed to be fine with Gav who, as soon as the previews had started, put his arm around her and pulled her close to snuggle.

"Will my fingers turn green if I play with your hair?" Grae heard a snicker in his voice and quickly gave his leg a hard pinch.

"Hey, that really hurt. Is that how you keep Whitey in line?"

Grae gave him a confused looked. "Whitey?" she whispered.

Gav laughed. "That's what we call Perry at the store. There is an older guy named Perry who works there, so we started calling him Whitey." Grae still looked confused. "Babe, it's your last name."

Grae felt two inches tall and hid her face. The gesture tickled Gav and he pulled her closer to him. "You're so cute."

As Gav began to get into the movie, an action-packed thriller, Grae's mind drifted from the plot. She couldn't help but be worried about what was happening to her. Her mind would take trips, and she had no idea where she went or how long she was gone. She was afraid that she would have one while she was driving and run off the road. Her hair turning green was embarrassing, but it was scary too. What could possibly be going on inside her body that she didn't know about? Had she caught some time travel bug or brought back some old influenza that her current century didn't have a cure for? Or was she being gradually drawn back into another journey?

She hadn't realized how long she had been thinking until Gav nudged her. The credits were rolling on the screen in front of them and the theater was almost empty.

"You weren't really watching the movie, were you?" Gav asked as they walked to his car.

"Oh, the movie was great!" Grae smiled. "I loved it."

"Uh huh, who did the main character murder?" Gav had stopped at the passenger side of his car to open the door for Grae, but he appeared to be holding the door shut until she answered his question.

"Um, it was, you know, that bad guy." Grae gave him a big smile.

"Nice try, but admit it, you weren't even in the theater tonight." Gav leaned against the car. "You know, you were like this before I left. I thought it was because you were so busy, working on the mountain and helping your mother put up all those endless baskets of green beans. But, now things have slowed down some. Are you going to tell me what's wrong? Why do you seem so preoccupied? Does it have anything to do with us?"

Grae moved in front of Gav. He was sort of sitting on the edge of the hood and it made him almost even to her height. She put her arms around his neck and leaned in for a kiss. As she felt his arms encircle her, she momentarily thought of dancing with Patrick. She could get lost in Patrick's arms, no Gav's. This inner war made her open her eyes and move slightly; interrupting what Gav probably thought was going to be a long kiss.

"It's happening again!" Gav moved away from her and walked around to his side of the car. He got in and slammed the door. Grae gently opened the passenger door and got inside.

"I'm sorry. I don't know what's wrong with me. I'm just not myself."

"No, you're not, and you're also not telling me why." Gav started the car and pulled out of the parking spot. "I'm moving to Blacksburg in just a few weeks. If you've got something going on with someone else, I want to know now."

"No, Gav, there isn't someone else."

"Yeah, well, it sure didn't feel like you were kissing me tonight." With those words, Grae realized her problem was bigger than she imagined.

"Mom," Grae said the next morning as she was fixing breakfast. Her mother seemed harried and nervous. "I was thinking that if you had time, I could drop by your office around eleven and bring you some lunch before I go to work."

Kat looked over her mug toward her daughter as she took her last drink of coffee. "Well, that would be a wonderful surprise."

"No, it wouldn't," Perry said, sitting down at the table.

"And why wouldn't it be?" Kat snapped at her son.

"She's told you she is coming, so it won't be a surprise."

"You inherited the sarcasm gene too! I'll never make it through your teen years."

Grae had stopped and gotten her mother's favorite meal at the local Chinese restaurant and arrived at Kat's office at the community college just a little before eleven. It would give them thirty minutes to eat at one of the picnic tables on the campus, before Grae would need to drive up Big Walker Mountain.

"What a treat!" Kat exclaimed opening the little square boxes. "I love Sesame Chicken!"

Grae smiled. It was nice to be able to treat her mother. She had sacrificed so much for her children.

As they both dug into their food, Kat cautiously looked at her daughter. "Is there something you want to talk to me about?"

Grae put down her chopsticks and looked into her mother's eyes. "You are the only person I can ask about this, but I don't want to upset you."

Kat reached over and took her daughter's hand. "Whatever it is, we will get through it together."

"Well, I really don't know how to even ask this question. What I'm about to say doesn't really make any sense."

Kat absentmindedly moved her set of chopsticks back and forth in her hand as if they were legs walking on the plate. It was a gesture that she had seen her mother do many times. Grae's father had said that something needed to be moving in Kat's hand for her to really think.

"Do you think it is cheating if I am in love with a version of Gav in the past?"

Kat laid down the chopsticks and tilted her head slightly as she absorbed what Grae had said. "I'm sorry, dear, but I don't think I understand what you just said."

Grae swallowed and began. "You see, when I was in 1786, I met this young man. He was the spitting image of Gav. They could have been brothers, twins. His name was Patrick McGavock and I guess he would have been an ancestor of Gav's. He would have to have been."

"And you became involved with him?" Kat's brow furrowed.

"Well, not exactly, I only knew him for one evening."

"Just one evening?"

"I met him at a party at a nearby farm on the same night that Joseph Baker later died. He shot Isaiah."

"He shot who? Were you there when that happened? Oh,

Grae, I don't like the sound of this."

"Oh, Mom, it was a very long night, and a lot happened, and most of it was pretty bad." Grae paused and pushed her food away from her, a glimpse of a red pepper strip in her meal sent a tremble through her. "But one good thing happened, I met Patrick, and it was just like Gav was with me there and it made me feel so much better. Patrick shot Isaiah because he thought that Isaiah was going to shoot me. Unfortunately that is what made Sam drop the ax aiming for Isaiah, but the ax hit Joseph Baker instead."

"Okay, you are going to have to explain that scenario to me later, slower. But going back to your question, you think you are in love with someone who lived in 1786? That's not very healthy, Grae."

"Well, it's like when I am with Gav, I get these flashbacks back to Patrick. When Gav kissed me last night, it was like Patrick was there. It's unnerving and Gav has noticed and he thinks that I am interested in someone else. The worst part is that is kind of true and it really has me messed up. I loved being with Patrick that night because it was like having Gav in 1786 with me. It was so comforting. It felt so safe. Now that I am back here, it's sort of like it is flipped."

Kat took a deep breath. "This can happen with time travel. People, experiences, can attach themselves to you. It is very dangerous. Oh, how I wish that you hadn't gone at all. I thought that I had made sure that everything that was attached to that portal was gone. I should have never let you make Clara's room your own, then you wouldn't have had such easy access to it."

"What? Clara's room? What are you talking about?"

"The closet in that room, the one she was kept in after she passed."

Grae continued to give her mother a blank stare.

"That was my time travel portal."

"Well, what do you know?" Grae shook her head.

"I don't understand your reaction."

"That's not how I got to 1786." Grae stood up and took their trash to a nearby receptacle.

"It's not?" Kat stood and walked toward her. "How did you get there?"

"Through the weird round closet in the foyer and that's where I came back to."

"Oh, no." Kat sat back down on the bench. She looked sick.

"Are you okay, Mom?"

"I wish your grandmother was here to help us with this. I hope Dad remembers the story. It's going to be hard to break the portal's grasp."

"Mom, you are scaring me!" A couple of students who were walking by glanced in their direction.

"Grae, this is hard for a mother to say to her child, but you should be scared."

SIX

The drive up the winding road to the top of Big Walker Mountain seemed to take a very long time that day. Grae's mother's stoic voice as she said, "you should be scared" rang in Grae's head like a broken record. She was beginning to become a little afraid of her life at Graham Mansion. She found herself longing for her previous life, the one she took for granted, even with the emotionally distant father who had his own versions of right and wrong.

While most people her age would want a job closer to town, Grae enjoyed working at the mountaintop attraction. It had an air of nostalgia and that was an authentic feeling; the business had been in operation for over sixty-five years. It had survived many twists and turns in its history and one of the reasons was the larger than life character who had run it for half of those years.

As Grae pulled in to the parking area, Mister Abbey waved at her as she parked. It amazed her how his mood never seemed to falter. In just the few short months she had worked there, she had seen several situations that would have given any boss reason to be grumpy. Staff showing up late, cantankerous customers, even a water leak that caused thousands of dollars in damage hadn't put him over the edge.

"Good afternoon, Grae!" A broom was in his hands and it was busy sweeping away dirt that Grae could not see. Mister Abbey was always sweeping the front porch of the general store.

"Hello, Mister Abbey. How are you today?" Grae stood back and waited, ready to mouth the words with him. They were always the same, his trademark.

"Wonderful and marvelous!" He said with a laugh. While Grae would never say it out loud, she thought Mister Abbey reminded her of a cross between Santa Claus and Otis from the Andy Griffith Show. Santa because he had a thick head of solid white hair and a moustache and beard to match. The similarity to Otis came from his walk; it had a little stagger to it as if he was drunk. Grae had never even smelled rubbing alcohol on him, but there was something about how he carried himself that gave that impression.

Grae walked into the store and to the back where employees kept their belongings. A straight row of hooks held the bright red aprons that all employees wore. Because most of her time was spent behind the ice cream counter, Grae also wore a small red and white checkered hat that screamed the wistfulness of days gone by. At first, she had hated the hat; it had to be attached to her hair with bobby pins. But after she saw herself in it and created her own style wearing it, tilted to one side, she began to enjoy the nostalgia of the very act of having it on her head. The customers loved it.

"Hi, Mary Lee. How's business been today?" Grae spoke to the store's oldest employee. She started working for the

Abbey family after her children started school and had been there for over forty-five years. She was the backbone of the operation.

"Business has been steady. Several families and a whole bunch of motorcycle riders. They all loved my sweet rolls." Now, in her early seventies, Mary Lee was still a striking woman. Her once long dark hair now barely touched her collar, but was always in a perfect style, never a hair out of place thanks to the stock she surely owned in Aqua Net. Not a gray hair either because of Mary Lee's personal friendship with Miss Clairol. Still trim and fashionable, she had the appearance that time had just stood still for her from about her mid-fifties onward. She had many duties at Big Walker, but her shining star was baking. Five days a week, she arrived at five in the morning and began baking. By the time the doors officially opened at nine, she would have baked several dozen of her famous sweet rolls, an equal amount of several kinds of cookies, and whatever she decided would be the "Bread of the Day." While the delicious goodies were loved by the travelers, as many locals made a trip up the mountain a part of their weekly shopping to get some of "Mary Lee's Marvelous Baked Goods," as Mister Abbey called her creations.

Grae began to replenish the coffee makers and get the aromatic smell going throughout the building. She had read an article online that said the smell of coffee was not only a comforting one, but that it could also stimulate the appetite. She had suggested that they keep coffee brewing during the summer because, while ice cream and cold beverage sales were good, people did not make as many food purchases when they were hot. That also translated into fewer sales of the canned goods, and Grae was counting on those sales to fill her gas tank.

"Those archaeology fellows from Virginia Tech who were in here this morning were pleasant."

Grae jumped as Mister Abbey spoke. She hadn't realized he was inside the store until he had loudly made that comment from behind her.

"I've gone and scared you again, haven't I?" He said with a chuckle. As pleasant as he was, he could also be a little devious.

"They were mighty interested in the Indians that lived around here, way back there." Mary Lee said as she slid another batch of oatmeal raisin cookies into the bakery case. She handed one to Grae with a wink before she turned to go back to the kitchen.

"They were indeed, and I guess they plan to do some digging at some different spots around here." Mister Abbey poured himself a fresh cup of coffee. He breathed in the aroma before adding cream and sweetener to the mug. "What'cha' got in the oven back there? I think Grae's theory about smelling coffee and being hungry is right." He smiled after taking the first drink. "You've created quite a good blend there, Grae. I'm glad I let you be our barista."

"Well, I would hardly call myself a barista, but if you get an expresso machine I would sure try." Since many of their travelers were from large cities, they weren't too keen on the regular store-bought coffee that had been served when Grae arrived. She suggested that they buy a variety of fresh beans in small quantities and start grinding and brewing their own blend. Mister Abbey loved the idea. With the help of her mother, Grae selected a few different types of beans to start with and ordered small batches online. After experimenting with a few versions, they finally created one that had a rich heartiness that well depicted the vast mountaintop on which the business stood. Big Walker Brew was now sold by the cup and the ground version could also be purchased by the bag. Grae was now experimenting on roasting coffee beans herself and creating fall and holiday versions of the brew.

"Maybe that is something you can put on your Christmas list," Mister Abbey said with a twinkle in his eye, reminding Grae again of Santa Claus. "I've seen small versions of those machines at the warehouse stores. Maybe we could start with a junior version and see how it goes." Mister Abbey turned to walk toward his office, after refilling his coffee mug. "Can you think of anything that I need more than a great cup of coffee?"

"Bran muffins!" Mary Lee yelled from the kitchen.

Mister Abbey and Grae howled with laughter when they realized Mary Lee had finally answered his question from several minutes earlier.

"You mentioned that those archaeologists who were in here this morning were going to do some local digs." Grae turned out the lights as Mister Abbey walked out through the front door. "What do they think they will find?"

Mister Abbey turned the key in the deadbolt lock and then rattled the door. "Well, they might find a lot of things if they dig in the right spots." It was just after eight and the sun had just begun setting a few minutes earlier. Grae gazed out over the panoramic view and saw the multicolored goodnight that Mother Nature was leaving. "But I imagine that they would be most interested in finding some evidence of the American Indians who once lived in these valleys."

"Hmm, I knew there were a lot of Indians in the North Carolina Mountains, but I never thought about there being any here."

"Oh my, you've never had the pleasure of hearing my group tour speech about our Native American history, have you? Well, we will have to remedy that, but you might be sorry you asked that question."

Grae shook her head. Mister Abbey had a speech for just about any subject. But the groups of travelers who came to the area via tour buses loved to journey to the top of the mountain and hear his tall tales. They were his captive audience and he could certainly entertain them. During Grae's first week of work, she had accompanied him on one of the rides and heard him recount the legend of the ride of Molly Tynes.

"Well, that might be good," Grae said with a grin. "And I want to hear about Molly Tynes again."

"Oh, my dear, that's a fine story. That young girl must have been a spitfire. Well, I bet she was a lot like you. Just rode on that horse miles and miles through the mountains to warn the good people of Wytheville that those old Yankee soldiers were on their way."

Grae opened her car door. "Is that true, Mister Abbey? Did she really do that?"

Mister Abbey stopped and looked up at the sky. "You know, they say that some of the stars we see on a clear dark night are so many light years away that they don't even exist by the time we see them." Mister Abbey paused and looked back at Grae. "I think history is kind of like that. A lot of things happened or didn't happen all those years ago. Molly might have made that ride that night or she might not have, but we know that those people were warned and they were ready when the Yankee soldiers came. So was the story once true, or something similar? Who knows? But just like looking at those stars that aren't there any more, we get some pleasure and enjoyment from that story, and really, who does that hurt?" Mister Abbey paused again as he opened his own car door. "Besides, short of going back in time, how would anyone really know what happened?"

His comment caught Grae off guard and she found herself feeling uneasy, like he knew something. But, looking up, she saw the same smile that greeted her every day. He had just made a statement, not an accusation. Grae thought for a moment about her journey and how she had learned the real story behind a mystery. Despite the circumstances, the thought made her smile. "Good night, Mister Abbey. See you tomorrow."

"Yes, indeed, and it will be another wonderful and marvelous day!"

SEVEN

It was the first Tuesday in August and pre-registration day at Wytheville Community College. Like many of the first year students from throughout the county, Grae would be receiving a special scholarship. A few years previously, a foundation had been created to provide two full years of paid tuition to any student who graduated from one of the local high schools. In Grae's old life, she probably would have headed off to become a Tar Heel or a Blue Devil or possibly even attend a private college somewhere. But that life was gone and she was just thankful that her mother didn't have to sell her soul for Grae to have an education. A community college education would be a great start for her, and she would get to have more time to figure out what she really wanted to do.

After she met with a counselor and signed up for her classes, Grae planned to have lunch with her mother. She didn't have to report to work until two that day, so they had plenty of time to have a non-rushed lunch. The next week would be Kat's birthday, so Grae wanted to start the celebrating early.

But the registration session ended before she planned and Grae had some time to kill. The counselor had advised her that condition of the scholarship included doing one hundred hours of community service work during the course of each year of classes. There were a variety of agencies that she could do this volunteer work for, but one location jumped off the list. Perhaps she could fulfill her scholarship responsibility and do a little digging into all of the Mansion's mysteries at the same time, by logging her time at the college's genealogy library.

Grae had not been inside the newest building on the college's campus. Smyth Hall was a large, open, modern building that gave off an air of twenty-first century in comparison with the other structures that had been used for decades. Although Grae had not been in too many college libraries, she had visited a few during her junior year of high school. Since she was in several advanced courses in her high school in Charlotte, she had been forced to seek out libraries of higher learning for research for many of the college-like papers she was required to write. She'd found them dark and dreary and sleep inducing no matter how interesting the research topic may have been. This library was bright and open and stimulating. She liked it.

The staff nodded politely as she entered, and she wandered up and down the aisles before she made her way to the genealogy section. Inside the room, she found a pleasant lady who introduced herself as Alice and offered to help her with her research.

"Well, actually, I'm sort of researching to work here," Grae said awkwardly. "I'm starting classes in a few weeks, and this is one of the places on the list where foundation scholarship recipients can volunteer."

Alice stood up and clapped her hands. "That would be

wonderful! The foundation program has been in place for several years, and you are the first student who has shown any interest in volunteering with us!"

Her enthusiasm was great, but Grae wondered if there was some not-so-obvious reason why no one was volunteering.

"I've imagined that most kids your age don't have much of a desire to work with old papers when there are jobs that allow them to interact with children or be outdoors. If you aren't interested in history, this might be a little dull for you."

"Oh, I love history." Grae replied. "It's a big part of my life." While the way Alice might perceive her comment was not Grae's true intent with the words, it was a true statement nonetheless.

"Oh, that's wonderful, but surprising at your age. Is it what you plan to major in?"

"No, not that I know of right now, but, well, part of my interest is because I live in Graham Mansion. My grandpa is the caretaker."

"Oh! You are Kat's daughter!"

"Yes, you know my mother?"

Alice sat back down at her desk. "Yes, I do. Of course, she works here at the college. But we knew each other years ago, since we went to school together for a while." Alice lowered her head and looked at some papers. The sudden movement appeared strange to Grae; she wondered if there was something that Alice was trying to keep from saying.

"Wow! A school friend of my mom's! That's great; I've never met anyone who she grew up with. I'll have to pick your brain about all the embarrassing stories I bet you have." Grae laughed to lighten the mood. It worked. The smile returned to Alice's face.

"So, what would I be doing here?" Grae walked around

the room looking at the bookcases and filing cabinets.

Alice stood up. "Well, there would be many different tasks through the two semesters. There is documenting donations and archiving special documents and, well," Alice picked up a huge stack of manila folders, "there's an endless amount of filing."

"So who comes in here to use the library? People writing research papers or something?" Grae absentmindedly opened and closed a very old book on Alice's desk. She thought that she saw Alice visibly flinch when she touched it.

"Well, sometimes that is the case, but most of the time people are researching their family history." Grae watched as Alice stood up from behind her desk and walked around to the front of it and leaned on it. It was a classic move that teachers made in the classroom. Grae wondered if Alice had been a teacher.

"You see, as immigrants came to this country, many began moving West in the hopes of carving out their own place and success in the new land. A good portion of them came through here because it was on the Great Road, which was one of the main roads that led west. Sometimes people would stop and stay for a while, and then move on again. Because of this, there are many family histories that can be traced back to Southwest Virginia. We are fortunate to have an extensive collection of records here."

"So people travel to here from other parts of the country just to search these records?"

"Yes, but also some will contact us and ask us to do some research for them. That may be one of the things I assign you to work on, if you decide to work here."

"Oh, I think I have already decided." Grae gave Alice a big smile.

"That's great, but there's one thing that I think we need to talk about." Alice sat down in front of Grae. "It's the color of your hair."

"Mom, it's getting greener." Grae sat across from her mother at lunch.

"What's getting greener, dear?" Kat was carefully chewing a bite of chef salad.

"My hair! Haven't you noticed?"

"Well, yes, I have, but I thought you might be experimenting with something, and I didn't want to upset you with any comments."

"No, my hair is turning green all on its own, and I think it has something to do with…" Grae stopped talking and looked around them at the neighboring tables. "Something to do with the trip I took."

Kat stopped chewing and looked at Grae. She swallowed, laid down her fork, and then bit her bottom lip. It was a sign that she was worried.

"Did you ever have anything like this happen to you?"

Kat looked deep into her daughter's eyes. Grae almost felt like she was trying to communicate telepathically. Kat resumed eating her salad. "My hair never changed color."

"Okay, but did anything ever happen to you?"

"Grae, I really don't think that we need to be talking about this."

"Well, if I don't talk to you about this, who am I going to talk to?" Grae stopped eating and looked out the window.

"I'm sorry. That was very insensitive of me. It just scares me so much for you to have experienced the travel." Kat put her fork down again and took a drink of her iced tea. "What time do you get off work this evening?"

"At six, it's a short day for me since I had to come and do registration."

"I'm going to wait at the college for you. You call me when you leave, and I will meet you at my car. I'll call Grandpa and tell him that you and I won't be there for dinner. He and Perry can go out for hamburgers. They will love that." Kat smiled nervously. "It's time we had a talk."

Grae gave her mother a weak smile. "I'm sorry, Mom. I know you probably don't want to think about your trips again, but there's so much I don't understand."

"We should have talked about it as soon as you returned."

Grae paused and watched her mother look in the mirror of her compact and apply lipstick.

"Oh, I decided where I am going to do my scholarship volunteer work."

Kat filled in her top lip before replying. "Where's that?"

"With Alice at the Genealogy Library."

Kat's hand trembled and she smeared lipstick on her cheek. When she lowered the compact and looked at Grae, she sort of resembled a circus clown. Grae started to laugh, but noticed that her mother had a strange look in her eyes.

"I'm not sure that is such a good idea."

"Why? I thought that during my free time, there's bound to be free time with that job, I could do some more research on the Mansion for our tour."

"Well, that's true, but…"

"Who knows? I might even decide to major in history."

Kat crinkled her brow. "You probably should think that through a little more. The options of using a history degree are rather limited."

"Whatever," Grae said. "But I still think that it will be a good scholarship job, and I like Alice."

"Yes, Alice is nice." Kat finished fixing her lipstick error and stood up from the table. "I'll see you after you get off work. Don't forget to text me."

EIGHT

"Grae, no one plans on this happening." Grae met her mother in the college parking lot that evening. It was especially warm, so they decided to get some milkshakes and have their talk in one of the local parks. Under the shade of a huge tree, they sat across from each other at a picnic table. Grae was relieved that an ever-so-slight breeze could now be felt. Even the normally cool air on top of the mountain hadn't been very cool that day. It was dog days, as Grandpa Mack called them, for sure.

Absentmindedly, Kat pulled the straw in and out of her chocolate milkshake several times. The straw against the lid made a creaking noise. It reminded Grae of the sound of the hinges on the door of her cell in 1786.

"Are you listening to me? Grae! Grae!"

Grae looked up at her mother and realized that she had been talking to her. The memory of her jail cell must have taken Grae back to wherever it was her mind was going these days.

"I'm sorry, what did you say?"

"You are having flashbacks, aren't you?" Kat's worried look intensified.

"I don't know that I would call them flashbacks. I don't really feel like I am going back there. It's just that something will trigger a memory from then and I will lose time somehow."

"You mentioned before about your feelings for Gav and the young man you met in 1786. Is that what those instances are like?"

Grae thought for a moment. "No, that's different. It's like when I am with Gav, I do sort of flashback to Patrick."

"This Patrick has a hold on you. You've carried him back with you. He was a McGavock?"

"Yes."

"Hmmm, that's interesting. He probably was indeed an ancestor of Gav's. That is what may be making this hold stronger."

"It's really starting to bother Gav, and I don't know what to do about it." Grae started pulling her straw up and down in her strawberry milkshake, and then heard the sound and stopped. "He thinks I am interested in someone else."

"I think you just need to reassure him. Pay more attention to him. His life is about to change; he's probably afraid you will change too."

"The sad thing is that I have changed, and I see him differently now, but I can't explain to him why."

"No, that wouldn't be a good idea. Even people, who you think will understand, really don't. They just think you are crazy."

Grae watched her mother. Kat seemed to be a million miles away in her thoughts. "Were you and Alice friends growing up?"

Kat looked at her daughter and gave a half grin. "For a while."

"Did she know about your journeys?"

"She was my best friend. She knew everything. It was a mistake."

"Is that why you don't want me to work at the library?"

"At first, yes, but now that I've had a chance to think about it, I was wrong. It will be a good opportunity for you to check into some of the Mansion's history and maybe it will change her opinion of our family." Kat became silent and began drinking her shake again.

"We're not going to discuss Alice anymore, are we?"

"Not if I can help it. But we will now talk about your hair." Kat got up and walked around behind Grae. She ran her fingers through Grae's hair. It was getting longer, but still just barely touched her shoulders.

"I've never seen anything quite like this. I thought it was just like a frost had appeared, but there is green down to the roots of your hair. I just can't imagine what this means. I wish your grandmother was here to see it."

"Really? Granny Belle? Did she travel too?"

"Oh no, this is purely a Graham trait; we get it from your grandfather's ancestry. But Mom knew a lot about it because of her closeness to Brenda Grace."

"Who was Brenda Grace? That's not a name I ever remember hearing before."

Kat sat back down at the table and drank some more of her shake. "Brenda Grace was your Grandpa's older sister, a lot older. She was about twenty years older than him. She was a traveler, and she liked it so much that she spent more time doing that than living her own life."

Grae's eyes got bigger as her mother continued to talk.

"Grae, the main reason I am so concerned about you travelling is that it is dangerous, pure and simple. You saw some of that. Even from what little you told me, I know that your life was in danger. People can go back in time and get lost." Kat bowed her head and paused. "Some people go back in time and die."

"How do you know that? I mean, where's the proof?"

"There are many rules in time travel." Grae started to interrupt and tell her mother about what The General had taught her, but decided to keep that information to herself for the time being.

"You can go back and experience another time period and make friends and have a good time, sometimes. But you have to be careful where you go and who you interact with and how deep you get into this other time."

"Brenda Grace babysat your grandmother long before she married Grandpa and apparently Brenda Grace had a flair for telling stories. But later, when Mother was older, Brenda Grace showed her a journal that she had kept about her travels. The stories she had told your grandmother were actually the adventures she had experienced in several different times."

"Wow! I would love to see that journal!" Grae paused. "Will I find it in Granny's boxes?"

"No, I am afraid you will not. It ceased to exist."

"Someone destroyed it?"

"No, it ceased to exist, just as Brenda Grace did."

"What?"

"That is one of the rules of time travel. We think that Brenda Grace died while she was back in time, because, according to your grandmother and grandfather, all of a sudden Brenda Grace was gone and so was all evidence that she had ever existed. Photographs of her disappeared, her personal belongings vanished, it was as if that someone came in one night, kidnapped her, and everything she was involved in." Kat reached over and took Grae's hand.

"That's why it concerns me so. I admit, I went on several journeys and had some interesting experiences. But, there were also some horrible things that occurred that I can never make right."

Grae started to speak, but her mother rose suddenly. "Okay! Enough of the glum! That milkshake only made me hungry. Let's go get some Mexican food and talk about maybe getting some special hair treatment."

Kat's conversation gave Grae many things to ponder, but it ended with the decision for Grae to visit Lucy the next day and ask for special treatment. Kat would rather have sent Grae to a more professional salon, but considering the circumstances it was decided that it was better to take green hair to someone who might not be as likely to discuss it throughout the community. Lucy might be crazy, but she was quiet crazy and wouldn't spread any rumors about Mack's family.

Grae's classes would start at the beginning of the following week. Gav was moving into his college dorm on Sunday. Grae needed to get something done to her hair soon, so the following morning she made a visit to Lucy.

"Well, Miss Grae White, how are you this beautiful Blue Ridge Mountain morning?" Grae found Lucy in her backyard, picking tomatoes. It reminded Grae that she must devote some time to getting tomatoes ready Friday, the day she and her mother had chosen to make spaghetti sauce.

"Hi, Lucy, your tomatoes are beautiful. Are you going to can some?"

"No, no, I'll leave that task to you, but I am going to

freeze some. It's much easier, and then they work great for soup or chili or sauce. But enough garden gab, did you come for me to give you a new 'do before you head to college?"

Grae followed Lucy through the back door into her kitchen. Before she could say anything, Lucy had turned around and looked at her hair. "Emerald City! Darling, what has happened to your hair?"

"Well, Lucy, I really don't know."

"I thought your hair was doing something mighty strange when I trimmed it back there in the spring, but goodness, this is seriously unfortunate." Lucy walked all around her, running her fingers through Grae's hair, then pulling on Grae's head to look at the roots. "We better get you in the chair quick."

Grae found herself back in Lucy's salon wishing that she could figure out something creative to tell Lucy about her hair. But versions of the truth weren't her specialty; her mother had taught her only to have one.

"Okay, now, we had the talk about drugs, and I believe you. You haven't been prescribed any new medication, have you?" Grae shook her head no.

"Didn't think so, too young for that. You've not been abducted by aliens lately either, have you?" Grae gave Lucy a strange look. "Hey, it can happen. We don't know what's out there." Lucy leaned Grae back and began washing her hair.

"Well, it must be time travel residue then."

Grae rose up straight in the chair, knocking the sprayer out of Lucy's hand and sending it wiggling out of control all over the sink. It took Lucy a couple of seconds to get it turned off. Both she and Grae got drenched in the meantime.

"What, what do you mean?" Grae stood up and shook some of the water off.

"You didn't have to get all excited. I'm going to have to go get the mop. Get some of those towels from over on the shelf and dry your chair off." Grae grabbed some towels and began working on the chair. Her mind was racing about Lucy's comment.

Lucy returned and began mopping the floor.

"I'm sorry, Lucy."

"Don't worry about it, darling, it's just a little water. Sit back down in that chair and let's get back to business." Grae returned to her chair and Lucy leaned her back again and shampooed and rinsed her hair. After she had toweled Grae's hair and turned her around to face the mirror, she began to speak.

"Your reaction pretty much answered my question." She looked at Grae in the mirror and winked. "So, now comes the hard part. How are we going to make that green disappear?"

"But…. Lucy, how?" Grae couldn't say the words.

"Honey, you don't grow up around this property and not know about time travel. There's been a Graham in just about every generation who went on a trip or two, and they all came back with trouble with their hair." Lucy turned the blow dryer on and began flipping Grae's hair with her fingers. After she dried it, she continued. "Now, I can't say that I have actually worked on the hair myself, before you, but my grandmother and her sisters and their mother, they were all hair people and, boy, did they have the stories."

Grae continued to stare straight ahead at Lucy's reflection in the mirror.

"You look about like that green in your hair." Lucy laughed and twirled Grae around to face her. She took hold of her hands.

"Listen, your secret is safe with me. I think it is a grand thing. I'm sure your mother has given you this speech already, but you are going to hear it again. Be careful. Most people go and come back just fine, but a few, well, it's not pretty. And, some people don't come back at all."

NINE

It was amazing what hair dye could accomplish. Lucy decided that a funky shag cut would leave Grae's hair length and a frosty highlight would probably mask the green. Her work was amazing. She gave Grae a special shampoo to use and had sent her on her way with a wink and a request. "If you ever take the notion to travel to Memphis any time in the last century before 1977, you just grab my hand before you go."

Grae thought about this request the next day, as she began to peel the fresh tomatoes that Grandpa had picked at sunrise. She knew that Lucy wanted to go back and meet Elvis and that made her smile, but the request also made her think. She wondered if you could take someone with you on a journey and what would happen if you did.

It wasn't every teenager's ideal way to spend a day off from work, but Grae had peeled about two bushels of tomatoes by lunch time.

"You've worked fast," Grandpa said when he came inside

to get a sandwich. "You did just what I told you, didn't you?"

"Yep, if it worked for Granny, it had to be a good tip." Her grandfather had told her to get a pot of boiling water going on the stove, and then another large bowl of ice water nearby. He told her to drop the washed tomatoes into the boiling water for about thirty seconds, and then quickly take them out and plunge them in the ice water.

"It worked like a charm. The tomato skins just slid right off. I've chopped the tomatoes up and put them in the extra fridge on the back porch. Later this afternoon, I will start chopping up the onion and peppers. Mom is getting some garlic at the market on her lunch break. We will start making Graghetti Sauce when she gets home."

"Gra what?" Grandpa reached for another handful of potato chips from the opened bag in front of him.

"We've been trying to give some of our canned goods some neat names. Instead of Graham Spaghetti Sauce, we are going to call it Graghetti. I thought it was cute."

"I wouldn't buy it." Perry walked through the back door. "People will call it Graghetti. Sounds gross."

"Well, I've not seen you buy any food for this house," Grandpa Mack said, with a hearty laugh. "So, let Grae see how the real consumers act."

Grandpa Mack winked at Grae and shook his head as he watched Perry make a sandwich. The turkey was two inches thick with at least three slices of cheese.

"Are you sure you just want two slices of bread there, son? You've got enough meat and cheese there for a couple of sandwiches."

"Gotta bulk up on my protein, Gramps. Football practice is in full swing. I got to be building some muscle."

Grae rolled her eyes and continued working on the

tomatoes. Soon everyone had left her alone in the kitchen. As she finished cleaning up, she decided that she would rest for a while and look through some of her grandmother's boxes. Grandpa had found a new one in his closet that she hadn't seen before. She was anxious to delve into its contents.

She went upstairs to her room to change her clothes. Upon entering the room, she looked at the panel that was still loose under the window and remembered that she hadn't finished looking at the box that she found inside it.

"I bet there is some information in that box about Squire David." She jumped as the window slammed shut again, the same one as before. "You can't scare me!" Grae looked around and shouted. "You better be careful, Squire David, I'll go back and haunt you." Stillness filled the room and ever, ever so faintly, Grae almost thought she heard a little shy giggle.

"There were three or four letters in the box that Grandpa found that were different — so formal." Grae began telling her mother about her afternoon discoveries as they worked on the spaghetti sauce that evening. Her mother hadn't seemed especially interested in the contents of the box until then. But now she seemed to perk up as Grae mentioned that letters were included.

"I love old letters. It's like this personal peek into someone else's life. There's always good stuff in letters, even boring ones."

"Well, I wouldn't exactly call these letters boring, but some parts are kind of dry. When I showed them to Grandpa, he said that there was a whole box of letters that was donated to the library about ten or fifteen years ago. I'm going to try and find those, too. There's got to be some good stuff for the tour in all these letters."

"I'm sure there is." Kat put a lid on the pot she was stirring. There were three large pots of spaghetti sauce now cooking on the stove. "This needs to simmer for about another hour before we jar it. Let's get something cold to drink and a snack and go sit on the back porch. It's sweltering in here."

Kat poured each of them a tall glass of iced tea. Setting the glasses and the pitcher on a tray, she also added a plate of cheese straws. It was another goodie that Grae had been experimenting with to sell at Big Walker. This was the last that was left of the perfection batch, as Grae had deemed it. "Bring some of those letters," Kat said. "You can read me a story."

As they settled on the porch and Kat began to munch on the cheese straws, Grae looked at the letters she had brought. "There are many letters in this box from Robert Graham, Squire's father, to a Major Joseph Graham in North Carolina. Apparently, Robert Graham held this Major in high regard. Let me read one to you, you'll love the language.

Robert Graham
Baltimore Waggon Road
Wythe County
Virginia

7 September, 1794

> *The Honourable Major Joseph Graham, Esq.*
> *Vesuvius Plantation*
> *Lincoln County*
> *North Carolina*

His Honourable Major Graham,

It is my hope that this correspondence finds you well, your family flourishing, and businesses prospering. I thank you for your letter of this December past as I read it with keen interest and admiration. God has surely blessed our lives and continues to set our course.

I write to accept your most generous invitation to visit your new mansion home with my sons Samuel, James, and John. Upon completion of the threshing and gathering these next two weeks we shall make our way to your new home. Son James is most eager to observe the forges under your ownership and management as he has apprenticed as a blacksmith. Sir you also give me undeserved credit by way of your thorough account of your newest family enterprise, Vesuvius Furnace, constructed on Anderson Creek. While the hills of Wythe County also possess an abundance of iron ore, coal, limestone, waterways, forests, and several successful iron furnaces, this iron-making process that you describe is beyond my small understanding of such things. We are in great anticipation of our visit there as we may further witness and learn from Yourself, Captain Brevard, and Major John Davidson. Once more his Excellency's generosity is only outweighed by his limitless sense of humility.

As I read your letters past, I note with awe your vast avocations as postmaster, Sheriff, Justice of the Peace, and State Legislator! Does your Honour also continue to set bones and stitch open wounds as you so skillfully performed on myself at the Battle of

Ramseur's Mill so long ago? As I speak of Ramseur's Mill, I ask do you recall a Captain Benjamin Newton from Rutherfordton, who fought valiantly beside us under General William Lee Davidson? To my everlasting appreciation Captain Newton gave chase and fired upon a most irritating Lobsterback who was about to use his bayonet upon my chest. I intend for my sons to meet Captain Newton upon our departing journey from Vesuvius Furnace as we have corresponded these many years since the War for Liberty.

Please allow me one additional indulgence your Honour. Would it be too assuming for me to make a humble request of Mrs. Graham? Perchance would Mrs. Graham do me the honour of permitting myself to join you for your traditional "mush and milk" evening meal? To my profound amazement, Mary, my wife of these four years past, has prepared a similar dish here for my nightly consumption and I find it the perfect accommodation to aid the digestion!

It is with the assurance of great confidence and esteem with which I have the honour to be Sir,

Yours Obediently,
Robert Graham

"That was delicious," Kat said with a smile as she sipped the last of her beverage.

"Are you still thirsty?"

Kat laughed. "No, I meant that the letter was delicious."

Grae smiled. It was her mother's southern-speak.

"Robert Graham sounds like a good man." Kat paused.

"You know, Grae, everything I have ever heard about Squire David Graham has portrayed him as a very hard, mean man. But you can't help but wonder what caused him to be that way. It doesn't sound like he had a cruel father. Children aren't born mean, something happens to make a person become hard and cruel. I hope you find something in those letters at the college that make us like him just a little bit more."

TEN

"Are you sure you don't want me to go with you and help you unpack?" It was their last full day together. In less than twenty-four hours, Gav would be moving into his dorm at Virginia Tech. Grae was worried that this distance would not make Gav's heart grow fonder.

"Nah, Mom will be there. She's the queen of unpacking. She's had some experience with my sisters, remember?"

"Yeah, but, I just thought…"

"You'd like to check out the coeds in my dorm. None of them are as pretty as you." Gav twirled her hair around his finger. "I'm not sure about this new hairstyle, but I'm glad the green is gone."

"For now," Grae said, under her breath.

"What?"

"Yeah, wow, Lucy did a good job, didn't she? I think it might have been a reaction to that tetanus shot I took."

"Yeah, I guess it could have been. You might mention that to your doctor."

Grae nodded her head and looked out across the back yard of the Mansion. She thought she saw a small animal darting behind one of the sheds.

"Well, are you going to get into the car?"

"Oh, yeah," Grae smiled and laughed nervously.

A worried look crossed Gav's face. They both got into the car simultaneously. Before turning the engine on, Gav turned to face her. "Listen, I've been doing a lot of thinking, and I am going to ask you a question and I want a straight answer. Not what you think I want to hear, just how you really feel. Can you do that?"

Grae shook her head and held her breath.

"Are you in love with someone other than me?"

At first, Grae felt a little torn as to how to respond. But, then, suddenly a realization came over her. In this century and two hundred years ago, it was really Gav that had stolen her heart. The other Gav just came in a slightly different package.

"No." Grae gave him a big smile. That was truly the truth, well mostly.

"Okay," Gav sighed. "Okay," he said again smiling. "That's the best answer I've gotten out of you in months and so I'm going to take it and not question it." He turned back toward the steering wheel and started the engine.

"Oh, and by the way," he said, as he turned around to watch as he backed out. "My answer to that question would be the same as yours."

There was a peace that washed over Grae. The past year had been horrible in many respects. Her father's trial and imprisonment, their move to Virginia; it was as if she, Perry, and her mother were being tested. Just when Grae thought that her life was developing a little normalcy again, she went on a trip. It wasn't long in minutes, but the travel had a depth in time beyond her imagination. What she had seen and experienced in 1786 had changed her.

As they drove down the driveway, Grae thought about how her journey had never really taken her very far off of this very property, but what a great distance it had truly felt like. It made her wonder what another couple of hundred years into the future would bring. How different life on this land would be when another century rolled over.

"I was thinking that we could go spend some time on the river," Gav said, jolting Grae back to the present situation. "Walk on the trail, take a dip in the river, maybe fish a little, just relax, are you surprised?"

"Shocked! You asked me to bring along a bathing suit, running shoes, fishing pole, and a picnic lunch, I thought we were going to the mall."

"Oh, there's my sarcastic girl! I've missed her."

"I've missed her, too. I promise to have a mouthful of sarcasm ready each time you call."

"What about when you visit? I've already arranged for you and Perry to have tickets to all the home games this fall."

"Oh, wow! Perry will love that!"

"Just Perry? I was hoping you would love that too."

"Well, sure, I just mean that he is so much more into the game. I look forward to seeing a very small version of you getting hit on the field."

"If I'm lucky, freshmen don't often get to set foot on the field. I will probably spend most of my time warming the bench."

"I don't know about that, they will recognize talent when they see it."

"Babe, you forget, I have been practicing for weeks. Maybe they will let me carry the ball out of the locker room."

They rode to the New River Trail State Park on U.S. 52. It was a great drive with lots of interesting houses and farms along the way. Grae wondered if the path was used in the late 1700s when Nannie Baker and her family moved to the area that later became known as Baker Island. She remembered Nannie's kindness toward her and how horrible it was for her husband to have been murdered.

Gav's voice singing with the radio brought her back to reality. She watched as he tapped the steering wheel like a drum, keeping beat with the tune. As the sun shone through the window, she saw the golden highlights of his hair glisten. His chiseled features gave him the look of a Greek god and amazingly he loved little mortal her. She had never imagined that she would find love in her teen years. Her life plan had always included marrying a career before a person. But, somehow, she could imagine herself in this seat next to him for a lifetime.

"You look so happy. What are you thinking about?" Gav stopped singing and reached over to take Grae's hand.

"You. You make me happy."

"That's what I want to do." Gav slowed down and pulled into the parking area. The vast New River rippled in green before them.

"Did you know that despite the name, this is one of the oldest rivers in the world?" Gav said as he got out of the car and headed to the trunk.

"No, I didn't know that." Grae got out of the car and walked toward the river as Gav got their stuff from the trunk. The bright sunlight reflecting on the water was almost blinding, so Grae walked under a tall oak that stood mightily on the riverbank. The rich green of the river mesmerized her. She felt as if she was looking into a deep hole, falling, falling…

"Grae!" Gav's hands on her arms shaking her brought her back. Grae looked at him wild-eyed. She could see that he was shouting, but his voice was distorted. She saw a glimpse of another man in front of her. He was looking at his hands and screaming.

"Grae! Grae! What is the matter? You're scaring me."

It was as much as she could take. It had happened one too many times. Grae surrendered. The tears flowed.

ELEVEN

Grae had been sitting on the blanket Gav had placed under the tree for half an hour. For a while, he had sat beside of her, trying to comfort her, but her tears kept flowing, so he decided it might be best to just leave her alone for a while.

"I'll be just down the river a few hundred feet. Okay?" Grae nodded and hiccupped. Crying made her do that. She thought of Joseph Baker and his sugar remedy.

She had to get control of herself. This was her last day with Gav. She just couldn't explain the feeling that came over her as she looked into the river. It transported her. Who was that man she saw and why was he looking at his hands that way? It almost looked as if he was crying out to God; the emotion on his face was terrifying.

Reaching into her tote bag, she retrieved her small pocketbook. Grae didn't wear much makeup, but she knew that her face was probably one big red whelp from crying. She reached for her mineral powder compact. She began hiding the redness with a thin layer of powder and was almost done before she looked at her eyes.

"I'm glad I didn't bother with mascara today," Grae said out loud to herself. "At least I don't look like a raccoon." Then she glimpsed her eyes and noticed that she hadn't put in her contacts. Two different colored eyes stared back at her and it hit her. Her eyes were the same as the man in her vision.

"Hey, baby! Are you feeling better?" Gav yelled from down the river.

Grae quickly closed the compact and threw it back in the bag. "This isn't going to ruin my day," she said to herself.

"I'm ready to fish!" she yelled at Gav and quickly ran in his direction.

It was a good day to fish. Gav reeled in several small muskies and a small mouth bass, but it was Grae who had the catch of the day, a huge catfish.

"Wow! That will make one great meal!" Gav said, as he helped Grae pull it out of the water. "I bet your mother could really cook that up."

"No, catfish is Grandpa Mack's specialty; Cajun catfish to be exact."

"Oh, that sounds like a wonderful going-away dinner!"

"I thought you and I were going out tonight." Grae sat down on the riverbank as Gav removed the hook from the catfish's mouth.

"That was before you reeled in dinner." A huge smile crossed his face, and Grae's stomach did a little flip. It was turning out to be a good day.

"Well, I better let Mom know. She will want to make all the sides that she usually does and her special hushpuppies." Grae began quickly typing a text message to her mother. At first, Kat had been very anti-texting, but later gave in once

Perry and Grae again had cell phones.

"Your mom makes special hushpuppies? Why am I just discovering this on my last day here?" Gav collapsed down next to Grae and pulled her into a hug on top of him. A feeling of nervousness began to overtake her. Their relationship had undergone many highs and lows over the last few months. Their busy schedules left little time together and even less time alone.

"We've never talked about this," Gav said. He looked deeply into Grae's eyes. After a few moments, Grae looked away, uncomfortably. It was hard to look away from someone when you were lying down face-to-face.

Gav ran his finger down the side of her cheek. "Look at me; we need to talk about this." Grae sighed.

"You know, you've been kind of distant, kind of strange this summer. At first, I thought that there might be someone else, but I asked around and no one had seen you with anyone. Perry didn't..."

Grae sat up and whirled around to face him. "You asked around?! Don't you trust me at all?"

"Hey, simmer down." Gav sat up next to her. "I trust you plenty, but every time I kiss you, I feel like there's a third person there with us. I hardly ever see you. You used to come by the store after you got off work." Gav stood up and began pacing in front of her.

"I've been working all summer, Gav. That part-time job on the mountain turned into almost full-time hours after Mister Abbey's niece decided to go to summer school; and Mom and I have worked night and day on all that canning." Grae stood up. "I've got to work, I have no choice."

"Yeah, well," Gav's voice began to sound angry. "Well, who's..." He paused, seemingly weighing his words. He turned around and faced Grae. "Who's Patrick?"

The words slapped Grae in the face, and she sank down to the ground. She put her face in her hands and unconsciously said, "Oh, no."

"Yeah, that's what I thought." Gav began gathering up their stuff and throwing it into the trunk. "I should have known you were too good to be true."

Hearing the anger in his voice and actions, Grae jumped up and ran to the car. "No, Gav, you don't understand."

"Oh, I understand! You're not the first girl to fool around on me. You're just the first one who I actually thought was different." Blankets and fishing rods and a tackle box seemed to be flying through the air like footballs. It would have been funny, if it wasn't so scary.

"Girls love dating the jock, Mister Popularity. But then they don't like it when they aren't the center of attention. They forget that being all-star in four sports takes hours of practice and working out every day." The tackle box didn't quite make its touchdown location in the trunk. The contents went everywhere on the graveled road.

"No, they are out cruising around and talking to every Tom, Dick, and Patrick they can find while you are trying to not fail calculus between push-ups. OUCH!" A fishing hook had punctured Gav's palm as he hurriedly picked it up.

Grae knelt down beside him and took his hand in hers and carefully removed the hook from his palm. "Patrick doesn't exist, Gav."

Gav jerked his hand away from her and wiped the blood on his t-shirt.

Red blood, white t-shirt, Grae began to sway. "No!" Grae screamed as she suddenly stood up, tears pouring down her face.

"Doesn't exist? Well, that's a new one. So you are interested in some imaginary guy. Give me a break, Grae."

"Gav, you don't understand." Grae grabbed Gav's arm. He stopped and turned to face her.

"Then explain it." He looked Grae straight in the eyes. It was a hard, hurt stare.

Grae took a deep breath. "If I tell you, you will think I am crazy and break up with me."

Gav removed his arm from Grae's grasp. "Well, the breakup part is probably going to happen unless you convince me that Patrick really never existed."

The words hit Grae hard. She knew it was true. But how in the world could she explain Patrick? "Take me home and I'll explain there. We've got to get this fish to Grandpa. He'll have to filet it first."

"I don't think I will be staying for dinner now." Gav got in the car.

"Mom's expecting you now. Don't make me undo it." Grae got into the car. "You may feel differently after we talk."

"I really hope that is true, Grae. But I don't see how."

As they approached the Mansion, Grae saw a truck that she didn't recognize parked in front of Lucy's house. "I bet that is Lucy's brother," Grae said, breaking the silence that had engulfed the car the whole way back.

"Who?" Gav said.

"Lucy's brother. She told me that her niece was going to come and stay with her for a little while." Idle chit-chat did not lure Gav into talking; he just kept driving and turned into the Mansion driveway. Grae noticed a young girl, maybe around twelve years old sitting on the porch. The instant that she saw Grae, she began waving and smiling. Grae smiled back and waved. It felt good to smile.

Grandpa Mack was waiting for them outside.

"I hear that my little Grae Belle has the makings of an angler," Grandpa said, slapping Gav on the back as they both walked to the trunk of the car.

"Yes, sir."

Grae looked back up on the hill, but the young girl was gone.

"Sakes alive, child, that is one nice fish. Did you catch these other little fellows in here, Gav?" Grandpa poked around the cooler, chuckling under his breath.

"No, Grae caught those too, sir." Gav's mood was not improving.

"Good thing you are sweet on her then. That would be hard to swallow if you weren't."

Grae couldn't listen any more. "Gav, I'm going to go inside and let Mom know we are here. You want something to drink?"

"Ah, maybe I should just..." Gav began to speak, looking at the ground.

"You are gonna have one of the best dinners of your life, son." Grandpa picked up the cooler and headed to the back of the house. "This will be some kind of send-off."

Grae wasn't about to meet Gav's eyes after Grandpa's last statement. She hurried up the steps. "I'll be right back."

"Mom! Mom!" Grae began yelling before she even got the door completely opened. She found Kat in the kitchen shredding cabbage.

"Oh, you're back already. Did you have a good..." Kat stopped mid-sentence when she saw her daughter's face. 'Good' had no place in the conversation. "What's wrong? What happened?"

"Don't hug me." Grae said, stopping her mother who was already walking toward her with arms outstretched. "I will start crying, and I don't have time to cry right now."

Kat sat down at the table. Grae did the same.

"Gav confronted me about Patrick." Kat's brow furrowed, but she remained silent.

"I must have mentioned him or called Gav, Patrick, or something. He thinks that I am involved with him. He's even asked around about him, maybe even asked Perry."

"Well, that explains that conversation." Kat shook her head.

"What conversation?"

"Your brother asked me if I knew if you were interested in someone else. I didn't think anything about it at the time. I just said no."

"What am I going to do? Gav's going to break up with me and go off to Tech. He is going to meet some great girl, and I'll just be the girl he went to prom with."

"Just tell him that there isn't anyone else. He'll believe you."

"No, he won't, not now. He knows that Patrick was real. He could see it on my face." Grae got up and went to the refrigerator and got out two bottles of soda. "This is going to be the worst day of my life."

Grae began to walk out of the kitchen.

"Wait, Grae, come back." Kat walked to the doorway as Grae turned around.

"Tell him the truth."

"How can I do that, Mom? He'll think I'm crazy."

"If your feelings for Gav could transcend time and make you love his great-great-whoever two hundred years ago.... If this Patrick risked his life for you because his feelings were so strong, then, well, some of that has got to be inside of Gav. If he loves you, he'll find a way to believe you. You've got to tell him the truth. The truth will set you free."

Grae heard the voice of Sal as her mother made that final statement. The comfort she felt at that moment gave her a strength that was beyond that moment in time. She smiled. It felt good to smile.

Grae found Gav in the barn, sitting on a hay bale. "I wanted some shade."

"I brought you a soda." Grae handed him the bottle. She noticed that one of the Gators sat nearby. "Let's go for a ride. I need to tell you something."

Grae thought he might object, but Gav just nodded and got into the driver's seat.

They'd driven across a couple of acres before Grae asked him to stop. Once again, they were gazing out onto water. This time it was the ripples of Cedar Run Creek. Somehow that was comforting, and Grae heard the words of her mother and Sal in her head.

"Gav, this is going to be hard for you to understand and even harder for you to believe, but please hear me out before you comment or pass judgment." They were still sitting side by side. Grae turned toward him, and he glanced at her and shook his head.

"Before we moved here, I never really thought much about the past. History wasn't one of my favorite subjects at all. I just thought it was all about a lot of old stuff and that today's world was so much better. Didn't think I had much reason to care about what happened before me." Grae got out of the cart and walked around.

"Then, I came here and everything is old. I found myself

living in a big house that has more lives in it than those who are living there." Gav's eyebrows raised and he shook his head.

"Yeah, I know you think I am talking about Carrie's haunted theories and you can believe what your mind lets you. But not every being fully leaves here when they pass and it's not about haunting." Grae sat down on an old tree stump beside the path and began to absentmindedly pick little wildflowers that were scattered around it.

"A house as old as Graham Mansion has lived a lot of lives and meant things to different people. For some, it was a showplace, to show others what wealth could buy. I lived in a house like that in Charlotte. For others, it was a place to work, paid or unpaid; more slaves than we want to know about broke their backs keeping this property up. Some found it to be a place of refuge, of safety, a home. They felt loved and cared for within the walls. They spent happy hours here." Grae stood up and walked toward the front of the cart. She looked Gav straight in the eye.

"For too many, this property was a place of sadness, heartache, tragedy. It was a prison."

Gav narrowed his eyes and tilted his head. "Grae, I don't understand what all this has to do with..."

"I asked you to hear me out." Grae heard the sternness in her voice. "Please, Gav."

He shook his head.

"I didn't know that this place would cast a spell on me. I didn't know that it would make me learn things about myself and my family that I wouldn't have dreamed in my wildest nightmares. I didn't know that I would take a journey that would change me forever. I didn't know that I would fall in love with you twice."

"What do you mean, journey? You've not been on any

trips since you have been here. Or, at least, none that I know about. Is that how you met that Patrick guy?"

He hadn't heard her last sentence at all.

"You're not going to listen to me, are you? You've already made up your mind. You probably never cared about me anyway." Grae began to walk down the path, away from Gav.

"Now, hold on a minute. I'm not the one who's cheated. You said you wanted to explain." Gav began to follow her.

"You said you would listen!" Grae swung around, not realizing how close Gav was behind here. She found that her face was now in his chest and again, she saw the buttons of Patrick's coat in front of her. "Oh, no, not again." Grae swayed and collapsed on the ground.

"What keeps happening to you, Grae?" Gav lifted her up. "I will listen."

Grae looked up and saw dark clouds approaching. "We better head back toward the house. It looks like there may be a storm approaching."

They jumped into the Gator and began driving toward the Mansion, but the storm was quicker than they were. They sought shelter in one of the many old buildings that were scattered across the property. This one was a very old barn that was still used to store hay for the cattle that grazed in the nearby pastures. It was one of the buildings that she and Perry had explored in the spring. She knew that it had a huge hay loft. They could watch the storm from there and she could finish her story.

"Perry and I found this building when we explored some of the property," Grae said as she climbed the ladder ahead of Gav to the loft. "There are a couple of mattresses up here that we can sit on. Grandpa says that the workers take breaks up here while they are baling hay."

Grae sat down on the mattress that was closest to the doors that Gav had just opened. It would be a while before the sun set, but the storm gave everything a dark ominous look.

"Continue your story."

"Gav, something happened to me in early May, just a few weeks before the prom." He didn't say anything, just continued to look at her.

Grae bit her bottom lip.

"Just say it."

"I found out...well, it all started with me getting dizzy."

"Oh, oh, I know what you are going to say now. Oh, it's worse than I thought." Gav stood up and walked to the ladder. "I never would have dreamed that about you."

"What? What? You can't possibly know what I am going to say." Grae stood up and walked toward him.

"I can't say it. Oh, I don't believe it!"

"Say it!"

"You're pregnant!"

At first, Grae laughed, and then she got mad. She rushed toward Gav and just barely pushed him not realizing that he was so close to the edge of the loft. Gav teetered on the edge. Grae reached to pull him back. This movement went back and forth a few seconds until they both went falling, falling down.

Gav landed on his back on a five-foot high stack of hay. Grae landed on top of him. When he realized that they were both okay, Gav started to laugh.

"I'm not pregnant," Grae said. "I've never even..."

"Okay, okay." Gav picked some pieces of hay out of Grae's hair. "Just tell me. Tell me how you met this Patrick. Tell me what he means to you."

Grae took a deep breath. She started to move, but decided that e her close position to him might work to her advantage.

"His name is Patrick McGavock. I only knew him for a few hours, in 1786."

Gav sprang up, pushing Grae off him. "McGavock! Is this some kind of joke?"

"I said 1786 and you reacted to McGavock? What did you think I meant?"

"Well, probably that you travelled back in time."

Grae's mouth flew open and her eyes bugged out.

"How, how…you said…how?" Her words were one long jumble.

"Did you meet some Indians back there?" Gav laughed. Grae wasn't laughing.

"Okay, bad joke. I'm trying to ease the tension." Grae's mouth was still open in shock.

"Everyone knows that the Grahams can travel in time."

"Everyone?" Grae began to pace.

"Well, maybe not everyone, but some people do. My grandfather used to talk about it." Gav sat down on a hay bale. "So the story goes, it really started with the McGavocks. One of the McGavock women married a Graham and had a daughter and she could travel in time, but then she also married a Graham and people forgot that it was actually through the McGavocks that the power had come from."

"What?"

"Yes, it really started with a McGavock from Ireland."

"What?" Grae didn't believe what she was hearing.

"I'll explain it to you later. So tell me more about this relative of mine. Did he try to make a move on you? Because I don't mind kicking an old guy's butt if he is messing with my girl."

"First of all, he wasn't old. He was about your age. And, second, why do you so easily believe I travelled back in time?"

"Like I said, everyone knows…"

"That the Grahams can time travel," Grae finished his sentence. "But, what made you believe that I had?"

"Well, I guess I didn't know for sure, but there were just things I observed that made me wonder." Gav began pulling pieces of hay out from the bale he was sitting on.

"Like?"

"Well, one day your hands were all smooth and girlie and the next day there were callouses on your palms," Gav stopped talking and reached for Grae's hands, turning them over to face palm up. "I know you live on a farm, but callouses take time to develop, it's not just from one day of hard work."

Grae looked down at her hands, while less visible, the callouses were still there. Hard labor side-by-side with the slaves had created them.

"A few weeks before the prom you just seemed different, like you had aged. I knew that you were more mature than most girls your age when I met you, but I thought that was mostly because of everything that your family had gone through with your father."

A lone tear ran down the side of Grae's face.

"In some ways, you just seemed, I don't know," Gav let go of Grae's hands. "You seemed hard, like you were on the other side of something that you wished you hadn't seen."

Grae turned away, not wanting Gav to see the many tears that had joined the lone one.

"I just don't see how you can just accept it, so matter-of-factly, like it happens every day."

"Well, when you have lived near this property as long as my family has, you learn a thing or two about your neighbors. Strange things happen here and it affects the people who live here. There are a lot of things that are hard to understand in this world, but if you are going to learn anything outside your own little universe, you better be willing to have a little room for acceptance." Gav walked over to the barn door. With the lightning bolts silhouetting his position, it brought back a surge of memories to Grae, memories of that horrible night when so much was lost.

"Besides, I'll take an ancient rival then a current one any day." Gav turned around and smiled. "I mean, what are the chances of you ever seeing him again?"

Grae smiled. She walked to Gav and put her arms around him. "Yeah, what are the chances?" The answer to that question was a very scary thought.

The storm ended and once again the sun shone bright and hot. When they arrived back at the Mansion, Grae and Gav were greeted with the aroma and sound of a big dinner in the works. This little slice of normalcy was comforting to Grae. Gav hadn't asked anything further about Patrick or her journey. Perhaps just the knowledge that she wasn't involved with someone else in the present was enough for him. Perhaps he thought she would share more when she was ready, or maybe he just didn't want to know.

Maybe it was because she caught the fish herself, but Grae didn't think that the dinner could have been any better. There they sat, on the side porch that overlooked Cedar Run, as the sun slowly set. A breeze still lingered from the storm, and she was surrounded by everything that was good in her life. The lines on her mother's forehead seemed to ease every day. Perry's interest had diverted from torturing her to sports and a girlfriend, Gav's redheaded sister. Grandpa's days of sadness and grief now had new purpose with his active family around. Grae loved her job and all the people she met and her new life in college was only days from beginning.

Her greatest joy and her greatest sadness sat beside her. Eating his third helping of catfish was this wonderful guy who one day joined her for lunch in that crowded high school cafeteria. She knew in her heart that her love for him had been channeled to Patrick. She knew that Gav had carried his love from another life. It terrified her that tomorrow he would move to a new world. She understood that he wouldn't seek to replace her, but she wasn't so naïve as not to believe that there wouldn't be easy reasons around every corner. She would have to live with that. She would have to hope that another journey wouldn't take her away and harden her even more.

As if he read her mind, he reached over and took her hand. "Don't be sad, Grae Belle," Gav said with that Hollywood smile. "I know my way home."

"You're not mad anymore?" she whispered.

He leaned over. She could feel his breath on her hair and every nerve in her body seemed to stand at attention. "It sounds like you cheated on me, with me. Can't blame that ancient cousin, he knew a good thing when he saw it." He kissed her head and reached for a peach cobbler that Kat had just passed to their side of the table. When Grae looked up, she saw her mother watching them. Her mother winked. For now, it would be okay.

TWELVE

She had to cry, she couldn't help it. Gav's mother didn't need to cry alone. Grae would join her. As she watched Gav's parents pull out of the driveway in a truck loaded with all of his belongings, his mother's face said it all, Gav was leaving. His mother helped a child off to college several times before, but it didn't change her feelings. It reminded Grae of the day that the police came to arrest her father. It was a Saturday afternoon, and she and her father were the only ones at home, no one knew that the police were coming. As the police cruiser pulled away, Grae remembered feeling finality to the moment. For some reason, she felt the same way today

"Don't you start too, buttercup." His parents had left a few minutes ahead of him to stop and get some gas, but Grae thought they really were just giving her and Gav a few minutes alone. Grae wiped her eyes.

"I'll be okay. You won't be that far. I'll be busy with school, too."

"Yes, you will, and we will text constantly, and I will call you every night." Grae gave him a smile.

"And promise me that if you, you know, go anywhere that you won't fall in love with one of my relatives and want to stay." Gav gave her a stern look that quickly turned into a smile as he pulled her into the tightest hug she may have ever gotten. He rested his head on top of hers; it was easy with their differences in height.

"I love you, Grae Belle, two hundred years and back, and two hundred more to come." There was no holding back the tears now, they streamed down her face, and Grae thought she might have felt some in her hair, too.

Eight o'clock in the morning was rather early for biology, but it was the only time available when she registered. So Grae sat in Fincastle Hall and waited, her watch said she was ten minutes early, but the classroom was only half full and the instructor was starting to look annoyed. Not a good sign for the first day.

Grae looked around the room and realized that this was one of the older classrooms on the campus. She'd heard that one by one, all of the buildings were being remodeled. From the looks of this room, this building might be a later one on the list. It surprised her that there was even an old green chalkboard in the front of the room. As she stared at it, it began to move and swirl and she felt as if...

"Young lady, what is wrong with...?" Grae could feel someone shaking her, but could not seem to focus on who it was. It was a man's voice. Was she dreaming?

"Young lady, are you okay?" Her vision cleared and she saw her instructor standing over top of her. She was lying on the floor next to her desk.

"I think so." Grae said as she sat up. "What happened?"

"You just fell over. Someone behind you said that you swayed a little at first, and then just fell over." The instructor helped Grae to her feet and she sat back down in her desk. "Have you been sick? Should we call an ambulance?"

"No, no, I will be fine. I didn't eat much breakfast, probably just low blood sugar."

The instructor didn't look convinced. "Well, why don't you go down the hallway and get a snack out of the vending machine? Something with some protein in it, you can eat it in class." He walked back to his desk. "But, for the rest of you, we aren't going to make a habit of eating in class."

Grae walked down the hall and bought a pack of peanuts from the vending machine. She knew it wasn't low blood sugar; her mother had insisted that she eat a full breakfast only an hour ago. Grae knew that she hadn't passed out, somehow she had been transported, but what she didn't know was to where. And she didn't know why the color green was haunting her.

The rest of the day was fairly normal. Grae was disappointed that the dreaded excitement hadn't involved multi-paged syllabuses and paper assignments. No, she had to pass out, and then have some of those same classmates show up in other classes and whisper.

After her three classes for that day had met, she went to the library to begin her volunteer work.

"Alice is in a staff meeting," Kelly, an assistant clerk, told her. "She said for you to start by familiarizing yourself with the contents of the genealogy section and that she would tell you more about what you would be doing on Wednesday."

So Grae went into the room and looked around. Liked the rest of the library, this room was very light and airy. Framed old maps could be seen on most walls, looking at one of them closely she saw the name Robert Graham on a homestead on the Great Wagon Road. Rows and rows of filing cabinets lined the walls and bookcases filled another portion. She put down her backpack on the floor and began to look through some of the books that were on the table in front of her. It seemed as if no time had passed, but when Grae looked at the clock on her phone she found that two hours had passed since she had arrived. After looking at the books and documents that were in piles on the table, she had found a filing cabinet that seemed to be full of letters. Many of the surnames did not register with her, although Crockett and Sayer seemed to be mentioned quite frequently.

She was about to close the cabinet when in the back of the drawer she saw a very aged manila folder. Its corners were worn and there looked to be notes written in pencil that had long faded. Underneath it was an old, handmade box and below that seemed to be an old ledger book. What incredible stories these documents had to tell, Grae imagined there were secrets waiting to be told.

As she turned the envelope over, she could see that it had a button on the back and a string wound around it. As Grae carefully unwound the string, she wondered who had been the original owner and where the contents had been. The first couple of papers appeared to be the will of someone named Isaiah Crockett. Seeing the name "Isaiah" startled Grae. The will was dated 1823, long after the Isaiah she had known had died in the Baker barn. Another document was a page from an old family Bible. The list of births was long, but, unfortunately, there were no last names to link the family heritage. Then Grae came to a letter with a familiar name at the top, Graham, she began to read.

Robert Graham
Philadelphia Waggon Road
Wythe County
Virginia

6 July, 1809

The Honourable Major Joseph Graham
Vesuvius Furnace
Lincoln County
North Carolina

Honourable Major Graham,

It is my utmost desire that this letter finds you and your dear family well. My sons and myself wish to thank Yourself and your lovely daughter, Sophia, for the kind hospitality this month past. Our every want and need being so thoughtfully tended to, you humble us with your gracious accommodation upon our visits to your fine plantation.

Sir, please forgive me if I speak too bluntly, as I entrust the consideration of your Honour's valuable opinion. I wish to ask your forbearance as I presume to have your approval to proceed for I am in need of your highly regarded and learned counsel for as my Papa said to me long ago, "The man who pays the piper calls the tune."

As you may recall my visit last to your fine home, I was accompanied by my son David. Though he is but nine years of age he is a remarkably advanced lad for his years. I assure you that I do not waste your

Honour's attentions with boastful exaggerations regarding David's adroit abilities. I have indeed been blessed with fourteen children in my fifty-nine years on God's Earth, yet I have no proper reference for a child such as David. If I may indulge your good favour, Sir, I shall attempt to make myself clear.

As a young boy David grew faster, learned his studies easily, was articulate, and managed himself far sooner than what is expected for his years. His mother, teachers, tutors, older brothers and sisters all present upon me example after example of his remarkable advanced proclivity for learning skills, memorizing volumes of writings of all sort, with a monumental talent for mathematics.

All of my children advance in their studies well, perform chores, and work in the fields and General Store here, yet I find David so quick-minded that when a sale or barter is completed, he often times has the totals figured before myself! At present David has reached the limits of our schooling opportunities here and I now employ tutors for his benefit. To further complicate my concerns I have observed David to have a uniquely industrious disposition and curiosity, particularly in respect to construction and design. To his credit David's temperment is forthright and direct, yet I have never, Sir, never observed him to join other children in light-hearted play. Indeed, David has always preferred the company of adults, and might I add persons whom he might learn or benefit from in their acquaintance. There is no need to hide my son's oddities, for in truth I am fearful that he will not be sympathetic to others less equal to himself.

This very situation presented itself upon our visit last at Vesuvius Furnace. I observed David to follow your grown son, Jackey, from Furnace Blast to Forge to Business Office as if he was Jackey's shrunken shadow. As David and I journeyed home, I listened to David as he reported in detail the specific operations of Vesuvius Furnace and I realized that there is every possibility that as his Father I will fail his brilliant mind and aptitude if I do not act.

Thus it is so my esteemed Friend. Forgive my forwardness, Sir, but you are indeed Friend to myself and my family all these years past. Your upright views and principles have served well as a compass in my hard-fought life and I find that I am in need once again of your sound advice and remedy.

With a humble heart and aged body I pray that Your Honour will take my son, David Graham, to live in your home or the home of your son, John Davidson Graham, upon his twelfth birthday until he is a man of eighteen. It is my supreme desire that David benefit from the tutelage of scholars as well as serve as an iron-maker apprentice alongside Your Honour and your son, Jackey.

You have my promise to deposit sums needed for his needs and I pledge also to assume all debt that David incurs while boarding here. If his Excellency is agreeable, we shall work out the particulars at a later time for I find myself much grieved presently regarding my inept position concerning these most unusual needs of my son David, whom I love dearly.

Sir, I am thankful every day for God's blessings upon my home and family and His Will be praised for only He knows our purpose.

I have the honour to be your obedient servant.
Robert Graham

Grae was amazed to find such a personal letter about Squire David. She looked at the clock and realized that it was almost time for the library to close. So she quickly went to the copy machine and scanned the document's several pages and emailed it to herself. There were more pages in the folder, but, for now, she would have to return them to their hiding place in the back of the drawer.

"It is the first document that I have seen that speaks of Squire David's childhood," Grae said to her mother that evening as they were preparing dinner. "It talks about how he was extremely smart and industrious, but not a very playful child."

"Well, I have never heard a story that portrays Squire David as lighthearted in any way," Kat replied, as she coated pork chops in breadcrumbs and seasonings. "I hope I got a big enough package of these, they look rather small and I bet Perry could eat six and still be hungry."

"I bet there is more information about him at the library. We should have some really good stuff to include in the tour." Grae had finished peeling potatoes and placed the rinsed pieces into a pot of boiling water.

"Yes, that's good. We need to start writing the script. Can you email me some of the research you have found so far? I think I will start working on it during my lunch hour each day."

"Sure, what do you have in mind for me to do with the tour?" Grae began gathering the dishes to take to the dining room.

"I was thinking that I would write the script so that I would be telling the overview of the history, and then you could relate some of the details about the people we include. Perhaps, as if you were someone who lived here or from that time."

"Oh, wow, that's a great idea!" Grae walked out of the kitchen toward the dining with the dishes, but turned around mid-trip and returned. "Hey! I could wear my dress. You know, the dress I came back in."

"Oh, Grae, I don't know. I don't feel very good about that dress." Kat turned toward Grae. "I really think we should destroy it."

"No! No! It is very special to me. Nannie and Mary worked hard to make it my dress, and I, I think it came back with me for a reason. And maybe this is the reason, so that it can help tell the history of this place."

"I don't know. You may be right. I just don't want it to take you anywhere else."

Grae again walked toward the dining room. She knew her mother's concerns; she understood the reality of them. But she also knew deep in her soul that there was a reason that dress had travelled over two hundred years with her and it wasn't just to be her prom gown. That dress had a purpose in the twenty-first century, and it was her job to find out what that was.

THIRTEEN

Grae wasn't hearing from Gav as much as she hoped and when she did, he sounded very tired. But, he had brushed off her comments asking about it by saying that classes and football practice were kicking his butt. It wasn't until a weekend visit with Carrie that Grae found out the rest of the story.

"His roommates are partying almost every night and some crazy girl is stalking him," Carrie said, as she watched Perry picking tomatoes with Grandpa Mack. She and Grae were sitting on the back porch. Grae had her nose in a biology book. Carrie was focused on Perry.

"What! A crazy girl is stalking him?!"

"Yeah," Carrie glanced at Grae. "Didn't he tell you?" Carrie paused. "I guess not, he probably didn't want to worry you, but he's had to get Mom and Dad involved. The girl sits outside of his dorm room."

"Who is she?" Grae closed her book and turned to give Carrie all her attention. She also reached for her phone and texted Gav.

"That's the really weird thing." Carrie stopped talking to wave at Perry. She signed. "Your brother is just wonderful."

"Yeah, yeah, he's a saint. But you are going off topic. What's weird about this girl? Besides the fact that she's a stalker?"

"Oh, yeah, well, it's like there are no real records on her at the college. Dad says that she's registered and everything, but like all the background records about her are gone."

"What do you mean no background?"

"Administration said that she has obviously been accepted to the college and enrolled in classes, but none of the background documents can be found about her. It's like she only exists at Tech, right now."

"Have they investigated her or questioned her?"

"Yes, but she keeps threatening that she will get a lawyer involved. That she has every right to be there and that there's no law against her hanging out in the hall since it is her dorm building too."

Grae got up and began to pace up and down the walkway. "What has she done to Gav?"

Carrie stood up and walked toward Grae. "I'm not sure if I should tell you. He'll be all mad at me that I even told you anything."

"Carrie, you can't rewind. Don't you think I should know?"

"Well, yeah, I guess. I'm sure he will tell you. He's just all caught up in it and it's affecting his classes and practice." Carrie looked out toward the garden. Perry and Grandpa were on the far end. "Well, one night, she hooked up with Gav's roommate, Taylor, and somehow she got a key to their room. The next weekend, Taylor went home on Friday evening because his cousin was getting married. When Gav woke up on Saturday morning, this girl was sitting in a chair watching him sleep."

"What? Wasn't that enough to get her in trouble?"

"No, she had a key. She said that Taylor gave it to her. Taylor's a jerk, so he took her side. But, now, he's been making Gav's life miserable because of it. It's like she cast a spell on him."

Carrie's last words sent a chill down Grae's spine.

"Mom and Dad didn't know I was listening, but the other night they had Gav on speaker phone and he was talking about how she always seems to know where he is. Not just where his classes are or when practice is, but unusual places he goes. One night one of his suitemates texted him and asked him to stop at a drug store for him and there she was. He gave one of his professors a ride to the other side of campus and she was standing in front of the building when he let the professor out. It is really playing with his head."

"Wow," Grae said, sitting back down on the porch. "I bet that is why he has discouraged me from visiting."

"Yeah, probably so. Dad went down there on Tuesday, and he and Gav went to several different offices on campus, and then out to lunch. But the whole time Dad was there, Gav never saw her. After Dad left, Gav went to eat dinner at the dining hall. He turned around while in line and she was about five people behind him."

"What does she say to him?"

"You know, that's another weird thing, she doesn't talk to him. She just stares and follows. I guess she thinks that silence is unnerving, or she's afraid to talk to him. Dad made some weird comment about some old movie because the girl's name is Eve."

"And he has never seen her before moving to Tech?"

"Mom asked the same thing, and Gav says that he doesn't

think so, but that there is something familiar about her." Carrie stood up and began walking toward Perry. Grandpa Mack was driving the truck toward the back of the house. Several bushel baskets of tomatoes were on the back.

"Mom said that maybe Gav knew her in a past life." Grae's tea glass hit the porch with a crash and Carrie almost tripped from the shock of the sound.

"Do you think this could have anything to do with me?" Grae had just finished telling her mother about Gav's stalker as she and her mother peeled tomatoes. Their latest creation with the end of the season tomatoes was going to be spicy tomato jam.

"Oh, Grae, I just don't know." Kat began chopping the tomatoes. It amazed Grae how young her mother looked in her 'Saturday night look' as she called it. Hair in a ponytail, all the makeup washed off her face, wearing an old t-shirt and cut-off jean shorts. She looked more like Grae's sister than her mother.

"I wish Mom was here. She knew a lot about the weirdness of the journeys and what they could result in. After my experiences, I didn't want to know anymore, and poor Mom didn't want to talk about it either."

"Are you ever going to tell me what you experienced on your trips?"

"It's not something that I care to relive." Kat looked straight at her daughter. "Grae, time travel is very serious. It's not just going off to another world and seeing what happened once. You can cause things that will forever change the present, and you may not realize it until it is too late."

"I think I saw enough on my last journey to realize the seriousness of it," Grae walked toward her mother. "I mean, I caused a murder."

"Grae, that murder was already going to happen. It was part of history. I caused the death of someone from the present. I deserve to be sitting in a prison cell even more than your father does, but very few people in this world know it."

"What in the world…" Grae stopped talking as her grandfather walked into the room.

"Lordy, aren't you girls sick of canning yet?" Grandpa paused and looked at Kat and Grae. "Seems mighty serious in here."

"Yeah, Dad, we were talking about consequences." An understanding look exchanged between father and daughter, a painful understanding.

"Everything we do has them. But we can't undo the results of our actions," he walked back to the door, and then stopped, "even if we try to redo them."

As she watched her mother turn back toward the sink and wipe tears from her face, Grae realized there were so many things about her own family she didn't know.

The front door opened and closed with a slam and the heavy stride of Perry's walk interrupted everyone's thoughts.

"Wow! That movie was awesome. The special effects were out of this world." Perry opened the refrigerator and began rummaging for a snack. "I think Carrie even liked it."

"What was the movie about?" Kat asked, as she resumed working on the tomatoes.

"This guy is like a normal police officer and he is in this strange accident, and then after that, he can like travel back through time." Kat drops her knife in the sink, but Perry keeps talking.

"So, this guy's grandfather had been wrongfully accused of murder like way before the officer was born, and he tries to find out who really did it." Perry began eating a meatloaf sandwich that he had quickly made while telling his story.

"So, does he find out?" Grae asked.

"Yes, he does. Only problem is that when he gets back to the present, he doesn't exist anymore. His grandfather not going to prison changed a bunch of things and it sort of wiped out his existence." Perry gulped a half of glass of milk. "These moviemaking people can really come up with some far out stuff."

Kat and Grae exchanged a look.

"It really got me to thinking though. It sure would be great to be able to go back and undo what Dad did," he paused and continued eating. "But I guess we wouldn't be living here then, and I like the things that have happened since we've been here. All this time with Grandpa and meeting Gav and Carrie, I like our life."

Kat walked over and stole a bite of her son's sandwich. "Things happen for a reason; it's not our place to question, but make the best of what life hands us."

"Yeah, and I'm glad that life handed me this meatloaf sandwich. It rocks!" They all broke out in a laugh.

FOURTEEN

The next two weeks passed quickly. Grae focused on getting into her new classes, her part-time job, and the research she did for the tour as part of her volunteer work at the library. Everything seemed to be in a fast mode and the days flew by quickly.

She decided not to confront Gav with what she knew about the stalker. As much as she worried about what was happening and who this person might be, she knew that she needed to give him space to deal with it. She kept their conversations lighthearted. When she and Perry went to a home game, she allowed him to have fun and enjoy their victory dinner without asking any questions.

The ladies of the historical society had met with Kat regarding the draft of her tour and were very excited about all the interesting stories that had been included about the Mansion. She and her mother had rehearsed almost every night for a week and were ready for the first weekend of tours to begin.

"I showed Miss Adelaide and Miss Bobbie Joe my dress," Grae said to her mother on the Friday evening before the first Saturday tour. "They think it is perfect for the tour."

"Oh, no, Grae, you didn't." Kat was busy dusting and straightening the downstairs rooms. "I told you that I didn't like the idea of that."

"I know, Mom. But I really feel like this is why I have this dress. It came back with me for this tour. It will make it magical."

"Well, it is certainly authentic," Kat shook her head in surrender. "I just hope it doesn't have any stories of its own to tell."

Grae looked out of her window and saw a steady stream of vehicles pulling into the Mansion driveway. It was a beautiful fall day. The summer heat had dissipated and a gentle breeze passed through the Mansion's tall windows. It would be a comfortable September day for a tour.

They had all been up since dawn for the last-minute preparations. Everything would begin outside with an informal viewing of the nearby grounds and some of Grandpa's stories of the property history. Then groups of twenty would be lead through the Mansion by Miss Adelaide and Miss Bobbie Joe, as Kat and Grae told the story of the Mansion's beginnings and the home's early master, Squire David Graham.

Grae looked at her own reflection in the mirror. The dress from 1786 still made her heart lurch whenever she saw it. Hands of love had carefully adapted it to fit her. The fabric was soft cotton. The background was an unusual shade of pink that leaned toward a light red. White flower motif designs softened the color and red and blue-green flowers seemed to jump off from every angle. The flowers were carnations and daisies in several sizes. The design of the dress fit at the waist with a square neck in front and back and puffy sleeves. From the waist, it flowed delicately to the floor and there were tiny bows at several points that pulled the fabric up from the floor and a larger bow in the back. Grae thought it was beautiful. It had weathered the journey through centuries amazingly well. Grae thought it had travelled through time on the love of Nannie Baker and her daughter-in-law, Mary. They had so carefully made this dress hers for that fateful night in 1786.

Knowing what she did now about the circumstances surrounding her return, and the small knife that Mary had carefully hidden in the dress, she wondered what its purpose really was. She had told her mother that she thought it was destined to be part of these tours, but she secretly wondered if there was a deeper meaning. She decided to keep with authenticity so she would return that knife to the secret pocket near the hem of the dress. If she were to discover its purpose, it needed to be in its proper place.

She had recently found a pair of lace-up dress shoes at a consignment store that seemed appropriate with the dress. They were made of worn light leather and had that fancy, but functional flair that dress shoes of another time seemed to offer. As she smoothed the skirt of the dress, she thought about Nannie and Sal and how those years on Baker Island must have been for them. Their shared heartache had resulted from the same crime. It must have been a great testament to the strength of their friendship that they could stand to endure the rest of their lives together.

"Grae, it's time!" Kat shouted from the foot of the stairs.

"Well, Squire David, it's all about you today. You should be happy," Grae said out loud as she walked toward the doorway. Grae felt a stronger breeze pass through the room and she turned back just as the front window slammed shut.

"Oh, Squire, you really need to behave today; you have guests."

Kat was also dressed in costume. She wore a pale blue long dress that was borrowed from the wife of a skilled re-enactor. This talented lady created beautiful handmade garments for the Civil War-era events that her husband and others participated in. The color was beautiful on Kat. Grae could imagine her serving mint juleps on the front porch of the Mansion.

"Welcome to Graham Mansion," Kat announced as she stood at the bottom of the staircase and began her introduction. "You will notice that I am not using the term 'Major Graham Mansion', as most of you have often heard. You might say that the Mansion has been misnamed in some respects. Major David Graham was the son of Squire David Graham. While Major David did make some significant additions to the Mansion during his years of ownership, it was his father, Squire David, who actually built the majority of this home and who left the most long-standing impression on this property."

From her vantage point above her mother on the staircase, Grae watched the group. They were mesmerized as Kat gave them a glimpse into the Mansion's mysterious history. There was something about a historical structure that was rarely opened to the public that made people desperate to get inside.

"My name is Katherine Graham White. Behind me on the staircase is my lovely daughter, Grae. As the ladies of the society lead you through the Mansion today, we shall be the narrators of the story, the legend, the history, and the mystery of Graham Mansion."

The ladies led the group through the foyer, into the dining

room, and then into the kitchen. Grae followed her mother to the kitchen doorway where Kat walked through the group and thus diverted their attention toward the fireplace and away from where Grae now stood.

"We shall begin in this portion of the house as these rooms are the humble beginnings of the later grandeur. To understand this Mansion, you must understand the man who built it. In many ways, even up until today, David Graham was this Mansion. The stages and phases of the development of this house in many ways are parallel to the levels of success that he attained for himself and generations after him. These phases also reflect the deep history of Virginia and of our nation."

Grae was amazed at how her mother had transformed all of the research that she had gathered from Granny Belle's papers and the files of information at the library. She was weaving quite a dramatic picture. Grae wondered if she was doing so only for this audience or also perhaps the star of the show, in the hopes that the story would appease Squire and keep him on good behavior.

"Before you learn about the house, you need to learn a little about the man," Kat continued. "David Graham was born in 1800 to Robert Graham and his second wife, Mary Cowan. Very little was recorded about David's young life, but we do know his father passed away when he was about eleven years old and that his mother passed when David was in his late teens. He was one of fourteen children and was an industrious sort of person from a young age. We are not sure how David became interested in the iron business, but some have speculated that after his father's passing, one of David's mentors was Joseph Graham of North Carolina. This Mister Graham was well-known for the Vesuvius Furnace he operated. Nonetheless, David's business began in 1826 when he purchased an iron business and the original parcels of this land from the heirs of James Crockett. The price was $10,000, and David must have worked night and day in some respects as he had that loan paid in full in five years." Someone in the group began sneezing; causing others to 'bless her' and a little general chatter about dust began.

"Yes, these older homes do have a special brand of dust all their own, but let's continue." Grae thought that her mother would have made a good teacher as she could regain control of even the most disruptive of groups in only a few moments. "David Graham did not marry until he was thirty-five. He was wed to Martha Peirce, the daughter of David and Mary Bell Peirce. Sometime around 1835, he began construction on the portion of the house in which we now stand."

"He must have really loved her a great deal to build her such a grand home," a middle-aged woman in the group interrupted. Almost instantly, a heavy glass that was on the counter behind the woman fell to the ground.

"Oh, I am so sorry. I hope it wasn't an antique."

"Oh, do not worry, it was not. Grae, will you get a dust pan? Don't try to pick those pieces of glass up."

Grae walked toward the closet, and as she reached the door to open it, her mother came running up behind her. "That woman insisted on picking up some of the glass and now she has a cut. Isn't our first aid kit in the closet, too?"

Grae opened the door. "I think so, it's in the back." Grae reached for the white and red first aid kit and a flash of memory streamed over her. Realizing that both of her feet were over the threshold, she turned to hand the kit to her mother. Their eyes locked, and, in an instant, mother and daughter both knew what was going to happen.

Grae saw the terror in her mother's eyes as a shrill sound

filled her ears. For a moment, she wondered if the experience would be less painful since the fear of what was happening was gone. Her answer came as the sound inside her head became louder, more powerful. Everything began to tilt, and Grae felt herself falling. The speed of the travel was pulling at her, from the outside, from the inside, like an unseen force gripping her soul. She knew the closet walls were not there, but it did not stop her from reaching, searching, for something to hold on to. She saw the swirls of green and purple mist engulfing her, but this time, the air smelled of pipe smoke. The ever-increasing shrieking in her ears began to sound like chanting, and the thump of a drum kept time with her racing heart. Just as she felt a horrible sickness in her stomach creep up into her throat, everything went black.

ANOTHER TIME

FIFTEEN

"You look a little lost, ma'am. I just saw that the stagecoach went by; it must be late if it dumped you out here." Grae looked down the dirt path to see that the voice was coming from a young man about the age of Perry, who was walking toward her.

"I…I…yes, I am a little lost." Grae looked at the young man. His outfit reminded her of watching *Little House on the Prairie*; boys his age just didn't wear suspenders in her time. She realized that she had once again landed in another century.

"Was the stagecoach running late?" The young man stopped a few feet away from her. He had lots of freckles across his nose and red hair. He reminded her of Opie Taylor.

"Yes, I believe it was. The driver said I could walk the rest of the way." Grae gave him a forlorn look.

"I would be glad to lead you to where you are going." The young man looked around. "Where are your bags?"

"Oh, dear, the driver forgot to give me my bags. That is unfortunate."

"May I be so bold as to ask if you are the new governess for the McGavock family?"

The word 'McGavock' struck Grae hard causing visions of Gav and Patrick to swirl through her mind. "How would you know that?"

"I work for Mister Graham, he is my uncle. He and Mister McGavock were speaking this morning about a new governess who had been hired. I do not believe they were expecting her to arrive until possibly November. But here you are!" The boy gave her a big smile. After a few moments of silence, Grae spoke.

"So, are we on the property of Mister Graham now?"

"Yes."

"And what would be Mister Graham's given name?"

"David, ma'am."

"And what is your given name?"

"Johnny, ma'am, I am John Montgomery Graham."

"Very nice to meet you," Grae smiled and shook her head. "Riding on the stagecoach for several days, I think I am a bit tired and confused. Could you tell me please what is the month and day?"

Johnny cocked his head to the right and furrowed his brow. Grae wondered if she might have been too hasty with that question.

"It is the thirteenth of September, 1830, ma'am. I had to think about that myself. It is easy to lose a day or two when you are working long hard days. I imagine if you are travelling, it would even be harder."

"Thank you very much, Johnny." Grae gave him a big smile. He didn't realize how valuable a piece of information he had just given her.

"Would you like me to take you there?"

"Yes, that would be very kind of you."

"First, we shall need to walk down this path to Mister Graham's barn. I will get a horse and wagon there; we shall then go to the McGavock property."

"Lead the way." Grae put out her hand for Johnny to go ahead.

The path they walked on was well worn and quite wide. All around, Grae saw beautiful trees and flowers, still lush from summer, but on the edge of changing colors for the fall. It seemed strange to her how the tall evergreens, the fields of golden rag weed, and the brilliant orange-green maple leaves that she saw around her looked so much like those that she had just seen outside her bedroom window that very morning.

As they came out of the woods, Grae gasped; there before her was the cabin of Joseph Baker. She could hear Sal's voice yelling for the men to come eat. She could see Aggie and Isaiah planting seeds in those long straight rows. Grae had been on this land every day since, but somehow none of these memories had returned to her this way. Seeing the little cabin brought it all back.

"Is something wrong? You seem troubled." Johnny said.

"Oh, no, I am fine. This place just reminds me of some-where. A place I knew long ago."

"Ah, I myself have never been anywhere but here. Would you like some water or something to eat before we move on to the McGavock's place?"

"Water would be nice. I am thirsty from the journey."

"Would you like to sit over there in the shade while I get you some water?" Johnny motioned to a bench under a large tree. Grae nodded and began walking toward it.

"This tree isn't here anymore," she said to herself as she sat down.

"No, it was cut down in 1910, after it was struck by lightning." The voice came from over her head. It was one she knew well.

"Oh, you are here. I was so hoping that you would be." Grae looked up to see her beloved friend, The General.

"I was hoping that you wouldn't make one of these journeys again." The General climbed down from the high vantage point and settled on a lower limb above Grae's head.

"So, why am I here?" Grae looked around the land. There were a few buildings that seemed new to her.

"I do not know. But, I am sure you will find a way to get yourself into trouble." The General climbed down the rest of the tree and sat next to Grae. She began to pet her friend, rubbing her hand along his back.

"Well, for now, I am going to the McGavock property. I am going to be the new governess."

"Oh, delightful. You know how I feel about you being off of the Graham property. We must figure out a reason for you to come back here so that you can travel back home." The General began to pace.

"You really pace a lot. Did you know that?"

"I'm a cat. Cats pace."

"Perhaps during this journey you will tell me who you are. I have really tried figuring it out, but I have no idea."

"My identity is of no concern to you. Just be glad that you have someone like me looking out for your interests."

"Here comes Johnny with my water. There's a man with him."

"Yes, you are about to meet the infamous Squire David Graham," The General whispered. "At least, an earlier version of him. You must be very careful! David is very sharp; he will suspect something if you are the least bit careless."

"Good day to you." David Graham bowed slightly. "Johnny tells me that the stagecoach was not very kind in delivering you to your destination. I shall write a letter of complaint to them. They must show more concern and kindness if they are to travel through our part of this country."

Johnny stepped closer to Grae handing Grae a cup of water.

"Thank you, sir. I appreciate your concern. I believe that they were falling behind on their journey. Since I was the only one getting off in this area, the driver decided that this would be their closest stop."

"It is his job to stop at the designated area. Where Johnny says he found you is quite far from that place. But my manners have left me; I am David Graham. This is my property." David bowed again, motioning for Grae to sit.

Her mind raced. She needed to introduce herself. She needed a name.

"The Honorable Joseph McGavock has hired a governess for his children. I do believe that her name is Arabella James. Would that be you?"

And, as if by magic, her identity was chosen; a name familiar to her yet one that she could answer without fear of forgetting.

"Yes, that is correct. It is so nice to be expected. One does not know how well a letter travels across this land. I am glad to know that my arrival has been anticipated."

"Indeed! I shall take you personally to the McGavock plantation. I shall make myself more presentable in the meantime. Johnny says that the driver did not leave your bags. What a dreadful one he was! I am sure the ladies of the McGavock home will provide you with some clothing items until others can be ordered or made for you."

David and Johnny both walked back toward the barn to get the wagon.

"David Graham seems very nice."

"I suppose he can be, but do not get used to it. This is not the man he will become. Nice shall not be a word used to describe him when he rules over his future mansion."

"No, I have not read many things that describe him as nice, but from what I have just seen, at one time his personality had those pleasantries."

"I hope that you are not around to see him change."

Grae and The General relaxed in silence for a time. The sun began its slow descent to the land. She began to miss her own time.

"I realize now that time stands still at home while I am gone on these journeys, but it does not make me miss it any less."

"That is understandable."

"I think my mother knew that I was going when the transition started. She was right behind me, and when I turned, it was as if I could see it in her eyes." Grae drank most of the water, then put the cup down on the ground for The General to finish.

"While only an instant in her time, this journey will be an eternity for her." The General lapped up the remaining drops of water. Grae picked up the cup and walked down the hill. David and Johnny were out front with the wagon.

"Will you go with me?" Grae asked quietly to The General.

"Of course, but I may have to travel another way."

"We shall see." Grae walked up to the wagon. Johnny took the cup out of her hand.

"We are ready to go, Miss James," David said, offering his

hand for her to climb into the front seat of the wagon.

"Mister Graham, does this animal belong to you?" Grae pointed to The General who was trying to scurry away before being seen.

"No, I do not believe I have seen that cat before. Was it bothering you? Johnny, catch that cat and we shall dispose of it."

"No. Oh no!" Grae said, running toward The General and picking him up. "I would like to take him with me. He is so friendly. I left a beautiful cat like this at my family home, a long time ago."

"Well, I doubt that my sister and her husband would object to such a comely creature. He can certainly accompany us. If they are not agreeable to his residence with them, I am sure he can be a mouser in one of our barns." David gave Grae a big smile and took The General and placed him on some hay in the back of the wagon.

"Your sister and her husband are the McGavocks?" Grae thought that she really wished she knew the family history a little better.

"Yes, Margaret is my older, half-sister. She is married to Joseph McGavock." David turned to Johnny. "I will be back at the edge of dark. See to it that the slaves finish the work in the north field."

David turned back to Grae. "Johnny is my foreman and my nephew. I am teaching him how to properly run a farm. He aspires to have his own one day.

"Yes, sir!" Johnny said. He smiled. "It was nice to meet you, Miss James."

"You were so kind to me, Johnny. I prefer for you and Mister Graham call me Arabella." Johnny smiled and bowed his head, but David had a different reaction.

"We should be going," he said rather curtly.

Grae took his hand and climbed onto the seat. With a word to the horses, they were on their way into a world that Grae could only imagine.

There did not seem to be a straight way for them to travel. The many turns confused Grae as to where she was in relation to the lay of the land she knew in her own time. The familiar landmarks were not in existence. It didn't help that David Graham was silent most of the way. Grae realized that perhaps she had made a misstep by offering to be called by her first name.

"You will have to forgive me, Mister Graham, if I have overstepped the bounds of decorum in my friendliness. I'm afraid that I am forgetting that I am not in the city life of which I am accustomed. I am sure there is more attention placed on the way to properly address each other in this part of the country." Grae wondered if what she had said made sense at all. She thought it did have a nice southern lilt to it. "I must engage you to help me though, as I do not want to make an improper first impression on the McGavocks. I do so want to be able to make my services useful here."

"It was not a serious infraction," David replied. "But a lady does not normally offer such familiarity to gentlemen with whom she has just met. It is proper for me to address you as Miss James and you to address me as Mister Graham. Should we become more friendly, over time and adequate social opportunities, our proper given names might be used later, but never a shortened version of that. Such a name is reserved for family members and your intended."

"I am so sorry to have made such a blunder. Thank you so much for explaining this to me." The rest of the ride, while less tense, was no more talkative.

Grae was awestruck at the grandeur, even considering the time. This was the kind of plantation that was written about as part of the Great South of the pre-Civil War era. This was the kind of farm that she knew David Graham aspired to have.

"It is grand, is it not?" David broke the silence and seemed to read Grae's thoughts. "My father's house was impressive, indeed for the time. But the McGavocks' have set a standard for our part of Virginia and just a few miles away there is another grand McGavock mansion being planned."

"It will last many years," Grae whispered to herself. It was just barely dark, but she could still see a scurry of activity. There were slaves and workers going in every direction as if they were preparing for a big event.

"Have we come upon a special event about to happen?" A feeling of apprehension came over Grae. It would be hard enough to adapt to these new surroundings; she remembered the night of the wedding party during her last visit…

"Good day, Massa Graham," a lanky young Negro man said as he took the reins of the wagon while David walked around to help Grae step down.

"Run and tell the house that the new governess has come."

The young man motioned to a boy behind him to go to the house. Grae stood beside the wagon as David began to walk toward the house. He turned and saw her still standing there and returned to her side.

"You are hesitant to enter?"

"I look like an orphan, arriving with only the clothes on my back and nothing else to identify me." Grae bowed her head. She needed for David to help make her transition into this house smooth. She needed for him to believe, so that others would also.

"We shall find your belongings and see to the dismissal of that negligent driver. But, until then, my word shall serve as the announcement of your arrival, you shall have no worries." David extended his arm to her, so that he could lead her to the door. "The McGavocks are anxious for a new governess. Their last tutor was a scoundrel of a young man whose only desire was to find a young, rich, southern lady and marry her family's money. The children learned nothing, except how not to behave."

The tall mahogany door opened. Grae was amazed at the brightness of the foyer. It seemed as if a hundred lamps and candles were lit, a golden hue hung there giving her a feeling of wealth. As she began to look beyond the light, she noticed that all around her the walls were green, a deep rich forest green. It was wallpaper that was covering them, embossed with a dark design; it looked like velvet and was so green, the same green she had been seeing for months that made her...

"Good evening, Joseph," David said. "I had the great fortune of rescuing your governess. She was left very rudely on the side of the road by the stagecoach."

Grae tried to focus on what David was saying and on the faces that were now filling the foyer to greet her, but all she could see was the green around her and it appeared to be closing in.

"I present to you, Miss Arabella James." David turned to Grae and barely caught her as she fainted.

SIXTEEN

Grae could hear voices softly whispering around her.

"It must have been the journey; she became overcome with exhaustion."

"Or lack of proper nourishment. Can you imagine what you would eat on a long stagecoach trip?"

"I hope she doesn't have the fever. It would kill us all."

"David said that she was left on the side of the road; perhaps it was the heat."

Grae tried to remember where she was and why she was here. She barely cracked open her eyes. All she could see was a dark hazy blur. She could distinguish the flicker of a lamp flame out of the corner of her eye. She felt someone touch her forehead so she gradually opened her eyes to see a black woman beside her.

"Sal?" Grae said softly.

"No, my name be Ruth, like in de Bible." Ruth came toward her with a cup of water. "You feel like you can sits up and sip a little water?"

Grae eased herself up and saw that another woman was standing at the foot of the bed. Grae took the cup from Ruth and sipped. It was ice cold and tasted good. She drank the whole cup and handed it back to her.

"More?"

"Yes, please." Grae smiled.

"How are you feeling, dear? You gave us quite a scare." The other woman sat down on the edge of the bed.

"I am sorry about that, but I do not understand what happened to me."

"Well, I think that you are just exhausted. Such a journey you have made to our remote corner of Virginia. I cannot imagine how many days you have been travelling from Massachusetts. The stagecoach must have travelled night and day since you have arrived so much earlier. It must have been horrible."

Ruth reached towards Grae and handed her more water. She drank it quickly.

"She is so thirsty," the woman said. "I imagine you must have swallowed so much dust along the way."

"The water," Grae said, drinking in the last swallow. "It is so refreshing. It is the best water I have ever tasted."

The woman smiled. "Boiling Springs, our water is delightful indeed, it just bubbles out of the ground as cold as you are tasting."

She turned to Ruth. "Go get our guest some food. If she is that thirsty, I am sure her hunger is not far behind."

"Where are my manners? I have not introduced myself. My name is Margaret McGavock, and this is my home. It is my children that you have come here to teach." As the woman stood, Grae could see that she was tall and slender, and her brown hair had beautiful glimmers of red and gold throughout it. Grae noted that it was pinned in an unusual bun that was rolled up at the nape of her neck. Her fair skin was almost translucent with tiny freckles that dotted her nose. She reminded Grae of Johnny.

"We are so glad that you have arrived safely." Margaret's voice had an Irish lilt to it. "It was my brother's son, Johnny, who came upon you on the road."

"Oh, he was so kind to me, he reminded me so much of my brother, Per…" Grae stopped suddenly realizing what she was about to say.

"Your brother? Oh, I am sure you must miss your family," Margaret said. "Perhaps that will lessen once you have become part of ours."

Ruth entered with a tray of food that she placed on Grae's lap. It had been a long time since she had been served a meal in bed; it felt strange to her. A hearty looking stew was in a china bowl with a large slice of buttered bread next to it. It appeared that a cup of hot tea was steaming in front of her. Grae began to eat as Margaret continued talking.

Grae saw a haunting sadness in the woman's eyes. It made her wonder what other sadness she would witness while in this time.

It was nightfall, so Grae was soon left to rest. She heard the hustle and bustle of the family moving about and thought she saw the door open a couple of times allowing little eyes to peer in at her. But when all the occupants were truly in their slumber and the house fell silent, Grae's restless sleep ceased. The enormity of her situation began to engulf her. On her previous journey, she had been an indentured servant, a slave. While the work was intense, she just had to keep her head down and do it. Her interaction was mainly with the slaves, they believed she was who she said; they didn't question her. Now, she was in a fairly wealthy southern home of 1830, and she would be conversing with many people, including several children who she was expected to teach.

Grae almost screamed as she felt something jump onto the bed. She quickly realized it was The General.

"How did you get in here?" By the light of the moon shining through the window, Grae saw The General look toward the door. It was closed.

"I meowed and meowed at the back door until someone let me in."

"How would they know you came with me?"

"David Graham told them before he left. They tried to send me to the barn, but I stayed around and let my presence be known." The General snuggled down into the covers on Grae's bed. "This will be a nice diversion from my most recent lodgings."

"Where was that?"

"The ground."

Grae smiled. How she had missed The General's quick wit. She lay back down and pulled the covers over her.

"What happened to me when I came into the house?"

"I am not sure. Did you feel anything?"

"I just remember seeing all the candles and lamps and that everything started getting fuzzy. And, oh, that green, it's everywhere!"

The General raised his head, "Green?"

"Yes, the walls downstairs have really dark green, wallpaper, I think. It was like they were closing in on me. I've been seeing green a lot lately. My hair was even turning green."

"Are you sure?"

"Yes, why?"

"Nothing, we will discuss more tomorrow. You must rest. Tomorrow is your first full day in 1830."

"Oh great, give me something else to keep me awake."

"Did you get good grades in school?"

"Yes."

"Then you will make a fine teacher. Just think of it as teaching old stuff as new stuff."

"Thanks, now you've given me something else to worry about. How am I supposed to know what has and hasn't happened yet?"

"You will figure it out. Good night, Grae; or should I say, Arabella?"

"Miss James to you," Grae said with a snicker as she rolled over and closed her eyes.

Grae was awakened by the sun making its morning entrance through the window. She opened her eyes and saw a tiny little girl standing quietly by her bed. She was staring at The General.

"What is your name?"

The little girl kept staring, but remained silent.

"Would you like to pet my friend?" By now, The General was stretching his limbs and back the way all cats do after a long snooze. His tail swished around him.

"Go ahead, just be gentle." The little girl timidly reached out her hand and touched The General's back. He purred and nuzzled her hand. The little girl giggled with delight and smiled at Grae. She sat down on the bed and began petting The General again as Grae rose from the bed.

"Cynthia," the little voice said.

"What?" Grae stretched and looked around the room for a mirror.

"My name is Cynthia."

"Oh, well, Cynthia, I need to go to the outhouse."

"I will show you." The little girl took Grae's hand and began walking toward the door. She looked back and said, "Come, kitty, do you need to go too?"

Grae laughed as The General followed them.

As they walked down the hallway, Grae realized that they were on the second floor. Since she only saw the foyer of the house before she collapsed, she did not know the layout. As Cynthia pulled Grae down the hallway toward a staircase, she saw that there were several rooms on each side of the passageway.

Walking down the staircase, they came into the foyer, Grae was lead toward the back of the house. She was almost in the kitchen before it hit her. "The walls..." she began to say.

"Cynthia, where are you pulling Miss James off to? I told you not to wake her up; she needs her rest." Margaret McGavock came toward them. Grae realized they were in a dining room, and through the doorway behind Margaret, she could see a small kitchen.

"Mama, she has to go!" Cynthia said defiantly. The shy voice from earlier was replaced by one that felt confident in the importance of what she was saying.

Margaret smiled. "Well, then, you must show her the way." Cynthia began leading Grae again.

"But bring her back," Margaret shouted after them. "We must feed Miss James some breakfast, and then begin to acquaint her with our household."

Out the back door they went. Grae looked around and noticed several out-buildings throughout the back of the property. The outhouse was located behind one of the larger barns. Close enough for convenience, but well hidden for looks. Cynthia opened the door and Grae stuck her head in, the odor was horrible. It was not one of her fonder experiences from her last journey. Grae stepped inside and closed the door.

"I will wait right here," Cynthia said. Grae smiled to herself; at least she had made a friend.

Back in the house Margaret asked, "Our hens have been very busy lately. Do you like eggs, Arabella?"

"Yes, ma'am, I do."

"I shall make you a hearty breakfast. Ruth has already gone to the big kitchen. Today is baking day. She will be baking bread and a few pies. I am not as good a cook, but you shall not go hungry." Grae saw that Margaret was cooking on a large woodstove. She watched as Margaret put a small amount of butter in a cast iron skillet. The pan was so hot that the butter melted faster than the woman could crack two eggs into a bowl. She gently poured them into the skillet, and the eggs began to sizzle.

"I hope that you rested well. You gave us quite a scare last night." Margaret poured Grae a cup of coal black coffee. Grae was glad to see a small pitcher of what appeared to be cream as well as a jar of honey on the table. The coffee looked strong enough to sit up without a cup.

"I am so sorry to have made such a dramatic introduction of myself," Grae watched as the coffee became a brown color, similar to toffee. "I suspect the long journey overcame me."

"Indeed, we were most distressed to learn that you were just left on the road," Margaret paused, and then lifted the eggs out of the skillet. They were placed next to a slice of ham. A small bowl of grits also appeared in front of Grae with a plate of biscuits.

"This shall make you feel better. There is nothing like a good hearty meal to get you back to yourself." Grae was starving. She dug into the meal immediately. The flavors were unbelievable. That was something that she remembered about her last journey, everything tasted delicious. So free of modern-day preservatives or extra ingredients that weren't necessary. In this time, nothing was too salty or too sweet, the flavors seemed perfect.

"Slow down, this is not a race. Take your time eating or you will make yourself sick."

"You sound like my mother."

"A mother, yes, I surely am. If I am nothing else, I am that." Grae detected a note of sadness in her voice.

"This is a wonderful breakfast. I am anxious to meet the rest of your children."

Margaret sat down at the table with Grae and began drinking a cup of coffee. "I believe you will find my children to be well-behaved, for the most part. My oldest is Mary. She is almost eighteen. She is very excited because we are going to be the host of one of her cousins' weddings this very weekend."

"Oh my, a wedding! Will it be held here?" Grae began to eat her second biscuit with honey slathered on top.

"Yes, the ceremony shall be held across the road at our Anchor of Hope Presbyterian Church, and then we shall have a grand wedding party here afterwards. I'm afraid that there will not be much time for teaching this week. Here we are, it is already Tuesday, there is much cooking and preparing to be done. We expected you to arrive after this event was over."

"I hope I can be of help then this week. Do not let the duties for which I have come deceive you; I was taught to work hard and am willing to do whatever needs to be done." Margaret smiled. "I can cook and clean and even do laborious work outside. There's only one thing you probably would not want to assign me."

"What would that be?" Margaret asked as she gathered the dishes.

"Sewing. I'm afraid that I even have trouble threading a needle."

Margaret laughed and Grae saw the face of the young bride she once was. "You and I share that trait. I confess that I have left most of the sewing and mending in my life to our slaves. But, my Mary loves to sew. She is taking lessons with a very talented woman a few miles away. She has only been learning for a year, but her skills have advanced so quickly that she was able to help this woman make the most beautiful wedding dress for my niece. It is breathtaking."

"Will Mary be one of my students?" Grae rose from the table, carrying her dishes.

"No, but you will have two of my children under your tutelage. There is Nancy; she is very excited about your arrival. Nancy is quite a student and I think she will convince her father to allow her a higher education when she is older. She is only thirteen, but she is very advanced in her studies. Your other student woke you up this morning," Margaret laughed. "Cynthia is ten. As you saw, she is very small and can be timid. But she has the curiosity of a cat, which is probably why we will find her aggravating your feline friend. My youngest is Lucinda. She is still a baby."

Grae followed Margaret through the small kitchen in the back of the house and to the outside. Grae got her first real look at the working part of the large farm. She noticed the porch they were standing on actually wrapped around the house. She wondered if that was unusual for the time. They walked down a few steps and onto a path that led to several barns, out-buildings, and two cabins. As they got closer to the first cabin, she could see that the door was open and Ruth was working inside. Two younger women slaves and several young girls were spinning yarn, shelling peas, or doing other tasks.

"Ruth, it does appear that our new governess is going to be fine. You should have seen the breakfast she ate. She might be able to eat more than some of our field hands," Margaret laughed.

"And that be your cookin', Miss Margaret. Imagine how much she eat if she be eatin' mine." Grae could see that Ruth was a spitfire.

"Hush now, Ruth. My cooking isn't that bad."

"No, but it not that good either." The rapport between the two women was evident. They were not just slave and master, they were friends. It reminded her of Nannie Baker and Sal. Grae wondered if either woman was still alive in 1830.

"I think it would be best to wait until later for you to have a tour of the farm," Margaret said to Grae. "Everyone is so busy this week. We expect our guests to begin to arrive on Thursday. We will have a pre-wedding dinner on Friday for both families and a few close friends."

Grae could see that Ruth had continued to work throughout the conversation. There were several rows of pans of bread rising on the stove behind her. Her hands were busy kneading more dough.

Margaret turned to Grae. "Now, this work is certainly not what you have been hired to do."

"Missus McGavock, I am not a stranger to work. I have come here to serve your family. I am glad to do whatever you need." Grae saw an apron lying on a nearby chair. She picked it up and tied it around her.

"Wonderful! We have certainly chosen a governess who

can help our children learn the practical things of life in this rural land. I will leave you with Ruth then. She has a full day of baking ahead and could use an extra set of hands." Margaret gave a nod to Ruth, and then left.

Ruth sized Grae up. "That be a mighty fancy dress you have on there."

Grae looked down at the beautiful dress that had been created for her in 1786. "It is my best dress. Since the stage-coach driver didn't leave my bags—it is my only dress now."

"Well, that be shameful. We shall need to do something about that. If you gonna work with me today, you gonna be gettin' dirty. We best go back to the big house and sees if we can find somethin' for you to wear."

SEVENTEEN

Ruth found Grae a dress that fit fairly well, even if it looked like it was for a widow in mourning. With an old pair of black shoes to match, she felt sure that she wouldn't worry about turning a man's head in the nineteen century. They returned to the cabin where Ruth had been working.

"This be our kitchen cabin. We do all the major cookin' in here. Just do small meals or heatin' up in da house kitchen. The slave cabin be the one behind dis here one. That be where we all sleep." Grae looked around the small cabin. There was a very large brick fireplace and chimney with a wide brick floor in front of it. Two black iron swing arms were attached to inside of the fireplace. A black iron pot was hanging on each one. Built into the bricks were shelves for baking. In one corner was a potbellied wood-burning iron stove with a couple of covered eyes. A large table and chairs were in another corner.

"I be making bread so far. We will need lots for all the peoples who be comin' for da wedding. If yous gonna be helpin' then I needs you to start cuttin' up them apples. We be makin' lots of apple pies dis mornin'. Later, we be making sweet tater pies. I's already got them cookin' up in that kettle. They's from da dried taters, I's…"

"Did you sew them and dry them?" Grae watched the shocked look on Ruth's face. "Did you sew them in the fall when they first were harvested or did you let them keep a while in the cellar and then sewed them in the spring?"

Ruth continued to have a shocked look on her face. "Spring, that's how my mammie taught me."

"That's how I learned to do them."

Ruth stared at Grae. "You talkin' like you is raised by a slave."

"No, that I was not. But, there sure was one who took good care of me when I needed it. I loved her very much."

Ruth shook her head and smiled. "Let's makes us some pies."

The morning flew by as Grae peeled as many apples for Ruth as she peeled sweet potatoes for Sal. It felt familiar. It was an excellent way to start her time there. Occasionally, she would see The General walk by with Cynthia behind him, chattering incessantly. Grae was sure she would hear about it later.

At noontime, a bell was rung. Grae watched as all the slaves ate at a long table near the cabin. Joseph McGavock and the rest of his McGavock family congregated at a similar table near the house. That morning, as she and Ruth worked on pies, Grae had watched the other slave women cook the mountains of food that was now on both tables.

"We cooks all our foods together. Most of the times, we all eats the same things, 'cept when the Massa has company or fancy relatives come. They be fairs to us. No one starves here."

Ruth talked to her as she rolled out another pie crust. "You best go eat at the house. The governess, she don't eat wit da slaves."

As she walked toward the house, she heard a male voice snicker behind her.

"What is so funny?" She quickly turned and found she was eye level with a row of brass buttons. A feeling of déjà vu passed over her. She followed the buttons up to the face. It was of a man who appeared to be in his early sixties. There was something about him that was familiar.

"I'm sorry. I thought I heard someone laughing." She quickly bowed her head, but then noticed that the man was clutching his chest. Looking back at his face, she saw the shock that engulfed him made him look like he was in pain.

"Are you having a heart attack? I know CPR." Grae covered her mouth quickly as she realized what she had said. By this point, the man had sat down on a small bench that was near the path they were following. Still clutching his chest, he appeared winded and his eyes were bulging.

"You! You!"

"Should I go get you some help?"

"No!" The man reached out and grabbed Grae's arm.

"Arabella! Is something wrong?" Margaret yelled as she ran from the house. Grae thought the man running behind her must be Joseph McGavock.

"Brother! You have arrived! Have you ridden too quickly? Or has seeing this fair young lady challenged your bachelor heart?"

The man kept hold of Grae's arm. Joseph walked up between them and gently removed his hand. "This is our new governess. She arrived yesterday."

Grae turned and smiled. This only made the man clutch

his heart more. Joseph looked at his wife for guidance.

"Patrick, this is our new governess. Her name is Arabella James."

"Patrick," Grae said softly. In a flash, she was back in 1786 and Patrick was leaning down from his horse to kiss her. That face, those eyes, the same face that now was before her.

"Arabella," Patrick said as he fell over on the ground.

Grae sat in the front foyer of the house. Some of the slaves had carried Patrick McGavock into the house. He was lying on a bed in one of the downstairs rooms. Grae tried to mentally figure out how old he would be.

"He was about nineteen or twenty in 1786. This is 1830. That was forty-four years ago. That would make him…"

"In his early sixties, now quit talking to yourself." The General slid under the high back chair Grae was sitting in. "You have got to make them believe you don't know him. You are her granddaughter or a niece, or you just look like her."

"What?"

"He's going to think you are Arabella."

"I am Arabella, then and now." Grae looked at the walls surrounding her. "I just realized something, this wallpaper is not green. I could have sworn that the night I arrived the wallpaper was green."

"Follow me."

"But, I need to wait here and find out how he is."

"Follow me!" The General was whispering, but his whispers sounded mad. Grae followed him. He went into a room that appeared to be a study. There was a large fireplace on one wall.

"Listen closely. We don't have much time. You cannot be Arabella from 1786. Patrick will think you are a witch and you will be hanged."

"Patrick would not have me hanged. He loved me."

"It wouldn't be his choice. There would be suspicions and, in this time, suspicions lead to hangings. Witches are not welcome here."

"But, I'm not a witch!"

"I know that, Grae, but make no mistake, you have powers like one. You can travel through time. You look like the girl he loved over forty years ago. You've got to convince him that you are not her. You may die here if you do not."

They heard footsteps go by and quickly left the room. Grae decided that perhaps she should return to the cooking cabin.

"Arabella."

Grae heard Margaret call her name. She turned and went back to the foyer.

"Oh, there you are. Patrick wants to talk to you." Grae bowed her head.

"I'm afraid I have scared the man. I do not know what I have done."

"He is fine. He should not have ridden his horse all this way. We told him to come by stagecoach." Margaret put her arm around Grae's shoulder. "Patrick is Joseph's older brother. He has lived away from here for over forty years. We wish that he would come and live here with us so that we can take care of him. Patrick never married. I'm afraid that you bear a strong resemblance to a girl he once loved. As Joseph tells it, it was the only girl that he ever loved. It has been quite a shock to him. We have told him that you just arrived here from Massachusetts. I believe he wishes to apologize for his behavior."

Grae nodded as her mind raced. Joseph McGavock came

out of the room as Grae waited to enter. Ruth was behind him carrying a basin of water.

"I am sorry, Miss James, if my brother frightened you," Joseph whispered. "He is getting on in years, and I suppose you resemble someone he once knew. I am sure he wishes to apologize for his behavior."

Joseph and Ruth left, and Grae slowly walked into the room. The bed was near the window, but the curtains were drawn.

"Miss James, is that you?" His voice sound gruffer, the price of time; but in the shadow of darkness, Grae could almost see the young Patrick, who risked his life to protect hers.

"I hope you are feeling better, Mister McGavock."

"I am a silly old man, so my brother says. Time can be a cruel companion. It seems that my heart has tricked me into thinking you are someone I once knew, while my mind knows that it is impossible."

"Perhaps you were just tired from your long journey."

"Perhaps, but strangely, you sound so much like the girl who has never left my memory."

Grae sat down in a chair as far from the bed as she could manage. Only one lamp shone in the corner. She was glad The General was not with her. Margaret had shooed him out of the house. He would hate what she was about to ask.

"You knew this girl when you were young?"

"Yes." Patrick was quiet for a moment. "It is really silly, but I only knew her for one day and not even an entire one. She came into my life. Then, she vanished."

Grae took a deep breath. "But you cared for her?"

"She captured my heart in a few short hours. Sadly, she took it with her." Tears ran down Grae's face. "Now, I am an old man, and I long so to see her that I imagined you were her.

I am sorry for any pain I have caused you today."

Grae tried to compose herself before she spoke. Her sniffles were hard to disguise in the quiet darkness. "Oh no, it is I who should apologize. The sight of me brought trouble to you."

"We must remedy this situation. I must overcome this. You are a guest in my brother's home and even after just one day, my brother's wife is so fond of you. Please, Miss James, go to the window and open the curtains. Let me see you again so that I can behold that you are but a beautiful young woman of this day, not my youth."

"Oh no, not now, you need your rest, sir. You can see me tomorrow." Grae walked toward the door.

"No, I am not a man of patience. Time has robbed that from me. I need to see you now, or I shall not rest until I do. Please humor this old man. Open the curtains and we shall have a proper meeting."

Grae thought for a moment. The only way that she could prevent him from seeing her is if she ran away from there entirely. That was not possible, and she would never get home if she did. Perhaps now that the shock had abated, his reaction would be different. This ugly black dress alone should make a difference.

Grae walked to the window and placed her hands on the curtains. Her hands began to tremble.

"Please," he said in a soft whisper. Her heart ached as she heard his young voice.

Grae drew back the curtains with both hands. The afternoon sun blazed through the cloudy window panes. It was blinding for a moment. Grae slowly turned around.

"You are shining like an angel, Miss James. Please step closer." Patrick had sat up on the edge of the bed. Grae stepped closer and out of the direct sunlight.

Patrick gasped. "My God! You are the spitting image of my dear Arabella!" Again, he clutched his heart. "It is as if the hands of time have turned back and she is here again."

Patrick held his face in his hands, sobbing. "She left me so long ago, but I never have let her go."

"I am sorry." Grae said softly.

"You shall not apologize for the shape of your face, the color of your hair. You must be her granddaughter. Is it true? Is your grandmother's name Arabella?"

Grae could not lie to him. "No."

"An aunt, perhaps, or a distant cousin."

"Not that I know of. The origin of my name is not known to me."

"Well then, I must just be mad. They shall lock me up and throw away the key." Grae's hand went to her neck. A key of freedom hung there. It would not free Patrick.

"I think I should leave you now, sir. You need to rest."

"Ah, yes, rest. I pray for an eternal rest to come and free my heart. I am sorry to have troubled you, Miss James. Please accept my humble apology."

"The fault rests with me, Mister McGavock. I am sorry to have caused you pain."

"Yous looks like yous been beat. Massa McGavock looks like he seen a ghost. What is your story, Miss? You got some secret you not be tellin'?" Ruth started asking Grae questions as soon as she walked back into the cabin.

"Could I have a cup of water, maybe a little something to eat?" Grae sat down on a chair next to the fire. It was seventy degrees outside, but she was cold, bone cold. Like she had been drained of every ounce of blood and could collapse.

"I guess you didn't get nothin' to eat. Massa and the missus just now eatin' themselves. Maggie, go fetch this girl a plate, hurry now."

For a moment, Grae thought Ruth had said Aggie and an even colder chill went down her spine. She dropped down off the chair and went into her "safe ball" position as Perry called it.

"What'sa matter with you? Shoulds I go gets Miss Margaret?"

Grae shook her head. "No! No! I will be okay. I am just…it is too much…I need a few minutes…I need some food."

Maggie brought Grae some water and a small plate of food. Grae began to eat in an automatic mode, but her mind was a thousand miles, or perhaps, hundreds of years, away. She needed to talk to The General.

"Ruth, I need to go use the outhouse and get a little air. Then, I will be back and ready to work." Ruth nodded at Grae as she left the cabin. Heading toward the outhouse, she scanned the horizon for her beloved friend. He would know what to do. As she turned the corner to go to the outhouse, she saw that Joseph and Margaret were standing to the side of the barn deep in conversation. They didn't see her so she stepped a little closer to listen to their conversation.

"I don't think she should stay in our house," Joseph said. "We will ask a neighbor to take her in. It will be too uncomfortable for Patrick."

Grae could only assume that she would now be sent to another farm. It might take her even further away from the Mansion property. She would never get home.

"It shouldn't bother Patrick," Margaret replied. "It was decades ago."

"But we don't know what she is capable of; someone else might get hurt."

Grae didn't realize that Joseph was so distrustful of her, or so protective of his older brother.

"She's just an old woman!" Margaret said scornfully. "Who could she possibly hurt?"

Grae's ears perked up. They weren't talking about her.

"She could hurt Arabella. You weren't around this family when Patrick stopped calling on her. She hung around the house every free moment. She had been certain that she was going to become Patrick's wife. All it took was one night for Patrick to change his mind. The first Arabella was an indentured servant at the Joseph Baker farm. After the murder, she disappeared. Patrick searched for years for her. But, she just simply vanished."

"And Evelyn Newton became a spinster," Margaret said.

"Yes. I think she had other opportunities. But, just as Patrick's heart was set on Arabella, Evelyn's heart was set on Patrick. The interest he had shown in her before meeting Arabella was all the ammunition she needed to insure she wasn't going to give up without a fight." Joseph paused and took hold of his wife's arm, whispering. "At the time, my mother heard that Evelyn even solicited the wiles of a witch to help her win back Patrick. When Evelyn did not get the results she wanted, she burned the woman's house down, with her in it."

"Oh, Joseph, that's preposterous. We don't believe in witches."

"You may not, but my mother did, and it was after learning this information that my mother sent her son away. She told Patrick to leave here and only come back on unannounced visits. He has heeded her words to this day."

Grae could see Margaret shaking her head in disbelief.

"Very well, you can have your way for now, but we must keep a close eye on Evelyn. If she sees Patrick's reaction to Miss James, it could affect our governess' safety. We are charged with her care while she is in our employment. I will be advising Patrick of Evelyn's impending arrival and that she will be staying in our house. Do not be surprised if my brother disappears in the night."

Grae decided that it was time to make her presence known. So she rounded the corner as if she was heading to the outhouse.

"Good afternoon," Grae said.

"Ah, Miss James, I trust you have now recovered from the frightful scene with my dear brother." Joseph tipped his hat.

"There was not any need for recovery on my part. I am dreadfully ashamed that my appearance incited such confusion for Mister McGavock."

"Well, perhaps that young woman's family tree crossed with yours at some point and allowed you to favor this woman from long ago. My brother is now an old man and looks longingly back at his youth. I was too young to know the first Arabella, but if you look anything like her, it is not wonder my brother is enamored," Joseph paused. "For now, I must get back to our preparations and seeing about the work in the fields. I will see you at dinner, Miss James."

Joseph and Margaret walked back toward the house as Grae entered the outhouse. She was about to sit down, when she saw something move.

"This is an atrocious place to hide," The General said. "Animals are much wiser in the elimination department. They don't congregate the contraband as this facility does."

"I suppose you heard that conversation," Grae replied.

"That was the only thing that kept me inside this odorous inferno. I did not know of Evelyn Newton, but I do know of the witch that she conspired with. That woman did indeed exist and she met the demise that Joseph described."

"I don't know that much about witches, but always thought they were immortal."

"All the tales you have heard about burning at the stake and hanging, they are basically true. This witch was burned and she died. Most believe that when a witch dies, her spells are undone; but this particular witch had mixed powers, white and black. You've heard about white witches and black witches?"

"Yes, basically white is good and black is evil. Glinda was a white witch, and the Wicked Witch of the West was evil."

"In a simplistic Hollywood way, yes, that is correct." Grae pushed open the outhouse door and they both walked toward the fields.

"Air, sweet clean air!" The General cried. "As I was saying, this witch had mixed powers. Because of this, some of her spells were suspended in a limbo state. They can only be broken by a very powerful white witch. This is one reason you need to be extra careful around this Evelyn Newton person. She may have been bestowed with some of this black witch's power. She may decide that she wants you to disappear again. I will be watching her closely."

The rest of the day was filled with cooking chores as Grae helped Ruth prepare many more pies. Dinner was held inside the house and Grae got her first glimpse of the formal dining room. The long table could seat twelve people. Adorned in beautiful linens, sparkling china, and ornate glassware, it held a mouthwatering feast to honor Patrick and to welcome her to the McGavock home.

Cynthia looked even smaller standing next to her tall father, but she chattered on about her many activities of the day with much detail about The General. Nancy, the studious one, seemed to be inheriting some of the McGavock height. Her features were very complementary to her mother's. She had a beautiful smile, but was less vocal than her sister. Patrick entered the room with Margaret and a gentleman who was introduced as the bride's uncle, William Austin, who had arrived earlier. Following them was David Graham.

"Good evening, Miss James," David said.

"Good evening, Mister Graham," Grae smiled remembering their conversation on formality.

"I trust that my sister has made you feel right at home."

"She is such a gracious hostess and a wonderful conversationalist. I am afraid that I have not been the best guest with my entrance last evening."

"Ah, that is perfectly understandable; your trip drained you and was unsettling at the end. I have, just a few hours ago, penned a harsh letter to the stagecoach company about their lack of service. They shall be wise to heed my words if they wish to continue to make one of their stops on my land. I have plans for a general store by which they may wish to pass."

"Where is Mary?" Joseph asked as everyone began to be seated.

"I am sure she will be along shortly," Margaret said. "I believe there have been some last minute changes to the wedding dress and Mary was intent on watching Missus Frederick make them."

"Did you send Big Jake in the wagon for her?" Joseph asked.

"Yes, I thought that was best. Let's begin our dinner."

Margaret had strategically placed both she and Patrick on

the same side of the table, but Grae could still feel his eyes watching her as she passed a plate or bowl to Nancy who sat beside her. She hoped that these encounters would be limited to dinner time during the rest of his visit. He would soon be engaged in a deep conversation with one of the other men at the table and hopefully forget about her presence.

Nancy was passing her a pitcher of milk when Grae saw someone quickly enter the room.

"Ah, our darling Mary. Miss James, may I present to you our eldest child, Mary Haller McGavock. Mary, this is our new governess, Miss James."

Grae turned toward the young woman as Mary also turned and smiled. Grae gasped in shock. She dropped the pitcher covering herself and her plate with milk. Grae had seen that face before, an older version in 1786.

EIGHTEEN

Grae was thankful that a dressing gown and robe had been left on her bed. As she peeled herself out of the milk-drenched dress, she thought in horror about the spectacle she had made. It renewed her sympathy for Patrick. Seeing someone from another timeframe was shocking. It was hard to mask a reaction.

There was no doubt in her mind. Mary Baker, the kind, pregnant wife of Charles Baker in 1786 was Mary Haller McGavock in 1830. The note that Mary had placed in the beautiful dress she had made Grae had indeed alluded to the truth. Mary was also a time traveler. But, from the blank look on this Mary's face a few minutes earlier, it was evident that young Mary did not know what her adult self would be encountering.

Grae knew that she didn't have long to come up with a reason for her shocked behavior. Margaret would surely come and check on her momentarily. In the meantime, The General slid through the unlatched door as the frustration of the moment made Grae begin to cry.

"Now, now, there's no need to cry over spilt milk." Grae thought she heard what could only be described as a snicker from her faithful friend. "I personally enjoyed the mishap until I was shooed away by that slave woman."

"It's not funny. Did you see her? Am I crazy?"

"No, I am afraid you are not." The General jumped up on the bed. "That is the Mary you knew in Joseph Baker's time. But, I do believe this younger version does not have a clue that she will be a traveler."

"Should I warn her?"

"I do not think that would be wise. You do not want to be deemed as a crazy person."

"But at least then when it happens she would not be scared."

"Grae, did she seem to be fairing alright in 1786?"

"Well, yes, she seemed quite happy being a part of the Baker family."

"Did she talk to you about time travel, even though it is now apparent that she knew of its existence?"

"No."

"Then, perhaps it is best if you do the same. Time travel is not discussed among people, even families. I'm sure your mother hardly wants to discuss it with you. Silence is an unwritten rule. It is a protection against those who would use it against you."

"It's just so strange. I remember her talking about her parents. I'm sure she said her father's name was Abner. He didn't like the red trim on the dress."

"Grae, have you not made up other versions of your life to fit your situation on your journeys?"

"Well, yes."

"And can you imagine why she might not want to say her parents were the McGavocks? That family was already established in the area. She had to be someone else."

Movement in the hallway ended the conversation. Cynthia gently knocked on the door as she opened it. Her little face lit up as she saw The General. His reaction to her was to slide under the bed. With all of the excitement downstairs, Grae hadn't realized that the little girl had been very dressed up for the evening with a pretty pink dress and her golden locks curled in ringlets. What little Grae had observed so far about the child's behavior lead her to believe that Cynthia had tendencies toward being a tomboy. Grae couldn't imagine how the person who had curled Cynthia's hair had managed to get her to sit still long enough.

"We brought you a tray of food," Margaret said, walking in behind her daughter and setting the food on the table next to Grae's bed.

"I am so sorry," Grae said. "The pitcher just slipped right out of my fingers."

"Nancy said that perhaps she had some butter on her fingers when she passed it to you. She apologizes."

"Oh, I am sure that the slippery fingers were all mine. I just cannot imagine what you and your family must think of me. I have caused nothing but disruption, and I have only been here one day."

"Oh no, my dear, do not feel that way. We are the ones who feel bad. You are most certainly still tired from your journey, and we have not even allowed you to have any proper rest. Now, Cynthia and I," Margaret paused to look for her daughter who was sitting on the floor peering under the bed for The General. Margaret shook her head and pulled her daughter up from the floor. "We will leave you alone so that you can enjoy your meal, and then get some rest. Hopefully, all will be better in the morning."

Grae ate her meal, giving bites to The General. Even though her mind was still racing, she stretched out on the bed and quickly went to sleep. She barely opened her eyes when a while later, two young slaves came into the room. They retrieved the dishes and her soiled dress. Another dress was hung up in its place.

The morning sun was up and bright. Grae could hear a rooster crowing. She sat up in the bed and looked around. The General was lying comfortably at her feet. On a hook on the wall hung a dress, it had a white collar and white sleeves, but the rest of it was one color. It was green, a rich green, like the color of modern money, like the color her hair had been. The General stood and stretched into a long cat.

"Good morning," he said.

Grae just pointed to the dress.

"Yes, that's a dress. You didn't expect to wear the milk dress today, did you?"

"What color is it?"

"Green."

"At least I am not imagining that. I swear the walls of the foyer when I came in the first night were green, a velvety green."

"Grae, green must be your predominant color for this trip. What did you see a lot of last time?"

"Red, definitely red, and that didn't end well."

"Indeed, so at least perhaps you will not witness a murder on this trip."

"But what in the world could green mean? That color has been haunting me for months."

"Green's meaning remains to be seen. Let's just concentrate on getting you back to the present day. I'm sure you have some homework to do."

"More like a tour to finish."

"Precisely."

Ruth brought Grae a pail of hot water and soap for bathing. "Yous looked at Miss Mary da way Massa Patrick looked at yous."

Ruth was sharp; Grae would have to watch her reactions better. "No, I dropped the pitcher of milk because my hand was slippery."

"Yessum, yous says so."

"What will I be doing with you today?"

"I hears Miss Margaret says she gonna sends you over to Massa David's with Miss Mary to picks berries. We be servin' berry dumplins ats the big dinner tomorra."

"When will the bride and groom arrive?"

"Whats you mean arrive? They both live less than a mile from here."

"Oh, I just thought that since the wedding party was here that they lived far away."

"No, this here farm be the center of all goings on. If there's goin' be a weddin' it be at that church over yonder. If there be a party, it be here."

Ruth left the room and Grae began bathing.

"What I wouldn't do for a shower!"

"Keep talking to yourself and you may have to invent one." The General slide back through the crack Ruth had left in the door.

"You scared me to death!" Grae squealed, splashing water on the floor.

"Oh, boo hoo, at least you don't have to worry about a little girl following you up the tree you just climbed to get away from her."

"Cynthia loves you." Grae went behind a screen in the corner of the room and began changing into the green dress. "Ruth says that Mary and I will be going to the David Graham property to pick berries today. Does that sound a little strange to you? Wouldn't this property have wild berries?"

"I overheard the conversation earlier and it was Mary that convinced her mother for you to go with her. I can only imagine that there is a motive behind this."

"Well, sooner or later, I need to find out why I am here."

"I vote for sooner."

One of the slaves drove Mary and Grae to the David Graham property that morning. Grae was delighted to have time alone with Mary.

"My sisters and I are so glad that you have come, Miss James," Mary seemed anxious to engage Grae in a conversation. "Our father told us that it might be as long as Thanksgiving before you might be able to come. We are so glad that you could leave Massachusetts sooner."

"It is my pleasure to be here. I am delighted that I did not miss this beautiful season." Grae noticed that the crisp vibrant colors of fall were beginning to be even more apparent. Southwest Virginia was a beautiful place in any season, but fall was her crowning glory, a multicolored collection of jewels glistened on every tree. Grae looked forward to her first fall season working on Big Walker. She had been told the views were like autumn paintings.

Grae swallowed a gasp as once again the Baker cabin came into view. Her memories of her time there were mixed. Her final moments permanently etched. She saw David Graham walk out of a building as they approached. She wondered about this man. It seemed surreal that this person she had researched for the Mansion tour was a real flesh and blood person. The kind nature she had seen in him was a stark contrast to the hard man that history portrayed. Grae wanted to know why.

"Good morning! How is my beautiful niece today?" David reached out his hand to help Mary from the back of the wagon where she and Grae had ridden. His white cotton shirt clung to David's skin with sweat. It appeared that the man had already put in a day's work, and it was only nine o'clock in the morning.

"Miss James, I hope that today brings better tidings to you. Have you adjusted to the comfortable ways of the McGavock family?" David gave his niece a hearty hug as he turned to speak to the slave who had driven them. "I shall bring the ladies home later. You can go back to the farm."

Grae pondered the word 'comfortable' from David's question. She wondered how he would view life in her time, in the twenty-first century. Squire David Graham might call modern life frivolous. The David before her might be fascinated with all of the technology and creative inventions that had graced the world since his passing.

"The McGavocks are gracious hosts. I am anxious to begin earning my keep by teaching their daughters."

"Great learners they are. My brother-in-law has insured that they are educated. He does no less for them then he would have done for sons."

"Miss James and I shall pick berries in the shade of the woods by the field, Uncle David." Mary's soft voice interrupted Grae's thoughts. Its youthful sound was a contrast to the voice of the Mary that Grae knew before. "Mother would like for

Ruth to make berry dumplings for the wedding dinner. It is a special favorite of the groom."

"I am surprised that Margaret did not want the berries picked from her own farm. There are surely young slave children who have idle hands."

"But the berries picked in the shade of your woods are sweeter and have not been picked over during the summer." Mary gave her uncle a large smile.

"And?" David replied.

"I should like to visit with Ama and her grandfather before the wedding activities consume my time."

"So, now we know the truth."

The words of Sal echoed in Grae's head. 'And the truth shall set us free.'

NINETEEN

Grae followed David and Mary as they walked down a path through the woods.

"Miss James, I imagine our rural lifestyle is foreign to what you have experienced up north," David dropped back to walk with Grae.

"I have lived in both a city and a rural environment." Grae was careful to tell the truth as much as possible. She did not know what the time travel punishment for lying might be.

"Have you experience then with farm life?"

"Some, but only in a limited amount."

"It is a time of growth! We are building businesses and our communities are expanding with new homes. Our Commonwealth shall shine with prosperity just as our departed President Jefferson showed us with his beloved home in Charlottesville."

"How has Ama been feeling?" Mary broke into the conversation as Grae glimpsed a very small cabin through the trees.

David's eyes darted back and forth from Mary to Grae. "She and her grandfather are well."

As they approached the cabin, Grae could see an old Indian man sitting on the stump of a tree stripping bark from a branch that appeared to be ten feet long.

"Greetings Wahulidoda!" The old man nodded as David walked toward him.

"What did he say?" Grae whispered to Mary.

"I can't pronounce it, but Ama says it means *Wise Father*."

"And Ama is?"

"His granddaughter. She is very special and very beautiful."

Mary began to walk inside the small structure and Grae was following behind when she felt a hand on her arm.

"Miss James, forgive me, but there is something I must say to you." Grae turned around and walked a few steps back with David.

"The young woman inside," David took a deep breath. "She is very important to me. For some reason you have very quickly gained the trust and respect of my sister and her family, that is why Mary has brought you here today. I hope that we can also trust one another."

Grae wondered if this conversation was in some sort of nineteen century code. She could not understand why he would be so concerned about her meeting this young Indian woman. Grae nodded.

"Thank you." David motioned for her to enter the cabin. Despite the time of day, the interior was very dark. The structure had only one small window. The dirt floor seemed primitive compared to what Grae had seen on the McGavock farm; where even the slaves' cabin had a wood floor. Grae imagined that this small structure might have existed in the

Baker days, but she did not remember seeing it.

Mary had her back to Grae and seemed to be standing in front of someone who was sitting in a chair. Grae assumed this was the young woman. Grae looked around the small space and saw that the cabin was just one room. A large floor mat was in the left back corner, it was most likely the grandfather's bed. A smaller one was in the left front corner. In the middle of the back wall was a good size fireplace with a large, black iron pot on a swinging iron rod in front of it. The food simmering within it had a rich earthy aroma that made Grae's mouth water. Another chair stood opposite the one that Mary was standing in front of and a small wooden table was placed on the right side of the room.

Grae didn't realize that David had come in behind her until she saw the glow of a lantern that he had lit behind her.

"Is this your new friend, Mary?" Grae heard a melodious voice over her shoulder and turned to see a beautiful young woman standing before her. She was petite in height, but her presence commanded attention. Her skin was softly dark, what Grae would liken to a modern day tan. Her long coal black hair shined with a silky beauty that made Grae desire to reach out and touch it. But, her eyes, they were her crowning glory and so strikingly out of place. They were ocean blue and they glistened, her spirit radiated behind those beautiful eyes; they were a window to her soul.

The young woman took Grae's hand. "You were found on the road, but you are not the lost one. You shall help others find their way."

Grae could feel the others watching them, but she could not break the gaze that held her to this young woman. It was as if they were communicating on another level and the voice without words was stronger than any she had heard before.

Ama took hold of Grae's other hand and tears began to run down Ama's cheeks.

"Ama, what is wrong?" David now stood beside them. Ama broke her hold on Grae's hands and turned toward David. It was then that Grae saw the lower half of the young woman's body. She was pregnant.

Ama grew silent and wiped her tears. "I am tired. The baby does not wish me to sleep at night."

Grae watched David. His whole demeanor changed. From his eyes, a deep love could be seen. There was no one else in the room but Ama. Grae wondered if this was why she was in 1830.

Mary and Grae left David and Ama in the cabin. Ama's grandfather was nowhere in sight. As they walked toward the spot where the berries were, Mary began talking.

"Ama has extraordinary abilities, she is very wise. She can see into someone and tell who they really are."

"Why are they here? Is their tribe nearby?" Mary and Grae began to pick the black fruits.

"Their tribe was struck with yellow fever many years ago and very few survived. Wise Father and his daughter, Ama's mother, found their way to Uncle David's farm while the previous owner was still here. Ama's mother's name was Singing Sunshine. She became involved with a white man, John Allison, who lived nearby. They were married; soon thereafter had Ama. When Ama was about five, she and her parents were out picking berries, just as we are, and were attacked by a large bear. The bear first attacked Singing Sunshine. Ama's father told her to run to her grandfather. He tried to get the bear off of his wife, not knowing that another bear was right behind him. He was very badly hurt, his clothes were in shreds, but he walked several miles carrying his wife. He got back to the farm and collapsed with Singing Sunshine in his arms. Neither one of them survived. Some say that he still walks the road in front of Uncle David's house trying to save his wife."

Grae snuck a few juicy and plump berries, as she listened to the story. She was about to ask Mary a question when she heard David call Mary's name.

"I will be right back," Mary said.

"I wonder if Ama's father is the man I keep seeing on the road in front of the Mansion." Grae said out loud after Mary had left.

"Possible." Grae about jumped out of her skin as she heard The General's voice.

"Good grief! I didn't know you had come with us."

"Do you think I would let you come back to the Mansion property without me? Remember, I am the one who wants you to leave."

"You know I will not be leaving until I learn what I am supposed to discover. I don't think that has happened yet." Grae offered The General a berry. He turned his nose up and walked away with a flip of his tail.

"But, I do think this journey has something to do with Ama. She is obviously a key person in David's life. I wonder why none of the research I have found mentions her."

"Really? You wonder? She's a teenage Indian girl living on a white man's farm. And she is pregnant with his child, and this is 1830. Really? You wonder?" The General climbed a nearby tree and lounged on a branch.

"Well, I realize this is a very different time than mine, but still, he loves her and this is his child, shouldn't history remember them?"

"Only if history knows they exist."

The buckets of berries were overflowing by the middle of the day when Ama invited them to share the stew she had been cooking. It was venison with root vegetables. It had a sweetness that Grae could not describe as she tasted it slowly.

"This bread is wonderful," Grae said, heartily taking another bite. Ama smiled and nodded.

"It is outstanding!" David said, as he ate his third or fourth piece. "Ama learned her baking skills from Ruth, Margaret's slave woman. But, she puts her own touch on it with all of the spices and herbs she includes. That talent came from her mother."

The grandfather spoke a long sentence in Indian and Ama made a hearty reply.

"My family's tribe lived in many parts of Virginia. Our people became wanderers when we left the mountain land of Carolina. My grandfather is a very skilled healer, what you call a medicine man. Herbs are a part of our medicine. They have many uses."

Grae was enthralled with Ama's story. "What is the herb in this bread? Could it be rosemary?"

"Yes!" Ama's face lit up. "Do you know herbs?"

Grae carefully chose her words. "Some, my mother is a…she's known for her cooking and likes to grow her own herbs."

Ama looked confused. "Who else would grow them for her?"

Grae tried to hide the panic that she was sure was crossing her face. "We have lived mostly in the city and there are farmers who sell their harvest in the streets."

David unknowingly came to her rescue. "The cities have many things that are foreign to our rural life. It is hard to imagine others growing your food, but there is no room for gardens in the cities."

Ama nodded and once again reached for Grae's hand. "My David calls you Miss James, but what shall I call you? I am Dekanogi'a Ama, it means Singing Water. But you shall call me Ama."

Her name sounded enchanting, as she was. "You can call me Arabella." Grae longed to tell Ama her real name.

"Arabella, I shall teach you about herbs the Indian way, as my mother and grandfather shared with me. Then you can share with your mother, when you return to your own world."

Grae stared deep into Ama's beautiful eyes after her last statement. She wondered if this exceptional young woman knew how close and how far away that world was.

They were sent back to the McGavock's with several loaves of the rosemary bread. Mary left a small bucket of the berries for Ama and her grandfather. As Grae began to board the wagon, David spoke to her.

"I am sure that you can understand, Miss James, that I will appreciate your discretion in regards to Ama."

"You can expect nothing less, Mister Graham." Grae knew she had now secured her way into the life of David Graham. This, she hoped, would lead her to the purpose of her journey.

TWENTY

"This house will be a crazy place for the next few days, Arabella. You will just have to bear with us; soon you shall see what normal is for our family." Margaret had a small sheet of paper in her hand. It appeared to be a list with a few items marked through.

"Mother, Ama has sent you some of her lovely rosemary bread," Mary smiled at Grae as she named it. "We shared some of the berries we picked with her. Ama served us a delicious lunch."

"That is very nice dear. I hope she and her grandfather are well." Margaret looked at Grae cautiously.

"Missus McGavock, I am aware of the situation with Ama and Mister Graham. Please be assured that I will be nothing but discrete with this knowledge and offer my assistance in any way to help when needed. A family's business is a family's business and should not be shared throughout the community."

Margaret walked to Grae and engulfed her in a hug. "I can tell you were raised by a loving family with sound judgment and honesty." Grae smirked to herself. "Your mother should be proud. She will be lucky if we let her have you back." Out of the corner of her eye she saw The General. Displeased with Margaret's last comment, he deliberately jumped up on a table and knocked over a small pitcher of milk.

"Oh, shoo cat." Margaret and Grae grabbed kitchen towels and began mopping up the milk.

"He must have been thirsty," Grae said timidly.

"Cats do like milk. We shall not cry over it," Margaret replied, causing both of them to laugh. Grae knew that The General was not laughing. She hoped Margaret's words were not prophetic.

The property was bustling with activity. There was a large flat area on the side of the house where many makeshift tables had been assembled with simple benches. Behind that, in front of the barn, it looked as if a small stage had been built. Grae wondered if musicians would congregate there and play as the wedding guests danced. Within the house, everything that was made of wood, floor to ceiling had been cleaned and polished. The silverware glistened, the crystal sparkled. Beds were adorned with beautiful, freshly cleaned linens and quilts. Even the chamber pots were given special attention.

Margaret gave Grae a detailed task that would allow her to snoop through the house. She was to go through every room of the house and check it for cleanliness and attractiveness. "You are perfect for this job!" Margaret exclaimed. "You have never been in these rooms before and can look at them as a guest would for the first time."

Grae was thrilled to have a reason to explore the house. Passing the massive polished staircase, she entered a parlor that was lavish with formal flair. While the southern exposed sitting room was decorated with velvet settees and ornate tables, it felt more inviting and comfortable than she would have expected. Perhaps it was the deep window seats under the large, tall windows. Grae fingered the braided silk drapes that served as window dressings. She wished she could take one of the many leather-bound books she saw and curl up in one of the window seats for a relaxing few hours.

The large dining room included hand-carved cherry furniture. There was a table to seat twelve with large chairs. Underneath there was a hand-woven rug that Grae imagined must have travelled via a big ship from a country in Europe. On the buffet server, she saw heavy silver serving dishes, silver utensils, and English bone china with a rose pattern.

Then, Grae began to inspect the bedrooms. There were three on the lower level. One was the master bedroom of Joseph and Margaret McGavock. A small nursery was located off of their room. Their youngest child, Lucinda, was found there taking a nap under the watchful eye of a slave girl who told Grae her name was Cissy. These quarters were not as grand as Grae expected after viewing the other rooms, but the canopy bed in the master bedroom was an impressive piece of furniture. It was large for the time and made of mahogany. The canopy itself was a hand crocheted islet with tiny pearls woven throughout. The quilt on their bed was made in the wedding ring pattern. Her mother had one of the same design that Granny Belle had made before her parents were married. It always remained in the guest room cedar chest.

The two other bedrooms served as guest rooms and were located on opposite sides of the house from each other. The first one was near the master bedroom and was the room where Grae had seen Patrick the previous day. She gently knocked on the door before entering. He was probably out helping his brother supervise preparations. As she walked into the small room, she felt as if she was disturbing his privacy.

The room was very simple. The walls were painted white and the bedspread mirrored them in color and simplicity. A small table was next to the window where Grae had opened the curtains. Those curtains were once again fully open and the window glass sparkled as the light beamed through. There was a chair next to the table and Grae noticed that Patrick's jacket was hung on the back. Grae touched the buttons at the top of the collar and smiled remembering how similar ones adorned Patrick's jacket over forty years earlier. The movement she made as she fingered the buttons caused her to see the glimpse of a red ribbon in the inside pocket. She took it out and instantly reached for the back of her head. It was the bow that Nannie and Mary had carefully placed to hide her short hair on the night she met Patrick. While she was in the prison cell, she had realized it was gone, but thought it had merely gotten lost in the shuffle of everything that transpired that night. But here it was, safely kept next to Patrick's heart all these years.

"It belonged to the only girl I ever loved." Grae turned to find Patrick standing just inside the doorway. "It is all I have to remember her by."

"Oh, I am sorry, I didn't mean to...when I moved your jacket, it almost fell out...I am so sorry." Grae laid the ribbon down on the table and quickly moved across the room. Patrick still stood in front of the doorway. "Missus McGavock has me inspecting all of the rooms to make sure they have been cleaned properly." Grae tried to change the subject and hoped that Patrick would soon move out of her way.

"An old man has many memories, some are clearer than others, some he would just as soon forget. But some things are never forgotten. He does not forget his first love, especially when she was also his only love."

Grae could not look at him. If their eyes met, she would not be able to hide the pain she now feels.

"You resemble her so closely that it is as if you were plucked up in time then and brought back here now."

Grae felt her face grow hot, but her hands were clammy. The green fog that she saw previously began to appear before her eyes. She reached for the bed post and Patrick moved away from the door. This movement caused a slight breeze and Grae felt she could walk on out of the room.

"Arabella, I will always love you." Grae heard as she turned the corner out of the room. She wondered if Patrick was speaking to her now or her then and realized that it really didn't matter. Time could stand still where love was concerned.

She stood in the hallway for a moment to catch her breath. She saw that an older woman watching her from the corner of the staircase. Grae took a deep breath and turned to the mirror on the wall beside her to straighten her dress and hair. In the reflection, she saw the same green fog and through it, behind her in the mirror, the face of the woman she just saw, a younger version. The woman's lips were moving and it seemed to Grae that she was saying, "I know."

"Arabella, how have the rooms been so far?" Margaret's voice startled Grae, forcing her attention away from the mirror.

"Very good, ma'am, I only have one more to inspect downstairs."

"Excellent. You should be finished then with plenty of time to rest before supper." As Margaret quickly moved on to her next task, Grae looked back at the mirror. There was nothing there, but her reflection.

Grae walked around the staircase and to the last room.

The door was wide open and Grae could see that it was almost as large as the master bedroom and more elaborate in its design and décor. Grae was immediately startled by the color. The walls were deep forest green wallpaper with a rich design that gave the covering the illusion of a velvety texture. These were the walls Grae had seen when she first entered the house. She reached out to touch them and her fingertips immediately drew back. It was the same feeling that you get in modern day after walking quickly across carpet and touching something, the electric feeling of a spark. Grae looked down at the floor; it was solid wood, no rugs.

To her left there was a large bed; an ornately carved flower design adorned the headboard. A large "M" was carved in the middle. This was a piece of family furniture. A matching dressing table and armoire stood on the opposite side of the room. As Grae walked deeper into the room, she realized that there was a sitting area in the far end. All at once the curtains were drawn back to reveal three large bay windows with brilliant streaks of sunlight beaming through, temporarily blinding Grae. When she had walked a few steps more, she realized that a young slave had drawn open the curtains.

"Go now." A voice told the slave, making Grae realize that they were not alone. The older woman who had watched her in the hallway, the same woman who appeared in the mirror was sitting in a chair.

As the older woman stood up, Grae could see that though small in stature, the woman had a commanding force in the room. Her silver hair stood high on her head in a tight bun and she was attired in a simple brown long dress with a white collar. She appeared to be in her early-sixties and her face showed that her life had not been as easy as it was in her current surroundings. Her only adornment was an amethyst broach at her throat. Long thin fingers reached for the broach and it occurred to Grae that her hands did not resemble the rest of her body. It seemed as if they should belong to someone else.

"We finally meet, Arabella." The woman's voice was silky and fluid, neither old nor young. Timeless.

"I'm sorry, but I am afraid I do not know your name."

"No, you would not, although our paths have crossed before."

Grae suddenly felt a cold breeze. She looked at the windows, they were all closed.

"Margaret has given you a task, a duty. The McGavocks are fond of you. The McGavocks were fond of me, a long time ago, the ones who slept in this bed. This should have been my bed."

The woman had walked around Grae; her hand was still on the broach.

"I am honored to be employed by them," Grae replied, trying to keep the conversation light. "I look forward to teaching their daughters."

The woman now stood in front of the dressing table. She sat down and gazed into the mirror.

"Yes, those young girls need to learn. They need to learn about the disappointments of life. I doubt you can teach them that."

Grae knew she needed to get to the door. As she walked behind the woman, she glanced into the mirror. The woman's reflection was the same as Grae had seen in the mirror a few minutes earlier and that green fog was all around her and the broach, it was…

The woman suddenly turned around and faced Grae. It was the face of the older woman.

"Leaving so soon?"

Grae ran, not looking behind her. As she was about to step over the threshold, she heard the voice behind her.

"I know." The door slammed shut.

TWENTY ONE

Cynthia found Grae standing at the foot of the staircase. Grae's hand was on the rail as if she was about to take the first step, but nothing about her was moving.

"Hello, Miss James, have you seen your cat?" Grae could hear the words, but could not form an answer in her head.

"I would so love to play with him. He is a him, isn't he? He doesn't seem like a her." Cynthia paused for a moment, thinking. "Does he have a name? I think that Jasper is a delightful name, don't you? Can we call him Jasper?"

Cynthia's sister, Nancy, came up behind them. Upon seeing that Grae wasn't moving, she began going up the steps around her and turned back to look at Grae.

"Miss James, are you feeling well? You look a little green." Those words snapped Grae out of the haze and she began running up the staircase, leaving both girls behind. They caught up with her as she reached the top where a long full-length mirror stood. It was a strange place to have a mirror, Grae thought. To use it, you had to have your back to the staircase.

One wrong move and you would fall backwards. But, a mirror it was and in it Grae saw herself clearly. She was pale, but the only green upon her was her long nineteenth century dress.

Despite the fact that two chattering girls followed her from room to room, Grae completed the task of inspecting the rooms upstairs. She turned and told the girls that she needed to rest and freshen up before dinner. She walked to her room and turned the latch on the door after closing it. The General sat in a relaxed pose on the bed. Grae collapsed on the bed beside him.

"Rough day?" The General asked, yawning and stretching.

"You would not believe it."

"Somehow Grae, I doubt that you can surprise me."

"Okay," Grae sat up. "Here's the abbreviated version. Patrick has carried a ribbon from Arabella's hair from the one night he knew her in his pocket for over forty years. Arabella was his one and only love. And, I think that the old woman across the hall from him is a witch."

"What?" The General stood up. "I leave you alone for one afternoon so that I can do a little exploring and what happens? You get in all sorts of trouble. And please quit referring to yourself in third person. You are Arabella, like it or not."

"But you know, I am realizing that I don't think I want to be."

"My dear, there are many of us who do not want to be who we currently are. You must make the best of it and work toward getting yourself back to your own time...and staying there."

Grae lay back down and tried to rest again, but her mind was spinning. She hoped the activities of the next few days kept her away from Patrick. She most certainly did not want to cross paths with the strange woman downstairs. She searched her memory for when their paths crossed and could only imagine that it was in 1786. The woman seemed old enough. She probably would have been about her age then.

"Do you think that woman could have been...?" Her question to The General was cut short as a loud knock came on the door.

"Miss James, it's time for dinner!" The enthusiasm of Cynthia could be felt through the door.

"Oh dear, it's the girl. I'm going to hide."

"She just adores you," Grae whispered. "And she wants to name you Jasper."

The General slid under the bed and into a corner before Grae unlocked the door.

"Thank you, Cynthia. I will be down in just a few minutes."

"Is Jasper in here?" Cynthia stretched to look around Grae.

"My cat is named The General. I don't think he would answer to Jasper."

"Oh, well, that's a nice name too." Cynthia turned and left.

"Thank you," The General said, not moving from his corner. "Please bring me some food. I think I need to stay out of her sight for a while. She is not a gentle petter."

"Well that just might have to be her first lesson then," Grae said, as she tidied up her hair and walked out of the room.

Dinner that evening was an interesting experience for Grae. She was seated with David Graham on her right and an uncle of the bridegroom, Mister Hathaway, on her left. Mary, the only one of the McGavock children who was allowed to dine with the adults that evening, was seated on David's right. Patrick was placed at one end of the table next to Margaret and the mysterious older woman was at the opposite end next to Joseph. An assortment of other wedding guests sat in between.

"I appreciate your kindness to Ama," David Graham whispered to Grae as he passed her a bowl of peas with pearl onions.

"She seems to be a simply delightful person," Grae replied, passing him a plate of ham.

"I hope you will come and let her teach you about herbs. She needs a friend. It is a difficult time for her."

Grae paused to think about what David had said as he began conversing with a gentleman across the table. For the rest of the meal, Grae listened to the buzz of conversation around her. She found that each time she looked at the mysterious woman, she appeared to be staring at her. Grae heard the hearty laugh of Patrick and she briefly saw the man he had become, strong, successful, satisfied with his life.

"Mister Graham," Grae whispered as the dessert was being served. "Who is the woman sitting next to Mister McGavock?"

"That is Evelyn Newton. She is a spinster who used to be the teacher at the school at Anchor & Hope Church."

"What is her connection to this family?"

"Well, she was a fixture in this community for decades; only in recent years did she move away to her sister's in the Shenandoah Valley. She is related in some fashion to the bride's mother. I can't remember how exactly."

Grae looked at the woman. She looked oddly at her plate of dessert, and then pushed it away. Her hand immediately went to the broach at her neck.

David leaned back toward Grae. "Oh, and Patrick McGavock was her beau once."

Grae almost choked on the piece of apple cake she had just put in her mouth.

"So the story goes, she and Patrick were almost engaged. I have been told that she was quite lovely in her youth, although no one could tell that now." Grae was a little shocked at David's bluntness.

"Apparently, one night he met a young woman at a wedding party. I believe she was visiting someone. He fell in love with her almost instantly. The woman just disappeared a few days later. No one knew what became of her. He spent the next year or more searching for her. He travelled on horseback and went from town to town. It's been said that Miss Newton waited for him, thinking that if he did not find the young woman he would come back to her. But, one day, Patrick came home, went to visit her and told her that he would never marry." David finished his last bite of dessert and took a long sip of coffee.

"I remember hearing that story when I was in my late teens and thinking how silly to be so caught up in one girl," David continued. "But now I know how he felt. Love can be a powerful force and can grip a man's heart with an unrelenting hold. My sister tells me that you favor this young woman of Patrick's. It must be hard on him. It must be hard for you."

There was such kindness, such gentleness in David's words. Grae wondered if she would learn what turned his heart so cold or if that would be something that happened in a later time. This David Graham she could see becoming her friend. This one was not the tunnel-visioned capitalist that history portrayed him to be.

"My best advice for you, my friend," David whispered as they both stood to leave the table, "is to keep your distance from Miss Newton. There was quite the talk, as I understand, about the lengths she went to in order to try and win him back. If she sees how he is looking at you, she may try for some revenge."

"Yes, I have already gotten that feeling. I wish I didn't have to be here these next few days."

David turned to her, smiling. "Well, I do believe that I might be able to help you with that."

True to his word, a solution to Grae's awkward position was found the following morning.

"Arabella, we realize that you have just stumbled into all of this wedding nonsense with our family this week. It must be quite boring and tiresome for you, since you do not know anyone involved." Margaret began the conversation with Grae after breakfast as the rest of the family dispersed to last minute duties. It was Thursday and by noontime, many guests would be arriving.

"Missus McGavock, I am happy to do whatever you wish. I realize that my tutoring duties will not commence until the wedding activities have completed and your family has recovered. I mean to earn my way here and am not afraid of work." Grae poured a large portion of cream and a dollop of honey into the cup of coffee before her. She had remembered that some had said that Granny Belle's coffee could stand up without a cup, but she thought that Ruth's was so strong it could walk to the table on its own.

"My brother David would like to be able to spend a couple of days here and help with the activities. But, he is concerned about leaving Ama since she is so far along. We have not talked about this, but I know that you are aware of this situation. I cannot say that I wholeheartedly approve of the arrangement, but my brother loves her and he plans to marry her, so I suppose I need to accept it."

Grae could tell that this was not an easy conversation for

Margaret. It was not a conversation that a Graham or a McGavock would find appropriate in most situations.

"David says that Ama was quite taken with you, so I thought that perhaps you could stay with her for the next few days while he is here with us. There is so much going on here, that I really can't spare Ruth or any of the other slaves."

"I would be delighted!" Grae tried to conceal a little of her enthusiasm, but she would do almost anything to get away from that scary Evelyn Newton and the sad looks of Patrick. She had a feeling that the reason for her journey had more to do with the Graham property than where she presently was sitting.

"Wonderful! Mary and I will find you some clothes and pack a bag for you. We have just got to get some new dresses made for you after all this wedding business is over. I will also have Ruth put together some food. I do not know how much that they have on hand. I'm sure that Ama is starting to have trouble keeping up with the cooking. David felt sure that you would agree, so he will be here in a couple of hours. Thank you so much, it will be a blessing for my brother."

"The pleasure is all mine."

"It pleases me greatly that you will be with my Ama. I hate to be away from her, but feel that I should help my family during these busy days." David had arrived by midmorning and they were now on their way back to his farm.

"I am happy to do this, Mister Graham. It will be delightful to spend a few days with her. I promise to take good care of her." Grae was sitting up in the wagon seat with David and The General was riding in the back. Grae thought that David might bring a slave along to drive her back so that he would stay at the McGavocks, but that was not the case.

"You now know my deepest secret and I am entrusting you with my most prized possession. I think that you should be privy to using my given name. Please call me David."

While Grae grimaced a little at him referring to Ama as his most prized possession, she also realized that it was a statement of the times and did not diminish his love for her.

"And you must call me Arabella."

"Now, Arabella, I must share with you a few pieces of information. The old man, Ama's grandfather, is strict in his Indian ways. We have barely convinced him to sleep in that cabin; he stays outside on the land rain or shine from sun-up to sunset. My slave man, Ezekiel, shall keep an eye on him. I have moved Ama to my cabin as she is due very soon. So you shall stay with her there. If anything happens, send one of the slaves to get me. I will bring Ruth right away."

"David, may I ask how old Ama is?"

"She is sixteen, but not far from the time of her seventeenth year. She is very old and wise for her age. She says that this is because of the other lives she has led." David laughed at his last comment, but Grae wondered how much truth there was in it.

"Ama is anxious to teach you about herbs and the phases of the moon and planting signs. I do believe that these things are true. Ama can grow a perfect garden."

On the horizon, Grae could once again see the Graham property. From her vantage point, it looked strange without the large Mansion there. "So, will you be building a large home soon for you and Ama and your family?" After the words had left her mouth, she wasn't sure it was an appropriate question to be asking.

"Oh no, I had once planned to make this property into a large plantation and to grow my iron business into the biggest in Virginia; but our union will not be accepted here. In the spring, we will move to North Carolina. There I have an uncle who is engaged in many businesses; specifically of interest to me is his Vesuvius Furnace. I spent many of my growing up years in that area with my father and will establish a home there and begin to grow a business again."

By this time, they had arrived on the property. David jumped down off the wagon and walked around to help Grae down, but she just sat there, staring off into space.

"Is there something wrong?" David asked.

Grae looked all around her and stopped her focus on the small cabin. She realized that it was indeed on the same soil as the Mansion now stood.

"You do not have any intention of building a large home here?" Grae asked, still sitting in the wagon seat.

"I had considered it, but that was before Ama came into my life, before the baby. I will build her something very grand, but not here. I have already been making inquiries about selling my entire property."

Grae stepped down from the wagon and gazed around her. David Graham died on this property, at a fairly old age for the time, in a grand mansion that he had built. Something was going to keep him here. David Graham was a planner and something was going to change his plan for his own life.

TWENTY TWO

Grae watched as Ama stood in the yard and waved until David was out of sight. She was whispering as she stood there, which had the cadence of a chant. Grae stayed behind her, not wanting to interrupt.

"It is a prayer for his safety. I learned much as a child about the ways of the white man, but thankfully my grandparents also made sure that I learned the ways of my Cherokee ancestors."

"I do hope you will teach me some of the Indian ways."

"Your mind is open to many things; it is because you have an old spirit. It has traveled much more than the years of your age."

Grae wondered if this wise young woman could see right through into her mind and soul. Did she know that she was from another time?

Ama turned and walked into the cabin and for the first time that morning, Grae was filled with dread. To her, this was the cabin of Joseph Baker and his family; the people may have left here, but the memories surely remain. She had hardly crossed the doorway when a powerful feeling hit her—everything around her began to move quickly like it was going in fast forward. She wasn't looking at the past because the Bakers were not in her vision. This was the future and something was very wrong. The green smoke was there, but this time there was fire, and a blood curdling scream.

"Arabella, ARABELLA!" Grae felt a hand shaking her arm and heard a name being loudly spoken. She had collapsed on the floor, and Ama had tried to stoop down to help her.

"Are you sick?"

"No, I'm sorry, I'm fine. I...I just got a little dizzy."

"You had a vision, did you not?"

Grae looked at Ama with shock in her eyes. She was amazed at her perceptiveness and simultaneously at her perfect English. The ways of the white race and the Indian weren't fragments of who Ama was, but clear portions of her. This had to be one of the reasons that David had been drawn to her. She was the best of both worlds in a beautiful package.

"Tell me about your childhood, Ama. How did you manage to learn both the white ways and the Indian ways so well?"

Ama handed Grae a glass of water, and then sat down in a rocking chair that was near the fireplace. She gently stroked her growing belly.

"My mother and her parents had lived on this land while it was still owned by the Crockett family. Most of the surviving tribe had travelled on to live elsewhere, but my grandfather liked it here and liked the Crocketts. We were not slaves, but we shared in the labor of the land. My grandfather can put any seed into the ground and it will grow. Some years the harvest may be more abundant than others, but I have never known him to fail to produce a crop. This was very valuable to old Mister Crockett; he saw that my grandfather had skills that could be profitable to him. So they reached an agreement."

Ama stood up and walked toward a basket in the corner that was filled with fall apples. She retrieved a large bowl from a shelf and began to place apples within it.

"What are we going to do?" Grae asked.

"I am going to peel some apples for drying. David picked these yesterday from an old tree behind the large barn. They will make good pies this winter." Ama clutched her stomach suddenly.

"Are you okay?" Grae asked, rushing to Ama's side.

"The baby is moving. I think he is preparing for his arrival."

"His?" Grae took the bowl out of Ama's hand and walked with her back to the chair. Placing the bowl on a table beside Ama, she handed her a paring knife.

"This baby is a boy; I know it to be so. He shall be given the Indian name Aginvda. This means My Sun, My Moon. Say it with me, you can learn, ah gee neh dah."

"Ah gee neh dah," Grae carefully repeated. Moving a chair near the basket, Grae had begun peeling apples as well.

"Continue to tell me about your family and the Crocketts."

"Old Missus Crockett very much loved my mother. She began teaching her to speak and read English. My mother was about twelve years old by this point, but learned rapidly. When she was about fifteen, she caught the eye of my father, John Allison. He was a young worker on the Crockett's farm. My mother became pregnant and they were married. Missus Crockett insisted that the ceremony occurred in a church and her influence made it so. This did not please my grandfather, he wanted my mother to honor the Indian ways, so they were also united in a traditional ceremony."

"I bet that was beautiful," Grae said, a pile of circular apple peels were beginning to form at her feet. She seemed to always be peeling something when she was in another time.

"I can only imagine." Ama looked toward the window, absorbed in thought.

"And then you were born!" Grae said, breaking the silence.

"Yes, I was born, and Missus Crockett convinced my mother that I should be taught all of the English ways. I went to school with white children and went to church and did all of the things that the other children nearby did. But it caused some sadness in my mother's heart, and I remember after my parents died, I wanted to remove myself from that life. I went to live with my grandfather and he began to teach me the Indian ways. I learned to make baskets and pottery, and even some of my grandfather's medicine secrets."

"What about your father's parents?"

"They did not want him to marry my mother. They removed themselves from his life after he married her. The only time I can ever remember seeing them is when my parents were buried. They stood far away and watched. Missus Crockett tried to take me over to them, but they got into their wagon and drove off."

"I am sorry, Ama. That must have been hard to experience."

"Love that was never ours is not lost love. We cannot grieve what we never knew."

Grae watched this young woman in awe. She had experienced so much loss, so much change in her short life. Grae imagined that her paternal grandparents were not the only ones who treated her with prejudice. Ama's union with David and the child she now carried would certainly result in more of the same. David felt that the opinion would be so strong locally that he had plans to move his young family away to start a new life. Grae could not help but wonder why he had returned to this property later in his life. She contemplated whether David may have led a double life with a family in North Carolina and one in Virginia. In his pursuit of his ambition, did he build two lives, one of prosperity and unhappiness in Virginia, and the other of love and simplicity in North Carolina? Somehow, she doubted that even the most extensive research would reveal the latter.

"Tell me more about Missus Crockett. She sounds like an important person in your life."

Ama smiled. "She was wonderful to me. She was the grandmother I was not allowed to have. It was her goal for me to learn all of the things she felt were proper. This continued after the passing of my parents, because my grandfather had great respect and honor for Mister and Missus Crockett. I learned to sew from Missus Crockett. I also learned about herbs; the Indian way for healing and preserving. Missus Crockett planted her garden by the signs and the phases of the moon, thus I also learned to do so. These were embraced by my grandfather when he realized that it was much the same as his own planting ways."

Ama and Grae spent the rest of the morning stringing the apples to be hung to dry. Ama's grandfather joined them as they ate a late lunch of fresh apples, ham, and some of Ama's wonderful bread, while they talked about all of the wedding activities that were taking place a few miles away. It was a light-hearted chat of details until Ama brought up Evelyn Newton. The mere mention of her name sent a chill down Grae's spine.

"This woman, her name is Miss Newton, I believe. David

tells me that she was long ago connected to Mister Patrick McGavock. David says that she cannot let go of this love that was never hers."

"Well that is about the way the story seems to go." Grae was unsure how much she should say.

"I see great love in Mister Patrick's eyes. This love is for a lifetime and the circumstances do not matter."

"You know Patrick?"

"Yes, since I was a child. Of course, I only see him occasionally when he visits. David holds him in high regard. He was here yesterday. He brought me some beautiful green fabric for a new English dress for myself and some blue fabric for a blanket for the baby."

"So Patrick knows that this child shall be a boy, too?" Grae laughed.

"Patrick knows many things, he is insightful. He has looked deeply into his own heart to be at peace with his life. He can look deeply into that of others. He carries the symbol of his love in his pocket. It is his redemption for a love that time ignored."

Grae began to feel light-headed. I need to get some air." Grae quickly rose, but Ama also stood and stopped her.

"You cannot run from the past, it shall find you. You are here for a purpose, so you must fulfill it. But you must stay away from that woman. She dabbled in powers that were not hers. She destroyed the one who gave them to her. Some of the dark power remained within her."

Ama's face began to fade from view, but Grae still turned and walked out the front door. She stopped in the yard and drank in a breath of fresh air. Her vision became clearer, and she saw The General on a stump nearby that was used for chopping wood.

"You will do well to listen to her. She may be young in years in this time, but her spirit is old in the universe. She knows of what she speaks."

Grae walked around outside, trying to clear her head. The General followed her, briefly chasing a mouse that scampered out of his grasp.

"What is this purpose that Ama speaks of? Must there always be a reason why I travel to another time? Can't I just come and visit, and go home like a vacation?"

"Grae, you know the answer to those questions. You know that you are a seeker of truth. You will go on many vacations in your life, in your own time. Your travels in time, of which I hope there are only a few, will be missions of discovery. On your last journey, you learned about the power of redemption. You learned that history sometimes paints a story that only includes one dimension of the facts and the real truth is hidden forever."

Grae sat down on a bench and held her head. "Will I ever lead a normal life? Will I ever not worry about tumbling into another time?"

"Grae, you have the power to stop these journeys, you know that. You have not yet chosen to prevent them."

The key felt heavy around Grae's neck as The General spoke. She reached for it and realized that she knew his words were true. She could have put it away in a box, but she chose to keep it around her neck in case a new adventure called her.

"Ama will be worried, you should go back inside. And I would like to have some milk." The General walked back toward the cabin and Grae followed smiling.

"You certainly have a way of putting things in perspective."

Grae helped Ama prepare the ingredients for another flavorful stew. Ama carefully chose a variety of herbs as ingredients and told Grae about healing uses for each one. "I am making some ginseng tea with a bit of mint," Ama said. "It will help relieve this dreadful headache that has overtaken me and calm my nerves. You will drink some too. Sweeten your cup with honey, if you must."

They drank their tea in silence as an afternoon breeze filtered through the open door and window. "It shall rain tomorrow, a large storm. I must wash the clothes today." Ama stood and staggered.

"You will go and lie down and rest. I shall take care of the washing." Grae led Ama to David's bedroom, the same one that had belonged to Joseph and Nannie Baker almost fifty years earlier. Grae recalled hearing their nighttime conversations from her nearby bed. She wished she could have warned them of what eventually ended their union. It was a rule she had dared not violate.

No one had to tell Grae how to wash clothes in 1830. She knew that no automated machine yet existed to make the task easy. She would do as Sal had taught her. Boiling water and lye soap, scrubbing until her hands were red and more boiling water to rinse. The warm breeze of the September afternoon would dry them on a simple line beside the barn.

Ama told Grae where the clothes could be found. Most were in a basket in the corner of the bedroom. This would normally have been the task of Sally, David's slave woman, but David had taken her and Ezekiel with him to the McGavocks' to help their slaves with the wedding party preparations.

"I believe that David left another shirt on the back of that chair," Ama said sleepily as she began to doze off. As Grae retrieved it, she noticed that an envelope was lying on the seat of the chair. It was addressed to a John Davidson Graham in North Carolina. Did Grae dare to read it?

"Go ahead," The General whispered. Grae did not realize that he had followed her in there. She carefully slipped it under the shirt and placed the shirt in the basket, tiptoeing out of the room. Ama was now fast asleep.

After Grae had begun to boil the water and placed the clothing in to soak, she sat down on a bench with the letter in her hand.

"Where has Wise Father gone?" Grae asked The General, who was grooming himself under the shade of a tree nearby.

"He went toward the North with his bow and arrow after the three of you ate earlier. I followed him for a while and realized that he was going deep into the woods. I believe he is in search of rabbits or squirrels. Sounds like a delicious meal for you later," The General replied, sarcastically.

"I will be glad to share."

Grae was thankful that the envelope had not been sealed. As she slid out the paper she wondered if she might find this letter in a research library somewhere, like the one at the college. It would be amazing to hold it in the present time after it had travelled through its years of life. She began to read.

David Graham, Esq.
Perry Mount Furnace
Cedar Run Farm
Wythe County
Virginia

3 September, 1830

Honourable John Davidson Graham, Esq.
Elm Wood Plantation
Catawba Springs
North Carolina

Dear Sir,

It is my fervent hope that this correspondence finds you and your family well. Your letter of July past states that you are indeed quite established in your new residence and your father continues in good health. We are blessed men my friend!

I write to you Sir with unexpected news and an equally surprising query. To my humble astonishment and undeserving amazement I find myself blessed with both the love and devotion of the most beautiful and diligent woman I have ever known. We have been well acquainted with one another these past four years, she was living and working with her grandfather here when I purchased Cedar Run Farm. But, before I reveal my sentimental self to you, allow me to digress with my business self, for it is both of these pieces meshed together that forms the whole of me, before God. It is with His Direction and your discernment that I must look to as I make difficult decisions for all parties involved.

As you are aware I began my acquisition of my present two thousand acres these four years past. The beautiful rolling hills of Cedar Run Farm are near the massive, oddly north-flowing and ancient Kanawha River. The property includes the Crockett family's productive iron furnace, Perry Mount, and the log cabins, barns, equipment, cultivated fields, and a slave couple who now have a young babe. As part of the contract a Mr. Ross claimed the crops in the ground the first year on the John Baker parcel, Baker's father being murdered on this very spot by his own slaves in 1786. Upon learning of this horror, I did wonder if it was cursed and perhaps I should have listened to my good senses and cancelled the transaction. Alas, I held to my ambitions and persevered, thank Goodness, for without this fateful decision I would have never met this wondrous woman who has captured my heart and my soul.

When I purchased Cedar Run Farm, there was the young slave couple and an old Cherokee Medicine Man and his granddaughter. It was my understanding that the recently deceased Mr. and Mrs. Crockett allowed the Indians to live on their massive farm when the Cherokee clan was stricken with the fever and driven west during the Indian hostilities with them both becoming as a part of the Crockett's own family. In fact, the granddaughter is educated with the knowledge of a fine plantation grower's offspring yet is clever with the raising of crops, cooking, has been baptized as Presbyterian, and sings like a bird.

Not unfamiliar to Yourself, I have labored and paid my debt in full these long four years past. I have lived and toiled beside the Cherokee man called " Wahulidoda" (which means "Wise Father") and his granddaughter "Dekanogi'a Ama" (meaning "Singing Water"), the man slave Ezekiel, and his wife, Sally, whose grandmother lived here fifty some years past, the wife I believe of one of the slaves who hanged for the murder of his Master here. Living and working as we have in close proximity to one another did slowly produce a most remarkable affect upon myself, one that both stuns and soothes my soul. You see, it is Dekanogi'a Ama, or "Ama" as I call her, to whom I have lost myself. I love her more than life my friend. Ama is the right side to my left. She is the air I breathe, and it is with profound happiness and fear that I report she will bear my child by the time of the hard freeze.

Sir, I wish to announce that we have decided to leave Cedar Run Farm and move to Mecklenburg County, not far from Vesuvius Furnace and Catawba Springs. I have several prospective buyers for my property and business and will be in a favorable financial position upon our move. Ama has relations living nearby, now part of the small Catawba Indian Tribe. Her cousin, Blue Moccasin, is happily married to a white man there who owns a tobacco plantation.

I understand your shock and possible dismay with my lack of moral character. I confess that your suspicions are not unfounded! I find that my very own heart, carefully hidden and protected all these years, has been overtaken along with my mind and sensibilities. Sir, I have never known the depth of this kind of happiness and it is my full intention to have a successful career and be happy, yet neither of us believe this is possible here. We do not feel we will be well received and our child will face overwhelming bias. Better to start a new!

Thus, I come to my question. May we impose upon your kindness and rent your previous home at Vesuvius Furnace? You mentioned in your letters that it is vacant but quite comfortable. We need only to live there while I investigate business opportunities, including iron-making, and search out property for sale in the area. I will also seek out my relatives living nearby, for my father's brother, Samuel, and sister, Margaret, remained in Mecklenburg County after coming to America with Papa so very long ago.

I will close now and pray to God for His Guidance for only He knows our Fate! I am anxious to receive your response since time is moving quickly now.

You have, Sir, my great confidence and esteem with which I have the honour to be your obedient servant,

David Graham

"It's amazing! He really does plan to sell this place and leave here. He is going to follow his heart instead of his fortune. This is not the David Graham that history portrays him to be." Grae returned the letter to its envelope and placed it securely under the basket that had held the laundry where The General was sunning himself next to the basket.

"As you know, he did not sell this land, as it stayed in his family for many years after his death." The General watched as Grae put the clothes from one big pot of water to another. Soon she would wring them out and hang them on the line.

"I wonder if he and Ama really moved to North Carolina after the birth of the baby. Perhaps he led a double life."

"Remember, while distance would keep folks here from knowing about such an arrangement, it would also hinder David from travelling back and forth very often. This is still a very rural part of this country in 1830 and for quite some time afterward. Transportation is an issue."

"I just don't understand how this all works out."

"Perhaps that is part of what you are here to find out. Now, I think you better go check on Ama and put that letter back before you hang the clothes. You don't want to lose that letter. David obviously intends to post it as soon as he can."

Grae went back into the cabin and looked in on Ama. The young girl was curled in a little ball of slumber. Grae returned the envelope to the seat of the chair and quietly left the room. As she walked back outside to take the clothes to the line, she saw Ama's grandfather walking toward her carrying two very long snakes. The sight made Grae's skin crawl, but she tried not to show it.

"Osiyo…uh…hello, where Ama?" The old man's voice was rough and deep. Grae did not realize that he spoke any English, but she hadn't really heard him speak any language very much.

"She is sleeping."

"Good, she and baby need." He seemed to realize that Grae was staying a safe distance away from him. "Agi'a inada, uh, you eat snake?"

"Oh, I…I have not…" The grandfather began to howl with laughter and wandered off into the barn.

"I'm not really going to have to eat snake, am I?" Grae walked toward the clothes line and began hanging the clothes.

"Remember, you are living with Indians for the weekend. They live off the land, so be happy they don't make you kill what you eat!" The General took off in a run toward a field of tall grass, and Grae wondered if he was going to go off to do just that.

TWENTY THREE

The days with Ama went by more quickly than Grae would have liked. Ama taught her much, including Missus Crockett's theories on planting by the signs.

"I called her Macrock, it was all I could say when I was little. Learning Tsalagi, the Cherokee language, and the English language at the same time was hard, I had trouble pronouncing Crockett. She was fine with me using that name, but anyone else got a stern look or a switch taken after them." Ama laughed as she and Grae shelled fall beans, it reminded Grae of doing the same task with Granny Belle.

"Macrock would say the moon is like a man, it changes every eight days. She said to never plant anything on the new moon; it was best to wait until the moon was full, and then plant from the full moon until it gets to its smallest point. She said that there are three dark nights in the last quarter moon, before the new moon, and that was the best time to plant anything that needed to go underground. It was important to pay attention to the signs of the body, too, and never, ever plant anything in the bowels."

"What would happen if you planted in that sign?" Grae asked.

"The plants would rot."

Grae rinsed the shelled beans in cold water, and then filled the big pot at the fireplace with water as Ama added the beans and seasoning. It was early Saturday morning, and the beans would cook all day.

"What a day this must be at the McGavock farm!" Grae said as she chopped cabbage that they would cook later to be eaten with the beans.

"I am so sorry that you have to be here with me. I am sure you would have enjoyed the party." Ama kept her head down as she said this.

"Oh no, that is not the case at all. I would much rather be here. The last time I had to go to a wedding party, several people died." Grae realized quickly that she had made a big slip.

"They died! What happened?"

'Think fast, think fast,' Grae thought to herself. She was so glad The General was out prowling around because he would lecture her severely for such a slip.

"It was influenza. So many people were exposed because this one person came to the party sick. Fortunately, I was vac ...visiting someone the next day and didn't stay at the event for very long." What was wrong with her? She almost told Ama that she was vaccinated! "Anyway, I am not that fond of parties. I would much rather be here with you."

Ama smiled. "Let's do something special. I am craving something sweet. Let's make a molasses cake and eat the whole thing before dinner."

Grae was glad to see Ama smile. She looked like the

teenager that she was.

Just as Ama had suggested, she and Grae ate almost the entire cake. They saved a piece for her grandfather, but the rest of it was gone, washed down with cold milk, every last crumb.

"I cannot believe how simple that was to make and so delicious. What in the world will we do with all of these beans?" Grae was gathering up the dishes to take them outside to wash.

"Grandfather will eat a lot of them. We can fry bean cakes tomorrow." Ama had a look of sleepiness again.

"Would you like to turn in early to get some extra rest? I will take your grandfather some food."

"Don't let him scare you with his snakes." Ama laughed as she walked towards the bedroom.

"He told you! I was afraid we would have to eat them."

"Oh, he will, but he enjoyed your reaction."

"My Ama happy you here," Wise Father said as he began to eat some of the beans. "She say—your spirit old, but your heart troubled."

Grae could see that there wasn't much you could hide from these Native Americans.

"You like lost bird not know where nest is. You find truth, but truth not welcome you." Grae gazed at the old man before her. His skin was brown, weathered with age and the elements. His hair was gray with long braids that hung on each side of his face. His hands trembled slightly causing the spoon to hit the plate. But his eyes, they were clear and bright and had a look of youthful vigor, a young brave. She wondered if his mind and heart shared that outlook.

"Na asgaya…the man say I go to the Catawba lands. My

people there, but I not go. Dekanogi'a, Ama not happy this life. Ama happiness come when Ama spirit reborn in another time." Wise Father ate the last bite of cake, surely savoring its lingering sweet flavor, then handed the plates back to Grae.

"Awohali...the great Eagle spirit shall bless you for your kindness to my granddaughter." He went back into the barn where he would sleep that night. A gentle rain started falling, but Grae stood and looked up into the darkening sky. Tomorrow, she must return to the McGavock house. She was not looking forward to what might be awaiting her there.

The sun had barely cracked the sky when David Graham's wagon arrived back at its home. Thankfully, Grae had awakened early and dressed before beginning to make biscuits and frying ham. A small pot of oats was also cooking since Ama liked to eat something soft in the morning.

"Good morning!" David said as he barreled into the cabin and walked straight back to his bedroom.

"It wouldn't have mattered if I was in my birthday suit," Grae mumbled as she laughed to herself.

"Oh, I think he would have noticed that," The General whispered.

David came back into the room quietly. "She still is sleeping. She sleeps a lot."

"She needs her rest; her time is drawing near."

"She was so strong before this child. It seems to have weakened her."

"A child growing inside draws a lot of her energy, her nourishment, even her very spirit. Don't forget, this is her first and she is still young." Grae poured David a cup of coffee.

David shook his head. "That's a mighty fine smelling breakfast there." He helped himself to several biscuits, a large piece of ham and red eye gravy. Grae placed two fried eggs on his plate. "That's sure to make her strong."

"If there is any left for me to eat." David and Grae turned to see Ama in the doorway, still in her nightgown. David jumped out of the chair and ran to her. He engulfed her in a hug, picking her up off the ground.

"Be careful with her." Grae didn't think it was such a good idea for David to be picking her up and swinging her around.

"I leave you alone with a governess for three days and she becomes a mother hen to you." Grae was still amazed that this was the same David Graham who ruled his home and his business with an iron fist. Could this be the same one who haunted Graham Mansion by slamming windows closed and scaring little girls?

Ama sat beside him at the table. He held her right hand with his left and ate with his right. It was almost comical to watch him try to cut the ham or butter biscuits. Ama slowly ate her oatmeal. Grae noticed that even after a full night's rest, she looked as if she had been up all night.

But the light in David's eyes seemed to sustain Ama as she perked up after breakfast. David finally remembered that Margaret had sent several plates of food home with him from the previous day's events. Ezekiel would be the one to drive Grae back to the McGavocks so after a warm hug, Ama allowed her new friend to depart.

The ride back to the McGavock property was quiet. Ezekiel only responded with "Yessum" to Grae's questions. He was a large man, strong from hard work, but he seemed to have a gentle side. That morning, as he had waited for their departure, she had watched him have a whispered conversation with the horse that was leading the wagon. He softly stroked its neck. It wasn't often that you got to see a personal side to the slaves, since they kept that for their chambers; but Grae thought that she saw a little of Ezekiel's personality in his caring interaction with his working companion. He had even petted The General when he slipped into the wagon to return with her.

The Sunday afternoon was beautiful and especially warm for the fall. As they approached the McGavock house, she saw that there was someone sitting on the porch and soon realized that it was Evelyn Newton. A knot began to form in Grae's stomach. She had hoped that Miss Newton would have already left.

Ezekiel carried her bag towards the house and as Grae walked through the lawn behind him, Evelyn Newton stood up from her chair. Grae noticed immediately that she looked different. Her dress was a deep burgundy, like the color of red wine, with delicate flowered rosettes on the collar and part of the bodice. Her hair was in a softer bun with beautiful combs. But there was something else different about her, but Grae could not put her finger on what that was.

"I have been waiting right here for you, Miss James, since church ended." Evelyn Newton's voice was calm and smooth, but more elderly in its sound than when Grae had previously heard it.

"Good afternoon, Miss Newton." Grae was not sure if she should pause there or go straight into the house and try to flee the conversation.

"May I speak with you a moment?" The knot grew tighter in Grae's stomach and a feeling of fear began to join it.

"Yes, ma'am."

"I want to apologize for my actions the other day. I am just a silly old woman who has held onto something for way too long." Evelyn's hand went up to her neck and Grae realized what was missing. The amethyst broach no longer adorned her neckline. Grae seized the opportunity to mention it.

"Your beautiful broach, you are not wearing it today. It would look lovely with the color of your dress."

Evelyn's hand lingered along her neck. "Yes, it would, but it is way too gaudy to wear to church. It would not be appropriate." Evelyn paused. "As I was saying, I am humbly sorry if my actions made you uncomfortable. I hope that you will forgive me for all the things I have done."

"Well, there's no need..."

"Oh, Patrick, look, our Miss James has returned. I was just telling her how we old folks can be so silly at times." Grae turned to see Patrick on the lawn behind her. He gave her a slight smile.

"Speak for yourself, Eve; I don't feel a day over twenty today. It's a beautiful Sunday afternoon, and I am hoping that Miss James will allow me the honor to take her on a walk."

Evelyn's eyes were on Patrick, Patrick's focus was on Grae, but Grae carefully watched Evelyn's reaction to Patrick's words. Her hand was still at her neck and her fingers slowly curved into a ball. Her grip became so tight that Grae wondered why her nails had not punctured the palm of her hand.

"Thank you, Mister McGavock, but I would like to get settled back in my room right now. I also feel that I should discuss my governess duties with Missus McGavock." Grae did not look back to see the disappointment on Patrick's face or to see Evelyn's reaction to her reply. She knew that she must avoid such confrontations at all costs. She wished they would both leave that day.

"Arabella, so lovely to have you back, did my anxious brother awaken you this morning?"

"No, Missus McGavock, thankfully, I was already up and working on breakfast. He seemed very happy to be returning home."

"I must say that seeing him mope around here for the last few days made me more fully realize the depth of his love for Ama. Joseph and I discussed last night that perhaps we should try to dissuade him from moving to North Carolina. We could encourage our neighbors to accept this union. It does not seem to be just a young man's notion."

"I am a little worried about Ama. She seems to be so tired and requiring so much rest."

"That is fairly normal, especially for her age. Growing a baby inside you takes a mountain of energy and nourishment. I have learned from my births that you must rest and you must eat. You are eating for two."

"Indeed. I believe I shall go to my room and get settled now if that is alright. May we talk later about when we shall begin the girls' studies?"

"Yes, that would be good. I imagine you have not had lunch."

"No, but I ate a good breakfast."

"Come back down in a little bit, and we shall give you a sampling of the wedding party foods. I saved you a bowl of berry dumplings."

"Oh, how kind of you; I'm sure they are delicious."

"Those berries you picked were so sweet. It was hard to save that portion from the groom." Margaret laughed as Grae began to climb the stairs.

The sound of little feet running soon met Grae. Cynthia was flying down the steps by her.

"Oh, Miss James, I am so glad you have returned. I have missed Jasper, I mean The General, greatly. Where is he?"

"I do not know, Cynthia. He may have gone to find a quiet spot to rest."

"Oh, I am sure I can find him. He will be so happy to have someone to play with him."

"Poor General," Grae said as she walked back into the room.

"The General is in hiding." The voice came from underneath the bed.

"How did you get up here so quickly?"

"I slid away while you were talking to Margaret. You handled yourself quite well during the conversation with Evelyn and Patrick. You did the right thing."

"She certainly seemed to be seeking redemption this morning. I am not sure what all she is apologizing for though as it seemed she was speaking of more than what has happened recently."

"It is hard to tell with that woman. The depth of her vengeance is immeasurable."

"You sound like you know more about her than you have shared."

"Let's just say that our paths have crossed in another time." The General jumped up on Grae's bed and stretched out. "What did Margaret have to say?"

"I'm glad you asked. Her opinion is softening about David marrying Ama. So much so that she and Joseph are going to try to convince David to stay here, I guess that explains why he didn't leave here."

"Perhaps."

"I think it explains a lot. Maybe even that Ama and her child continued to live on the property. Maybe the historical accounts were influenced to leave her out."

"You need to go back downstairs before that little girl

comes looking for you. I think I am going to take a nap."

During that afternoon, Grae spent some time with Margaret reviewing how the girls' studies would proceed the following week. It was decided that Mary would have some lessons in the work of French and English clothing designers of the eighteenth century and that she would practice on a special dress created for her eighteenth birthday. Nancy's writing abilities would be further encouraged with assignments in poetry and short stories on themes chosen by Grae. Cynthia's math skills needed work, and she needed to practice her handwriting.

When dinner time arrived, Grae found that she was seated next to a young man she had not seen before. He was introduced as George Watson. A cadet at the United States Military Academy, he was scheduled to graduate with the Class of 1832. He also happened to be the cousin of the groom and had come to serve as the best man. It was obvious to both she and George that they had been seated next to each other for a reason. Grae was relieved that, while attentive, George did not seem to show the slightest interest in her. Grae would remark to The General later that George seemed to have the air of a minister and she wondered why a military academy education had been chosen for him.

Evelyn had decided to have her meal in her room. Patrick had a seat next to Joseph and only glanced in Grae's direction. She was sure that he was not pleased with her rejection of his offer for a walk, but it was best that he keep his distance for the remainder of his stay. She learned from the table conversation that he planned to be there another week to take care of business dealings regarding some land that he still owned there.

"John Evans has offered me a fair price for the land. I

think it is time that I let it go." Patrick made an obvious glance in Grae's direction, which was noticed by Margaret who quickly changed the subject.

"All this wedding nonsense did not stop the coming of a new life onto this property." All eyes quickly turned to Margaret. Seemingly embarrassed by the reaction, she continued. "Our slave girl, Lena, gave birth to a baby boy last night. The night before, another slave, Esther, had a stillborn child, a girl."

"Indeed, another strong young man to till the fields," Joseph said with a hearty laugh.

Grae looked around the table and saw there was no reaction to Joseph's words. It was another example of how different this time was. This young child was considered McGavock property. What would the child of David Graham be considered?

TWENTY FOUR

The days during the following week were filled with the normal tasks of life on a growing southern farm. Crops were harvested, livestock attended to, fences built and repaired. Everyone always seemed to be busy. There were no idle hands. Even the new mother, Lena, was shelling fall beans for drying as her new son slept in a basket at her feet.

Grae found her way to Ruth's kitchen, as most of the slaves called it. Ruth was baking pies again, all kinds of pies for a church social that would be occurring the following day. Grae stopped by the kitchen while she allowed her students to have a recess since it was Friday afternoon and they had worked hard all week on their lessons.

"Zeke says that the girl be starting to haves pains and it be early. Miss Margaret done says that I needs to go on over there." Grae walked in as Ruth was talking to the women around her.

"Yous sees her justs a few days ago; Miss James, how she seems?"

"Tired, very tired. She wanted to sleep most of the time that I was there."

"I thinks she gonna have trouble. She be little through the hips and only one way that baby gonna come out. I has delivered many babies into this here world, they come when they wants to and don't care who they hurts coming out. I hopes she gots enough strength to push that one out. Lena, she usually the one whos helps me, but she stills too weak herself."

Grae turned to go out the door and find the children, but something stopped her and she turned back around.

"Ruth, I do not know anything about childbirth. I have not even seen an animal come into this world, but Ama trusts me and I think Mister Graham does too. I could ask Missus McGavock if I could go with you. I can try to be as much help as I can. I would do whatever you told me to do."

Ruth stopped what she was doing and walked over to Grae. "That would be mighty good. I sees that you knows how to work. You just have to understand that childbirth ain't pretty, not even when that baby comes out and gives its first cry. Nothing pretty about the whole process. It be the closest to death any woman come to before her dying day. You gots to be ready to makes fast choices."

Grae nodded and left the cabin. She was walking so fast toward the main house that she failed to notice the rock that caused her to land face first on the ground. It knocked the wind out of her for a moment and she laid there until she felt a hand turning her over and saw that the face of Patrick McGavock was inches from her own.

"Mister McGavock, you always seem to be nearby when I need assistance." Grae tried to make light of her fall, even though she was certain that her knees would be black and blue. Nothing felt broken which would have been dire and disastrous, as The General would say, in this time period.

"Do I? Only recently, or has this happened in a previous time?" Patrick's bold question shocked Grae and reaffirmed that she needed to get away from this property.

"Where were you heading in such a hurry?"

"I was going to find Missus McGavock. I understand that Ama is near time for childbirth and that Ruth is being sent. I am going to offer my assistance."

"Oh, I do not think that is a good idea." Patrick helped Grae up. "Childbirth can be a messy experience and might be too much for someone of your delicate nature."

"Delicate nature?! I will have you know, Mister McGavock, that I have experienced plenty of messy experiences as you call them. While childbirth has not been one of them, I do not shy away from something just because it may be unpleasant for me to see."

A large smile broke out on Patrick's face. "Tell me how you did it? Where have you been all these years? I would have moved heaven and earth to have been with you."

Grae saw such tenderness in his eyes that her own almost revealed the truth. She would have to do something to stop this. "Mister McGavock, will you please stop confusing me with someone else? I would think that a person of your means could get himself some sort of help for your condition. These delusions are quite unhealthy. I have tried to be a lady in my dealings with you, because of my new status in the McGavock home, but I must say that these conversations are making me very uncomfortable and I wish for them to cease."

Patrick stood stunned before her. She could not bear to watch it any further, so she turned and continued walking toward the house.

As Grae made the offer to Margaret, she saw the concern in the woman's face. David was obviously a special brother to her.

"I do not know how David will handle it if something happens to this baby. He is so infatuated with the thought of being a father. Joseph went over there yesterday and talked to David about considering staying in Virginia. I think that he may change his mind if he can see that his child will be accepted as a Graham."

Seeing her take the tumble, The General had scampered into the house and followed her to her bedroom after she spoke with Margaret.

"We are going back to the Graham property. Surely a childbirth cannot be as bad as seeing a murder." The General was silent. "What are you thinking?" Grae stopped her packing and sat next to her friend.

"I'm thinking that you should make sure that key is securely around your neck and that you should realize that birth is a lot like death -- it is a dramatic moment in life. You need to get back to your time as soon as possible. Being off of the Graham property has made me very concerned. You cannot travel back unless you are there. You don't need to get any further away."

Grae closed her bag of belongings and reached for the key around her neck.

"Let's go."

She was met at the top of the stairs by Mary. The young woman seemed very distressed.

"I am so worried about Ama, Miss James. Mother tells me that you are going to accompany Ruth to help her. I have begged and begged Mother to let me go as well. I could be so much help."

"Do not worry about your friend. I am sure she will be fine. Perhaps your mother will allow you to come as Ama is recovering. Your presence will be such a comfort to her." They both began to walk down the stairs. "In the meantime, you must continue designing your pattern. This dress for your eighteenth birthday must be very special."

"Oh, I have already been working on the design. Last year, father travelled to the home of our late President Jefferson to learn about the planting methods that they used there and about his famous winemaking. He went to a very grand general store in Charlottesville and brought back several bolts of beautiful fabric. Father said he knew that he had pretty daughters that would soon need fancy dresses." Mary giggled. "I had almost forgotten about it until you gave me my assignment. Some of the fabric is a very beautiful pink color with little flowers. How I would love to trim it in red! Father will think that is scandalous!"

Grae stopped on the bottom step and looked into this young woman's eyes. She had just learned the origin of the dress she had brought back from her first journey. The dress that had so lovingly been made to fit her in 1786 by an older version of the girl before her. Mary would wear it on her eighteenth birthday and be the belle of the party. Grae wondered if that would be the day when Mary would make her own journey through time. The older Mary knew exactly what she was doing when she gave the dress to Grae. She may well have sealed her fate to stay in 1786 with Charles and the grieving Baker family along with the life that Grae had seen Mary carrying within her. She longed to ask her why she hid the small knife in the dress, but she knew that the girl before her would not know.

She was surprised to find that Patrick was the one who

was waiting to drive them to the Graham property. Before she could say a word, he took out a white handkerchief from his pocket and waved it in front of her. The gesture was lighthearted, especially considering the blunt manner in which she had earlier talked to him.

"I come in peace, not to cause you further aggravation, but to offer my humble services as a means of repentance. No matter how young I feel at times, I am but an old man who has allowed his emotions to cloud his better judgment. I shall be silent as we make this important journey."

There are people in your life who can always win their way back into your good graces, no matter what they do. Grae knew that like her dear Gav, Patrick would be one of those people, if even for the short periods of time that she saw him. Despite her better judgment, she accepted his hand into the seat next to him on the front of the wagon. If she made a fuss about the arrangement, it would only draw attention to the situation. It would only prolong the time to get to Ama.

The drive was silent until Grae asked Patrick a very innocent question.

"Mister McGavock."

"Oh, please call me Patrick. I dare say that I have earned the right for you to call me by such a respectful name. Mister McGavock was my father, a much more honorable man that I will ever aspire to be."

"Mister McGavock." Patrick let out a loud sigh, and Grae heard a snort of laughter from Ruth sitting behind them. "May I ask where it is that you live?"

"Ah, I live in the land of Carolina. I have lived many places since I left my Virginia home. I was in Tennessee for a time, around the great city of Nashville, as well as further west where the mighty Mississippi touches the state. I had the great fortune to be in Memphis as it was being founded in 1819 by our current President, the Honorable Mister Andrew Jackson." Patrick swerved the wagon slightly to miss a large hole in the road, causing Ruth to suddenly slide to the opposite side of the wagon.

"I am sorry about that, Ruth, but I was afraid the horses might break a leg or this wagon might lose a wheel if we hit that hole." Getting back on the path, Patrick continued his story. "But a few years ago, I met a distant relative of Margaret and David's, Mister John Davidson Graham at his beautiful plantation in Catawba Springs, North Carolina. It occurred to me that it was a beautiful part of our country, and, in many ways, very similar to my old Virginia home. So I made some inquiries about purchasing some land in the area, and I have made my home there ever since."

John Davidson Graham. Grae was sure that was the name on David's letter.

"If I am not mistaken, is that not the area where Mister David Graham plans to move his family?" Grae knew it was bold of her to acknowledge that she knew such a private detail, but she doubted that Patrick would dare repeat that she had made mention of it.

Patrick cleared his throat, seeming a little uncomfortable with the question. "What makes you think that?"

"David told me that was his intention. He obviously feels that his union with Ama will not be accepted in this community."

"Indeed, there is a low tolerance for many things, including bachelors." Grae dared not let that topic continue.

"So, shall his family be accepted more easily in North Carolina?"

"The Cherokee have long been an abundant part of the Carolina mountain heritage. There are many marriages of white men and Indian women there, and those unions that are led by a prosperous business man and landholder, as I am sure David will be, are not looked down upon. Ama may not be asked to tea on the largest plantations, but she shall also not be shunned when she enters church on Sunday."

As they approached the Graham property, Grae could see Wise Father dancing around a large fire. He was dressed in full Indian garb. Getting closer, they heard him chanting and saw him raise his hands to the sky as if appealing to the gods for favor. David paced in front of the cabin, one suspender down and the tail of his shirt hanging out. He looked as if he had not slept for days.

"Thank God, you have come. Please Ruth, she cries out in such pain." David did not even wait for the wagon to come to a complete stop before he reached in the back and picked Ruth up and set her down on the ground. Ruth grabbed her birthing bag, as she had called it, and ran into the cabin with David following on her heels. The piercing cries of Ama could now be heard by both Patrick and Grae. He jumped out of the wagon and helped Grae down. She paused to say something, but he just motioned for her to go on.

Grae opened the door to the cabin. For several days the previous week she did this simple task numerous times and not once did she have the feeling that now gripped every inch of her body. Ama's screams were Nannie's screams, the past was replaying in the present. Blood was being shed and ironically, again, someone wanted their freedom.

She dropped her own bag as she saw Sally walk towards her. This young woman looked a lot more like Aggie than she had first noticed. She was dripping in sweat and had two empty buckets in her hands.

"All I needs is to get me a glass of water and sits down for a minute. I has been on my feet with poor Miss Ama for two days, this pain gots to leave her. Ruth, she done say that you will help me, Miss James." Grae started rolling up her sleeves.

"You sit down and drink something. Tell me what to do."

"Ruth needs us to boil more water. She says she brought a pile of clean sheets. Theys be in the wagon she says."

"Here, eat a biscuit, you need strength, too." Grae looked at the plate of biscuits she was handing Sally. "I guess they are okay."

"Yes 'mam, I made these yesterday. Thank you, Miss…"

"You can call me Arabella. We are soldiers in the same war now."

Grae found Patrick with two of the slaves. They were watering the horses. "I need two buckets of water." Handing the buckets to one of the slaves, she turned back to Patrick. "Ruth brought a big basket full of sheets and rags. Can you bring that inside? I've got to get more water boiling."

Patrick touched her arm as she turned to leave. "Is it bad?"

"It is not good. I am afraid for the baby. If Ama is in this much pain, it may be in distress."

"It will be a hard thing for David to bear if the baby is lost. He will blame himself because he is not married to its mother. He will think that the baby was punished for that."

"You speak as if you know this from experience," Grae stood beside him as he lifted the basket out of the wagon.

"Men succumb to their urges more so than women do, I fear. I know of more than one man who has left behind a child. Some men can cast women and children aside, others cannot."

"The water, ma'am." The slave boy came with two full buckets, Grae lead him inside. Patrick followed with the basket.

Ruth came out of the bedroom.

"Go talk to the old man," Ruth said to Grae. "Gets him to makes her a sleep tonic. He knows, he mades it for us slaves when we hads our first babies. She needs some rest. There's somethin' wrong in there. I'm goin' to try and reach insides and sees if the baby's head be right."

Grae and Patrick left the cabin and went to where Wise Father was still chanting.

"Ruth says that Ama needs the special tonic you have made for the slave women." The grandfather looked like he was in deep meditation but there was fear in his eyes.

"She says it is for rest, for the women having difficulty." Grae could almost see the light bulb go off in his head.

"Yes, yes. Awenasa…my home…my herbs there."

"I will take you," Patrick said. The grandfather looked at the wagon and gave Patrick a confused look.

"We shall go on horseback. We will take one of David's best horses." The grandfather followed Patrick into the barn and soon they were on their way through the woods. The sun was just beginning to set for the night.

Grae boiled water and began to prepare some food. David helped Ruth and Sally move Ama so that they could change the bed. They waited impatiently for Patrick and Wise Father to return. When they did, Ama's grandfather insisted that he give the tonic to Ama and everyone left them alone. Patrick took David outside.

In the cool breeze of an early October night, David and Patrick sat underneath the stars in silence. Grae brought David a plate of food and some strong coffee. He took the coffee, but tried to push the food away.

"You better eat, David," Patrick said. "This is going to take a while and you need to be strong, too."

Grae could tell that David held Patrick in high regard. He took the plate and slowly began to take a few bites.

"We call women weak. We are wrong. I could not bear the pain she is in, and it has only just begun." David gulped down the last few bites eating more than he realized and handed the plate back to Grae.

Ruth came outside and David rushed toward her. "She be sleeping. The old man's tonic be powerful stuff. All of us, we dranks it whens our first baby not wanna come out. He takes care of us, we takes care of Ama. She rest now. I say you should too."

"You heard the woman," Patrick said, taking David by the arm. "We will find you a soft spot in the hay loft. You sleep while she does. Ruth will let us know when Ama wakes."

The grandfather went back to his chanting, refusing to eat the plate Grae offered him. Exhausted from the previous two days, Sally curled up on the small bed that Grae had slept on the previous week. With Patrick and David in the barn, that left Ruth and Grae to stay and watch Ama.

Ruth placed Ama's rocking chair in the doorway between the two rooms so that she could see Ama but not be standing over top of her. "Yous cannot rests with someone standing over yous."

"What do you think, Ruth? Will the baby be alright?"

"I reached up inside her and I feels the baby. The head be coming just fine, like it 'spose to. I tries to feels its neck and I thinks I did and I not feel the cord. That be good, maybe it be where it 'spose to be too."

Ruth took a long drink of coffee. "Yous makes good coffee, most white women they makes it too weak. This here be strong coffee, strong like the girl who makes it." Ruth smiled at Grae and Grae noticed that her teeth were perfect, a rare thing to see on anyone in 1830.

"In this world, there be a fine line between living and dying, and that line moves while you not looking. You cans fall one way or 'nother and not know it till it be done."

Grae looked out the window and saw the moon almost full. "The moon will be full tomorrow night. Mister McGavock said this morning that there were two full moons this month. It is a rare thing."

"Oh, lordy, mercy," Ruth held her head.

"What?"

"Tomorrow night be a full moon then and the next one be a blue moon. My mammie say, blue moon rare, shine like the sun, blue moon come when the crying done." Ruth got up and walked toward the front door. "Something tell me that this not gonna end well."

TWENTY FIVE

The day was long and filled with pain. Ama's labor would increase with intensity, and then subside. The smell of fear grew in the cabin.

"A baby be able to stand nine months inside its mammie," Ruth said as the sun was setting. It was the second day of October, 1830. "Them signs is not good. Them signs, theys just not good. I be scared 'bout what be happening. I thinks we should tell Mister Graham."

Patrick and Grae exchanged glances. David was outside in the barn with Wise Father.

"I will talk to him," Patrick said, rising and walking toward the door.

Grae was not sure, but from somewhere deep inside, a voice of strength came to her. "No, I shall tell him. You are too close." Grae walked out the door with Patrick following her. They were silent.

"What? Is the baby coming?" David met them at the barn door and started to run past them. Patrick grabbed his arm.

Wise Father was sitting on the ground, propped up by a hay bale in the corner. He lowered his head.

"The labor has been long and hard, David," Grae began. "You must prepare yourself. Ruth fears that it will be too much for the baby."

"NOOOOO! No!" It was an agonizing wail. "Ama is strong, she will keep our child safe. Nothing will happen to my family." David stormed past them and toward the cabin. Patrick walked over to Wise Father and helped him up.

"Woman speaks truth. Sadness and anger will fill the night." Grae watched as Ama's grandfather went outside and began building a large fire in the middle of the front yard. She was spellbound watching as Patrick helped the old man gather logs and branches. The smell of cigar smoke lingered behind her as David and the grandfather had been smoking when they found them.

In no time, it seemed, a roaring fire was reaching toward the sky. The old man began to slowly walk around the fire, chanting. He reached into his pocket and pulled out a small pouch. From it, he sprinkled a powder onto the fire and Grae watched as green flames rose. The smell of cigars. Green flames. Green smoke. Green. Grae was mesmerized by it all. Perhaps this night was what her journey was all about.

Ruth stopped giving Ama the special brew that her grandfather made. "She must be awake and alert now. She must bear the pain." For the remainder of the evening, David sat by Ama's side, holding her hand, stroking her hair, kissing her forehead. They had whispered conversations.

Through the pain, Ama smiled as Grae offered her a cool cup of water while David walked outside for a moment.

"I am glad you are here," Ama said slowly. "We will need

your strength." Ama took Grae's hand. "Do not worry about what you know; it cannot help us in this time." Grae looked at her strangely and started to speak, but Ama shook her head as David came back into the room.

The time was close. David sat on one side of Ama with Grae on the other. They would need to support her arms and back as she pushed. The contractions came and Ama strained and moaned and cried out. Her screams were filled with pain and exhaustion. The determination in David's face, his encouraging words, did not hide the fear. Ama began to tremble as she rose to push. Grae looked down and saw the reason; the mattress under Ama was soaked in bright red blood. Red blood, white cloth, again, this image would haunt her.

As the full moon brightened the sky, Ama arched her back and bore down one last time, pushing her baby into the world. Ruth pulled it out and gave it a slap and a loud cry was heard. David rushed to Ruth's side, smiling with joy. He took the child in his hands as Sally took a rag and rubbed inside its mouth. She wiped the infant's face clean as Ruth cut the cord.

"My son! My son! He is so beautiful." David's eyes were glued to the child as Grae turned and looked back at Ama. She was laying very still, eyes closed. Grae looked at Ruth. The woman was frantically packing rags between Ama's legs; but the mound of cloth was quickly turning red. Their eyes met and she saw Ruth's fear.

"Ama!" Grae knelt beside her and shook her. No response. The room was suddenly very quiet.

David took his focus off his son and looked toward Ama. He almost dropped the baby as he handed him to Sally.

"Ama! AMA!" David scooped her upper body in his arms, shaking her as Ruth continued to try to stop the bleeding.

"DO SOMETHING!" He cried angrily at Ruth.

Grae thought of what would happen in her time. The modern delivery room with doctors and nurses everywhere, equipment and medicines and emergency surgeries that could make the dark presence of death disappear. She thought of her own training in CPR, and then remembered Ama's words from just a little while earlier. "Do not worry about what you know, it cannot help us in this time."

A cold realization engulfed the room. David rocked back and forth with Ama in his arms, the tears poured down his face. Patrick and Wise Father entered the room. The old man touched the baby's forehead and then walked toward the bed.

"Ama ega...Ama gone. Let her go," the old man said. David clutched Ama tightly. He sobbed, but did not release her. Her lifeless body looked like a rag doll clutched in his grip.

"LET HER GO!" The grandfather's powerful voice shook the room and caused everyone to step back, including David. He released his grasp and gently laid Ama on the bed.

Without saying a word, everyone knew to leave the room. David ran out of the cabin, knocking things over and slamming the door as he left. Patrick looked briefly at Grae and he turned to follow David. Sally, who had been clutching the cooing baby throughout the whole ordeal, gently put him in Grae's arms. He was sleeping soundly, unaware that his whole existence had just changed.

The rest of the night passed in a blur. A slave girl, Esther, who had recently given birth to a stillborn infant, was brought to the Graham property from the McGavocks. She would nurse the baby. David's face and body were frozen as if he was a concrete statue. He just stared at Ama's body. He did not move from the chair beside her bed. He did not hold his child.

Grae had forgotten that burial in this time would be done very quickly. There was no real way to preserve the body and in the heat of the fall, it would quickly deteriorate. Patrick had taken the grandfather back to the cabin he shared with Ama while some of the slaves began building a box, Ama's coffin.

Hours later, Grae was outside washing some dishes when Patrick returned. He was alone on horseback without the wagon or the grandfather. He stopped in front of the hitching post and slowly got off the horse. She had estimated that Patrick was in his mid-sixties, a much older age in that century than it was in her own. Today, he looked it.

"Where is Wise Father?" Grae walked toward Patrick, who was taking a satchel off the back of the horse. Patrick just stood there, shaking his head.

"I suppose a man's heart can only take so much grief. I left him alone for a while and tended to their few animals. When I went back into the cabin, he was lying on the bed and this garment for Ama was beside him. I thought at first he was just resting, but soon realized that he was not breathing. His strong heart had enough, I suppose."

Grae began to cry. "He was the last of his people here. Everyone he knew and loved were gone. His days of strength were over. May he rest in peace."

As Patrick told David and Ruth what had transpired, Grae looked at the garment that the grandfather had selected for Ama's burial. It was a traditional Indian dress of tanned leather the color of soft beige. Intricate stitching across the top, front, back, and arms gave the look of an eagle's wings if the wearer's arms were extended on each side. The stitching was white and gold and red and black with tiny beads delicately intermingled in the stitches. Fringe with larger beads graced the bottom of the dress and sleeves. It was beautiful.

"Well, that decides it," David said, drinking his last sip of coffee. Grae was not sure how many pots he had consumed in the last few days. His thirty years looked much older and deep lines seemed to be forming on his face before her very eyes. "We had planned to take the old man with us when we moved to North Carolina. Ama dearly loved him." David stopped. It was as if the very uttering of her name tore through his heart. But the tears were now changing to anger and he clinched both fists.

"I will take the child to North Carolina. He will not know a life here. He will not be raised a half-breed. He will be raised a Graham, by a Graham."

"What do you mean, David?" Patrick asked.

"I sent a letter to John Davidson Graham of Catawba Springs beseeching him to allow me to rent his former home to start a new life for my family. You know this," David nodded to Patrick. "Now, my family is gone, but I will not let this child suffer for the sins of his parents." He turned and with both hands gripped the mantle over the simple rock fireplace.

"But, David, surely you are not thinking that you caused this?" Patrick walked toward David.

"I know that I should never have dreamed of a life of love! I should have known that taking my sight off of work would only lead to heartache and disaster. To have as my ambition a life of happiness was a silly folly for me." He turned and faced all of them. "I shall not make that mistake again. My son shall not grow up with a father who looks at him wishing that his mother was there instead. God forgive me, but that is my heart!" David walked over to the cabin door and opened it. He stood in the doorway facing outside.

"Patrick, send two slaves to the cabin and have them bury

the old man. Old Jeremiah worked the Crockett place; he will know a good spot, where the others are buried. And get...get her ready. I have chosen the spot. Ama must see the sun and the moon from where she rests. We will place her at sunset." David jumped on the horse that Patrick had ridden and tore out of the yard causing a sea of dust to follow behind him.

"I have never done this before," Grae said to Ruth as they began to dress Ama. Ruth had carefully undressed and bathed Ama. It was obvious from the amount of blood on the sheets, her clothes, and all those rags that something had gone terribly wrong inside of Ama and she had hemorrhaged. Red again had a new meaning to Grae, blood shed while giving life this time. The end result was still the same, a good soul was gone.

Grae gently rolled Ama to one side, and then the other after she was dressed. Ruth arranged her hair into two long dark braids. Even in death, she was breathtaking. Two slave men had made a simple wooden box to place her in. They now waited in the cabin's main room.

Patrick came into the room and gasped when he saw Ama. "How you have honored her with the care you have taken, she just looks like she is sleeping."

"I thinks we should wait for Mister Graham befores we put her in the box." Ruth was wringing her hands in worry. It was almost sunset.

Patrick nodded and went outside. Grae heard a wagon and saw that it was Joseph, Margaret, and Mary McGavock. Behind them on horseback was David. Mary's eyes were red and swollen. Margaret's face had a pinched, uncomfortable look. Joseph looked stiff and out of place.

"Is she ready?" David barked, there was no other word to describe the sound of his voice. It was cold and very serious.

"Yes David, Ruth and Grae have taken good care of her. I think you should see her before she is placed in the box." Patrick put his arm around his friend. What a caring man Gav will be, Grae thought, if he only inherits a fraction of this man's compassion.

"No! I have seen enough!" David shrugged Patrick's arm off him. Glances exchanged between Patrick and Margaret and she walked toward her brother and touched his arm.

"I think you should, David." Something softened in him momentarily and he allowed his sister and her husband to lead him into the cabin. Mary followed behind, winding a handkerchief over and over around her fingers. Grae had a flashback of Sal doing the same thing when she came to visit Grae in the cell. Her heart pained for the sadness of then and now.

Grae, Patrick, and Ruth stayed outside with the two men who had made the coffin. Esther quickly came outside with the baby after David and his family had passed by her. Only a few minutes passed before they again heard the pained outcries of David. Joseph and Margaret led him out, supporting him on each side. He was staggering.

"He keeps a bottle of whiskey in the barn," Joseph said to Patrick.

"Yes, I know where," Patrick replied.

They took him to the barn as Margaret and Mary came out of the cabin. Mary rushed to Grae who engulfed the young woman, this friend from long ago, in a comforting embrace.

"She had so much more to teach us," Mary sobbed. "She was my best friend."

Ruth led the two slave men into the cabin. Still comforting Mary, Grae caught glimpses over the girl's shoulder as the two men carried Ama to the box. Ruth knelt down and made some adjustments to her hair and appeared to say a short prayer. The men placed the lid on top of the box and nailed it shut. A shiver went down Grae's spine as she heard the hammer hit the wood a final time.

They walked in a solemn line behind the wagon that was driven by two slaves. David, with Margaret and Joseph on each side, followed by Mary and Grae, with Patrick bringing up the rear, no minister or neighbors, no one else knew what had happened. At some point it had been decided that Patrick would say a few words. He spoke of Ama's graciousness and beauty, her love for the land, and for her family. He remembered Ama's talent and skills in ancient ways that gave her the sight to peer into the soul of another and see their goodness and strength. In closing, he pulled out a piece of paper from his pocket.

"I found this next to Wise Father with the dress that he chose for his only granddaughter."

Grae glanced at David and saw that he was mesmerized by what Patrick had just said and waited anxiously for him to read the paper.

"Pieces of sun on the lake of my spirits;
Pieces of sun on waters of eagle and hawk;
Pieces of sun lie broken on the waters of the lake
From which come the voice to all my singing,
the eyes to all my beauty,
the peace to all my longing.
Above all is the long-living spirit which is the thread
from generation to generation,
as long as the land we live on is everlasting
and our children have a place to lie down.

All as it was, love.
All as it was, beauty.
All as it was, order.
All as it was, in exactly the right place.
This place of the sun trail
The buffalo-grass plain
The hummingbird spring
The grass hat
The frog mesa
And the Big House in the lake where good spirits live.
This place of my people
This place of my grandsons still unborn.
All as it was, peace.
Everything good is to be found here.
Everything good is to be kept here."

Everyone stood in silence - taking in the meaning of the words. The old man's final gift to his granddaughter was ancient words to honor her passing. Patrick nodded to the two slave men and they gently lowered the wooden box by two ropes down into the ground. A rumble of thunder was heard off in the distance. A hot fall storm was coming shortly.

The slaves took turns shoveling the dirt into the grave until it was level with the ground. The storm drew closer and Margaret and Joseph tried to get David to walk back to the wagon for the ride home, but he refused to go.

"I will stay with him," Patrick said. "You all go on back to the cabin before the storm comes."

Joseph, Margaret and Mary followed the two men to the wagon. "Miss James?" Mary said.

Grae stood a few feet away from where David was

standing. He was staring at the grave below him.

"I would like to stay as well," Grae said to Patrick. He nodded and motioned for the wagon to go on. A few moments later, there was a crack of lightning, the clouds opened up and water flowed down in sheets.

"My God, why have you forsaken me?" Before they knew what was happening, David's arms were moving up to the sky, his hands clinched into fists. "Why have you taken her from me?" He screamed and slowly sank to the ground as the storm raged on. Grae realized that this was the image from her vision. What she had seen in her time was now occurring before her eyes.

Thunder boomed and lightning cracked through the sky. It was as if Mother Nature herself were attacking them or an unspoken evil that now might forever linger with them. By now, the grave was a sea of red mud and David laid down up it. Grae screamed as she saw that he sank a little.

Patrick was at her side in a flash. "It's just his weight, the dirt is not settled. The rain is causing it to sink."

"David, Ama has left a part of herself in your son, you shall draw comfort from him." The words were no sooner out of Grae's mouth than she regretted them as she saw David rise up on his hands and knees. He was covered in red mud. Dark red mud intermingled with blades of green grass.

"I shall not know him. He will live a life free from my influence. He will never know where he came from. I will be dead to him as his mother is." David again raised his hands to the sky, palms open this time. "I shall work and work and build. My dreams shall be wood and metal, not flesh and bone. I shall make all matters of my life business, even the children that come after him shall be for a purpose. My heart is closed to love."

David began to walk back toward the cabin. Patrick and Grae followed him. The storm quickly burned itself out and passed as quickly as it was violent and the rain stopped. Grae had discovered the purpose of her journey. She now knew what turned David Graham's heart into stone. She could go home now

TWENTY SIX

"We shall leave day after tomorrow," David announced upon returning to the cabin. Joseph, Margaret and Mary had waited out the storm there. Ruth was cooking some stew and a pan of hot biscuits was ready. All the evidence of what had transpired the night before was gone, except for the baby nursing at the breast of a slave woman in the corner.

"But, David, that is too soon. You need some rest. The baby should be a little older. That trip takes many days." Margaret was drinking a cup of coffee, but rose to meet her brother as he came through the door. "What in God's name has happened to you?" She said, as she saw he was covered in mud.

"I must deliver the child and return to my work. The slave girl will have to stay there until the child is weaned." Everyone looked at Esther, but she kept her head down. The baby was lying in her lap.

"I want all of you to go home and leave me in peace."

"Perhaps that is best, you get some rest. Ruth has cooked

you a good meal. We will come back tomorrow." It was the first words that Joseph had said the entire time.

David sat down in the rocking chair next to the fireplace. It was the same chair in which Ama sat just a few days earlier. David began to rock back and forth and he started to laugh, first softly, and then it grew louder.

"Peace! Leave me in peace. I shall never have peace again. Long after I am dead perhaps, but in this life I shall never have peace. Peace has abandoned me."

"It must be time for me to make my journey back." It was late that same night as Grae returned to her room at the McGavock house. All was dark upon their return, but Grae found The General there.

"Were you at the cabin? I never saw you there."

"I was nearby. It was best for me to stay out of the way." The General moved to one side of the bed as Grae collapsed beside him. "Why, do you think it is time for your return?"

"Because I have seen what changed David Graham. That was the truth I was seeking."

"If that is true, then indeed your journey should soon be over."

"You seem resistant to this idea. It is you who are always preaching for me to go home."

"And that I do, I did not want you to come in the first place. I am not resistant, I am unsure as to whether this is the only truth for which you seek."

"What else can there be?"

"You shall have to wait and find out."

"We are so grateful to you, Arabella, for everything you have done for David." Margaret met Grae in the dining room.

It was late Monday morning, the day after the burial. Grae had slept the sleep of exhaustion and no one had disturbed her. She had risen, bathed and went downstairs as the noon day meal was being served.

"I did nothing extraordinary. I wish I could have done more to…"

"Yes, dear, we all feel that way. I fear my brother will never be the man he once was." Margaret sat down beside Grae. "Before the others arrive, I would like to ask another favor of you. It would be an enormous inconvenience and a serious sacrifice; but, we are willing to double your wages if you will agree to help my family, my brother." Grae sat in silence, waiting for Margaret to continue. She feared that The General's prophecy might be coming to fruition.

"David is determined to leave tomorrow for North Carolina. No amount of argument from my husband or Patrick seems to be able to dissuade him. Esther shall go, of course, to nurse the child. Patrick shall go, and then return to his own home. What I fear is what shall happen upon David's trip back. I fear that he will not take care and something shall befall him. I cannot ask Patrick to make the return journey, he is not a young man and his health may have issues he has not shared." Margaret poured Grae a glass of water.

"I need for someone to go with them, someone who needs to make it safely back here." Grae began to feel sick on her stomach.

"I know it is a great deal to ask, but Mister McGavock and I are willing to pay you twice your salary for the month."

"A month?" Grae could not control her outburst.

"I am sure that David will get every possible traveling moment out of each day, but most of the area that must be passed through will not allow for night travel. It will take almost two weeks to get there." A crash was heard in the kitchen and Margaret rose to check on it. The General skirted by Margaret in passing and made a piercing meow in Grae's direction.

"I know," Grae whispered.

"That cat should be very glad that it came with you," Margaret said as she returned to the room. According to Ruth, it seemed to deliberately knock over a pitcher of milk. I suppose it was thirsty," Margaret laughed.

"Arabella, I know that I have put a heavy burden on your shoulders, but I really feel it would help David for you to be with him. He seems quite fond of you. Who knows, after he has gotten through his grief, he might even…"

"Something smells wonderful!" Joseph McGavock burst into the room. "It's just what this family needs, one of Ruth's good hearty meals." Joseph nodded approvingly as Ruth and another slave placed several large platters of food on the table. Joseph did not wait for the rest of the table to be seated. He began filling his plate with food.

"Eat up, Miss James; you will not see food like this on your journey to North Carolina." Margaret immediately looked uncomfortable after her husband's statement.

"Joseph, I was just now talking with Arabella about the possibility…"

"Possibility? This young woman is in our employment. She shall do as we say or she shall seek employment elsewhere."

"But, Joseph, this is outside the realm of what we…"

"We hired Miss James to be of service to our family. This trip certainly is that, David is our family, his needs are ours. I'm sure that Miss James understands me." Joseph gave Grae a pleasant, but stern look. Grae bowed her head. Joseph let out a yelp.

"That blessed cat just bit me on the leg. Get out of here!" The General ran out of the dining room and under Ruth's feet to the kitchen door.

"Do we understand one another, Miss James?" Joseph asked. Evelyn Newton had arrived in the room and sat down next to Joseph. She turned her attention toward Grae, but it was soon obvious who she was really looking at."

"Understand what?" Patrick asked, he was behind Grae's chair and his voice startled her.

"Understand that she shall be accompanying you and David on your journey to Catawba Springs and will be David's travel companion on the return trip.

"She cannot travel back alone with David, it would be highly unacceptable, a young single lady travelling alone with a man." Patrick sat down on the other side of Joseph seemingly unaware that Evelyn was seated across from him and was staring a hole through his soul. The broach was again prominently displayed at her neck and her hand was fingering it.

"They will not be alone. There will be two slave men going along to help with the driving," Joseph answered between bites of beef stew.

"Really, Joseph, two slave men? How shall that improve the situation?"

"They will not be alone. This is not seventeenth century England; we are in a rural location in a new land. We cannot conform to every single rule of proper behavior. It is not possible!" Joseph's voice had risen and he set his fork down until he regained his composure.

"Miss James has proven to us that she has the ability and tolerance to adapt to different situations. I realize that this situation may not be what her mother in Massachusetts would approve for her daughter; but, she would also not have approved for her to witness the death of an Indian princess either as she brought the half breed son of my brother-in-law into the world!"

"Joseph, don't speak of the child in that manner!" Margaret's voice had risen and was almost matching the volume of her husband's.

"Margaret, I mean no disrespect to the child, but the truth remains the same. His heritage cannot be argued. His mother's heritage could not be either." Joseph took a long drink from the glass of water before him. "Miss James has shown us that she is not a stranger to work, that she can be a valuable part of this household. She shows no fear of the uncomfortable. She shall help us watch over David and she shall be abundantly rewarded for it upon her return, both monetarily and in good favor from this family."

All eyes were on Grae and she knew in her heart that this would be the most dangerous thing she had encountered thus far. It was unlikely that she would experience any physical harm; but, her ability to return to her own time might be compromised because of the distance she would be from the Graham property. Her mind raced. If she did not go, she would surely be sent away to who knew where. Either decision was placing her future in the twenty-first century in jeopardy. At least being with David would have the possibility of returning and not force her to rely on the kindness of strangers. She didn't see that she had really any choice.

"I will go." Grae released a long sigh with this statement. Looking around the table, she saw concerned relief on the face of Margaret. Joseph seemed very satisfied that his speech had rendered such an outcome. He gave her a hearty smile. The lines of worry only deepened in Patrick's forehead, but his eyes acknowledged his understanding. Grae glanced at Evelyn as Margaret passed her a bowl of sweet potatoes. Their eyes met and Grae saw darkness, almost anger, as if she could almost not control what she was feeling inside.

"Joseph and Margaret, I would like to thank you for your hospitality," Evelyn began; her voice was very deliberate and controlled. "I do believe that I shall begin my journey home tomorrow as well."

"You will have good weather for it, Eve." It was the second time that Grae had heard Patrick address this woman by the shortened version of her name. A habit from their youth Grae was sure, but there was something about the name that triggered Grae's memory and she couldn't figure out why.

"Indeed, Patrick. But, I do intend to visit another friend or two before I begin my journey home. I have many friends here." Evelyn seemed delighted that Patrick was speaking to her, even if it was about the weather. "My beloved Shenandoah shall be waiting for me in all the splendid colors of fall. You should come and visit my beautiful part of Virginia."

"I have travelled through there in the fall. The area is indeed beautiful. Almost as beautiful as our own Southwest Virginia, we cannot deny that the home of our families cannot compare to any other place." Evelyn's face visibly fell at Patrick's reply.

"I think I shall retire to my room and rest up." Joseph and Patrick rose briefly as Evelyn departed the table. Patrick glanced at Grae and raised his eyebrows at her departure causing Grae to almost laugh out loud.

"Miss James, I suggest you do the same thing. David will wish to leave at sunrise. We will make sure that you have several items of clothing to take with you. Upon your return, we shall hire the services of this community's best seamstress to provide you with several new dresses of your own. We have not forgotten what needs to be replaced by the stagecoach driver's irresponsible behavior." Joseph rose from the table. He kissed his wife on the forehead as he passed her. "There was no need to worry, my dear, I knew that Miss James would not let us down." With a nod to Grae, he walked out of the room and toward the front door.

Margaret left the table and began giving orders to Ruth before she even reached the kitchen. "We must prepare as much food as we can that will not perish on their journey. Perhaps, we could…"

"You do not have to do this," Patrick said once everyone else had left the room. "I can make the journey back with David, or perhaps even convince him to stay on at my place for a month or so. It would help him clear his head."

"That is not how his sister wishes for it to be, Mister McGavock."

"Would you please just call me Patrick?"

"I do not think that would be the proper thing to do."

"You call David by his given name."

"Well, considering the circumstances with Ama, he felt that it was…"

"Have I not been by your side throughout most of this ordeal as well?" Patrick was not going to let her get out of this question.

"I suppose that is true, but…"

"You have some personal tie to David that I am not aware of?"

"No! There is no such tie, other than friendship. I just feel that since you are an older man, that I…"

"I haven't always been." And there it was again; the evidence that he still was not convinced that she was not the

Arabella from his youth. "But, I understand, you are being polite to an old man." Patrick rose and walked toward the doorway. He stopped with his back facing her. "I should consider it a distinct honor if you would humor this old man and give him the pleasure of hearing his name, his personal name, spoken by you. It would do my heart good. Good afternoon, Miss James."

Grae sat alone at the big table, feeling very small. The emotions of everything experienced coming down on her in one silent blow. "I want to, Patrick," she whispered. "I really need a friend."

TWENTY SEVEN

"I will say it once again, because you do not seem to be hearing me. You have lost your mind!" The General paced back and forth across Grae's bed. It was the hour just before sunrise the following morning, and he had awakened Grae again to try and convince her not to make the trip.

"What choice do I have?" Grae was putting the last of her meager belongings into a satchel that had been brought to her the night before. Grae would take the green dress, her own dress from 1786, and an ugly light or faded brown one that was currently on her back. It was all the space allowed.

"This is the most dire and disastrous situation you have found yourself in yet. Grae, let me speak clearly, you could be stuck in this century permanently. Your life as you know it could be over!"

Grae took a deep breath. "I know that, but I don't know what else I can do. I can't exactly tell them that I have to stay near the Graham property so that I can travel back to the twenty-first century. You heard Joseph! If I don't go, I will be sent away. At least I can have you with me."

"No, you cannot." The General sat down.

"Oh, I'm sure that David will allow me to take you in the wagon…"

"It doesn't matter what he allows you to do."

"You don't want to go with me?" Grae's lower lip began to tremble.

"It's not a matter of wanting. I am not allowed to travel that far away from the Graham property."

"But, wait, you travelled back and forth over a couple of hundred years at least. This is only a few weeks."

"You are speaking of time. I am speaking of distance. I am not restricted by time, but my feet will not allow me to travel more than twenty miles away from the property in any one direction."

Grae sank down onto the bed. "And what would happen if you did?" She was afraid to hear the answer, yet she knew she had to know."

"I would cease to exist."

"So what makes you think that I can travel away from here safely? What makes me different from you?"

"You are not under a spell."

"What? You've alluded to this before."

"Grae, I cannot discuss it, and it really is too long of a story for the time we have. The distance you travel is not limited, but you cannot travel back to your time unless you are on Graham Mansion soil. Of that, there is no dispute." A knock at the door interrupted their conversation.

"Arabella, are you ready? We have a big breakfast prepared. David should be arriving shortly." It was Margaret.

"Yes, ma'am. I will be down in a few minutes." Once she thought Margaret had gone, Grae continued.

"You have been a good friend, and I appreciate all you have done. I know you are concerned, but I am going to just have to take this leap of faith. Perhaps there is further truth that this trip shall reveal to me and upon my return, my mission will be complete." Grae stroked The General's soft fur. "I will return. One way or another, I will find a way back here. I will not give up on my life."

"Very well, I wish you Godspeed. Remember, Grae, rely on your instincts. Don't try to change the course of things, and remember that Patrick could be your downfall or your savior, choose wisely."

As the light of sunrise was breaking, the wagon was on the way. David was in the wagon seat with one of the slave men, his name was Jacob. Grae learned that the other slave was John and was the equivalent of Esther's husband. It was a small kindness that he was being brought along. John and Esther would be left in Catawba Springs to help care for the child. Grae sat beside Esther under the wagon's covering and watched as Patrick followed them on horseback. The baby, as yet unnamed as far as Grae knew, was very quiet. Perhaps even at his young age, he knew better than to make too much of a fuss. Esther called him Sweetness and hummed to him when he would start to wake.

"Is this hard for you?" Grae asked. "I know you lost your own child." Tears welled up in the woman's eyes before she answered.

"There ain't never been nothing easy in my life. That babe I carried, it weren't Johns, it be some other slave that work on the farm for less than a month. He hold a knife to my throat as he made me lie with him. Massa McGavock, he see the trouble in 'im and sold 'im away. I would have loved that babe no

matter, but I cants say that I wasn't some glad to sees it go."
There was hardness in the woman's eyes. Grae thought it was a
testimony to her strength that there was life in her eyes at all.
"This here babe would have had all the loves in the world if his
mammie done lived. Now he gots to settle for seconds. But ole
Esther, she gonna see to it that he gets some firsts. I wills love
him as long as they lets me. This be a new life for me and John,
maybe our new Massa be kind like Massa McGavock try to be.
We can pray so."

The road was nothing but bumps as far as Grae could tell.
Sometimes the path hardly looked passible for a horse, much
less a wagon, but somehow they kept going. Patrick shouted
out the name Kanawha as they crossed the New River. Perhaps
it was his humble acknowledgement of the woman who caused
this journey. As they stopped to water the horses, David spoke
directly to Grae for the first time that day.

"One of the horses has thrown a shoe, so we will have to
stop early at the farm of David Peirce. It's not far from here. I
want to make sure you understand a few things." David and
Patrick stood with Grae on the riverbank; it reminded her of
Gav's last day before he left for college.

"It was not my idea for you to be on this trip, but I know
how persuasive my sister and her husband can be. I am
thankful for your sacrifice to come with us, but I do expect you
to help me with appearances." David and Patrick exchanged
looks and Patrick nodded.

"We will tell the Peirces and anyone else who we
encounter until we get to Catawba Springs that this child is
yours." Grae's eyes grew wide.

"You have married into our family, and your husband had
an unfortunate accident that took his life before your child was
born. We are helping you get to relatives in North Carolina."

"What is my name?"

"We can make that easy for you, Arabella Graham." Grae noticed the look that crossed Patrick's face. Neither of them realized how many different names she had in her travels.

"And what is the baby's name?" David looked at her as if she had uttered something horrible.

"Choose whatever name you like, I will be giving a name to John Davidson Graham that shall be only known to me." Grae was shocked at his answer, but knew that David must deal with this in his own way.

Esther and John napped on the way to the Peirce farm. Grae saw the edge of a piece of paper showing at the opened part of David's bag. She gently lifted it out and saw that it was an envelope, another letter addressed to John Davidson Graham. She could only imagine that it contained information that she might need to know. So she carefully opened it and began to read.

David Graham, Esq.
Perry Mount Furnace
Cedar Run Farm
Wythe County
Virginia

3 October, 1830

Honourable John Davidson Graham, Esq.
Elm Wood Plantation
Catawba Springs
North Carolina

Dear Sir,

I write to you this day with a profound heaviness of heart. I am consumed with a paralyzing pain that impedes my every breath; it arrests all rational thought, each step seemingly lost in a numbing, stumbling grief. I beg Your forgiveness and patience as You read these, my words, before You here, although mere phrases cannot convey the vast pit of emptiness and sorrow that I feel. Sir, I shall attempt a full report to You here for only Yourself will read or hear this confession of my very soul. Heaven help me.

Was it just last month that Ama and I made our arrangements with Yourself? Yes, of course, but it seems so long ago now. Ama was happy about the promise of our new home in North Carolina, near her people living now among the Catawba Tribe, a blessing from the Almighty Himself. What supreme joy we did share this last month together, planning our new life and waiting for the birth of our child. This, Sir, was an ill-fated euphoria! God has chosen to take Ama from this Life, from her healthy newborn son, and from my world!

For despite our most vigorous interventions Ama died as she gave life to our son. I wonder now, if my dearest Ama did not sense her coming death, for in the hours before her death, she told me of a vision. That she saw our son in the future as a man, and it is this vision that directs my heart and hand as I write to you this day, just hours after her passing.

With a peaceful smile and loving eyes, Ama spoke of her wishes to me. She spoke his Cherokee name,

Aginvda, which means "my sun and moon". Did I ever tell you she named our home here *Sagwanvda*? In Cherokee it means "one sun and one moon". The name has been our secret epithet for our one, true love. But, she revealed that this would not be known to him, that we must only use an English name of my choosing.

She said that our precious son would grow and thrive in North Carolina, but she did not mention us as being there with him. I now know why and I know that it was her way of telling me that he must not be raised under the stigma of his birth. It is our wish that our son be raised in Your home, as Your adopted son, arriving from a distant, deceased relative.

Rest assured, my dear Sir, that I will always provide for his needs and will bring slaves to care for him and to supplement your household. I know now that I must protect my son always from the secret of his birth. Always. God save me!

I must confess that I know in my heart I am to blame for Ama's death. The fault resting entirely at the feet of my sins! For it has been my monumental Ambition and Pride, Sir, that has cursed our love and our lives together. Sir, I confess to you now that I had yet to wed Ama, our son indeed illegitimate in the eyes of God. It was Ama who refused to marry me here, demanding that I must preserve my position and my upstanding reputation in this community. I know now that I should never have permitted this! I should have insisted upon our immediate marriage once we knew she was with child! But, I was blind! I was blind to my true obligations to her, my son, and to God, for I was filled with my own selfish pride. These, my disgraceful actions, I now lay before Yourself and before God to judge. How can I ever forgive myself? How can I continue to live with this shame and go on with life?

Sir, now my full confession is known to You. I stand before You stripped of all arrogance and prideful vanity and ask that You will talk with your dear wife, Betsy, about this most unusual thing. I humbly beg You to take my son and raise him as your own! You have my pledge to provide for his every financial need.

Can you bring Yourself to put aside my disreputable behavior and assist me? It is only the hope of Your supreme kindness that sustains my unworthy soul as I write these agonizing words to You. Praise God. I have said what I thought impossible. With His Grace and Your Blessing, may I now go forward and do what is unthinkable.

I shall begin the journey to your home within the day and shall humbly beseech you in person to take into your home this small soul who must now grow up without the daily beauty of the one who gave him life. It is a cross I will always bear.

You have every assurance of my great confidence and esteem with which I have the honour to be Your obedient servant,

David Graham

That night, they slept in a warm house on soft beds. Grae wondered how many nights she would be able to say this when the trip was over. The Peirce home was comparable to that of the McGavocks'. David Peirce was quite up in years, and Grae learned that he had been a mentor of David's in the years since his father's death. His wife, Mary Bell Peirce, was many years his junior and had a quiet, reserved presence. It was apparent that the Peirces had several children, but only three were at home during the visit.

The story was easily accepted and Grae was treated with the utmost hospitality. Esther was allowed to stay in an adjoining room to Grae's that once served as a nursery. The other slaves were given shelter in the slaves' quarters.

Grae was happy to be seated across from Martha Bell Peirce at dinner. Grae remembered that Martha would later become the wife of David Graham and also live a painful life with him. She was intrigued to watch their interaction, as they were seated next to each other at the dinner table. David was polite, but obviously very uninterested. This did not dissuade Martha from glancing at him throughout the meal. Grae noticed that each time she would pick up her napkin, cover her mouth, and make a soft noise. It was almost like a giggle.

Grae found herself seated between Mister David Peirce and his son, Alexander. The Peirce's youngest son, James, was seated next to Patrick.

"James," David Graham said. "I understand that, at times, you serve your father as a messenger. The young man had beautiful coal black hair and the features to be a handsome one when grown.

"Yes, sir. I enjoy this work very much."

"He is good at it," Mister Peirce said. "He knows to travel as fast as possible, to be diligent about his assignment."

"Splendid," David replied. "Then, tomorrow morning, I would like for you to travel with a letter for John Davidson Graham of Catawba Springs, North Carolina. Patrick will draw you a map. It needs to arrive at least a couple of days ahead of us. Can you do that? I shall pay your wage and a bonus."

"Indeed, sir!" James smiled and he resumed eating heartily. "I shall prepare my horse right after dinner and retire early for plenty of rest."

Grae knew the contents of this letter. It was the one she had read earlier in the wagon. It would seal the fate of David's child.

"Alexander, I was sorry to hear of Rebekah's passing," Patrick said. Appearing to be in his early thirties, Alexander seemed to be the life of the party. Grae could detect an odor that indicated that he liked to start the party earlier in the day, and he tried to refill Grae's wineglass on several occasions.

"Yes, sad, very sad. Rebekah was my second wife," Alexander replied, leaning over to Grae. "I love my wives as King Henry the Eighth did...briefly." Alexander chuckled. Grae noticed that David's jaw had clenched at the comment.

"My dear son has just not found the right woman," Missus Peirce replied quietly.

"I do not find women, they find me," Alexander added. "It is a curse." He leaned back towards Grae's direction. "You shall fall in love with me before the night is over, Miss Graham."

"It is Missus Graham, Alexander. She is still in mourning for her husband." David's reply was stern.

"Where is her black then?"

"It is not practical for her to wear her mourning attire on such a long journey," David replied. It was obvious that he did not care much for Alexander.

"Pay my son no mind, Missus Graham." Mister Peirce's voice was hoarse and deep. "He has never learned the art of standing on one's own two feet. He keeps trying to marry his way to good fortune."

"I shall not be like my sisters," Martha joined the

conversation. "I shall marry for love, when the right gentleman comes along."

While pleasant and comfortable, the visit seemed hardly memorable, with the exception of the interesting dinner conversation. Grae wondered if the next few weeks would just be one long day followed by one boring evening. After a restful night, they once again rose early and left at dawn.

During the next two days, they traveled through rolling hills. They saw very few people. They were fortunate to find several springs and streams to water the horses, and even to find some late fall apples. Grae managed to impress David and Patrick by frying them for a delicious breakfast with the last of the biscuits that Ruth had packed for them.

As the sun prepared to sit on the third day, they made it to the small town of Taylorsville. Grae was surprised to see that there was a Main Street with an ordinary. She somehow missed the history lesson that would tell her that, in this time, an ordinary was an inn that also served meals. It was a delightful surprise as it meant she and Esther would sleep on something other than the hard floor of the wagon.

The name of the inn was MacKenzie's, and there was plenty of ale and Irish grub. While Grae was not entirely sure what the meat was in the stew she was served, she recognized that the cook had a talent with spices and ate two hearty bowls with the delicious wheat bread. A balladeer named Emerson serenaded them while they ate and told colorful stories as the evening turned into night.

Esther had experienced an especially rough time the previous night with the baby, so after she nursed him, Grae encouraged her to go on to bed. Holding the newborn in her arms reminded Grae of her old neighborhood in Charlotte and their next door neighbor who had twins the year Grae turned twelve. The young mother was overwhelmed and anxiously accepted Grae's offers to help. The woman's husband was away frequently on business, and Kat would allow Grae to stay overnight in case Janice needed an extra set of hands to rock or change one of the infants.

Grae hummed one of the songs that Emerson had sung earlier; the Irish lilt was a fitting lullaby. The baby opened his eyes and tried to focus on Grae. His little fists balled in determination as she had seen his father do.

Grae continued to rock him back and forth and soon he was fast asleep. She placed him in a small basket that served as his bed. She moved to the window and watched the stars in the clear October sky. Below, she saw Emerson walking away from the inn, his guitar slung on his back.

They crossed over into North Carolina on the fourth day and camped that night on the banks of the mighty Dan River. Their evening and night were not the most comforting. The previous cool days had been replaced by a second southern summer bringing too much heat. Grae and Esther found a massive oak tree that shaded them and the baby, but Patrick and David waded into the water to cast their makeshift poles.

"They look like little boys out there, don't they?" Grae said to Esther.

Esther laughed and pointed. Grae saw that Patrick had pulled in an aggressive fish and had fallen backward in the water. One of the slave men tending to the horses had run over to help David pull Patrick up. Grae also ran over and realized that Patrick did not look well, he looked overheated.

"I think you need to go sit in the shade for a while," Grae said to him as he struggled to climb the bank, his clothes dripping wet. Patrick was breathing heavily and sweat was pouring off his forehead.

"No, I am fine. We need to catch some more fish."

"Well, you go over there and sit with Esther and watch me really catch some fish." Patrick looked at her in disbelief. "Go on, you'll see."

For as long as Grae could remember, she had fished, with her father, her mother, her grandparents, and her brother, and most recently with Gav. David stood in shock as almost as quickly as she could recast her line, another fish was biting. Within an hour, she had enough fish for all of them to eat a hearty meal.

Returning to the campsite with the fish, she saw that a roaring fire was now ready on which to cook them. She handed the fish to the slaves, and turned to walk away as Patrick asked her where she was going. "Well, certainly, you do not expect me to cook them, too."

After the last fish was eaten, Patrick and David began talking about the route they would cover over the following days. Hearing them speak of the trails and waterways in place of interstates and highways made Grae appreciate the world of GPS and Google maps on her cell phone.

"We should reach Germanton by afternoon tomorrow," Patrick said. "There are a few farms there, but I don't recall that the owners are that friendly to travelers. It is where we can pick up the Great Wagon Road. I imagine that there are more travelling it now than most farmers wish to see."

"Ah, that road shall serve us well for several days. It will not be as treacherous as our last few days have been." David stared at Esther, who was bouncing the baby up and down. "How quickly a man's life can change? Last week this time, I was full of happiness and anticipation. Today, my heart is dark, and I have no desire for it to be anything different for the rest of my days."

"My friend, time shall heal your wounds. You shall love again and make a new life," Patrick took a long swig from a bottle of whiskey that was passed between him and David.

"Like you did?" David said with a chuckle. Grae pretended to be nodding off hoping that they would continue the conversation.

"There is a vast difference in you and me, David," Patrick replied.

"And what is that difference? We both loved women who left us."

"But the difference is that you know yours is gone; she will not be coming back and it was not her choice to leave you. I know none of that. She may be living; she may be dead. She may be five miles away or five hundred. She may have left by no choice of her own; or she might have just decided that she didn't want me." Patrick took another swig from the bottle. "I mean no disrespect, but in some ways I envy you. You had Ama's unconditional love with no doubt. And you know where she is and why she is there."

David pondered what Patrick had said for a moment. "I understand your words, my friend, but I don't agree with all of them. I know where she is, indeed, and that time will forever keep her there. But, I do not know why. Why she was taken from me? That is what has closed my heart. I had no desire for love before I met her. The female being was of only one use to me and I could take what I wanted from some slave girl and be satisfied." Grae felt Esther flinch beside her.

"All I wanted was to succeed; to be a man of ambition like my father. Ah, Robert Graham always had some coins in his pockets they would say. His wealth was in his pocket, in a steel box, under the mattress and over the vast land of his success. That was what I aspired for also, and that is what I shall serve for the rest of my days."

Grae wondered if with each day that passed she would see more of the David that history portrayed. Would he be true to his words and never seek love again?

The nights were long in the wilderness. Whether she was settled inside the wagon or on the ground, the noises of the night made her sleep fitful. Being her mother's daughter, she had never enjoyed camping. There was a reason why civilized people didn't live outside anymore, and they should honor it. She thought a lot about her mother and how the previous year had changed her. Financial struggles were a daily part of Kat's life, but somehow there was calmness around her mother's being that Grae had not seen before.

As they rode from dawn to dusk, Grae would often think of her father. When she and Perry were barely in school, their father occasionally would take them on a Sunday afternoon ride. Looking back, Grae imagined that it was a way to give her mother a little freedom, a break from all the "mommy time." Grae also thought that it was like a mini-adventure to him though; he would just start driving, no destination, and no map. He would always find the most interesting little places, and they would never feel the anxiety of being lost, even though they most surely were at times.

Despite the fact that she and Perry had little contact with their father, Tom, since he was incarcerated, Grae knew eventually they would resurrect some sort of relationship with him. As screwed up as life had gotten, there were still many happy memories with him. He was paying for his mistakes; she would allow him a smidgen of redemption when his debt to society was paid.

The further south they journeyed, the hotter it got. Grae wondered if it would be considered one of the hottest Octobers of that century. They got on the Great Wagon Road as Patrick had predicted, and a twinge of excitement passed through Grae as she thought about all the settlers that had let this road be their compass to their new home.

On the sixth day, they passed through the German and Moravian settlements of Salem and Bathabara and with it came several inns, taverns, and ordinaries. She realized that this was close to the area now known as Winston-Salem in her time, and remembered a trip in elementary school where they visited the historic area called Old Salem. But, in this century, it was a bustle of activity in comparison to most of their trip.

"I'm sure this has been a difficult trip for a lady," Patrick said, as he helped her down from the wagon. "They only have one room with a bathtub," he whispered. "I have arranged for you to have it." Music to her ears was these words; she would see a bathtub on this trip.

"I might just have to sleep in it," Grae smiled and before she realized it, she had kissed Patrick on the cheek. He looked stunned and humbled, and sadly, old all at once.

"You have given an old man quite a thrill," he said, holding his heart. "It pleases me to make you so happy." Grae immediately wished that she had not let her excitement take over her emotions.

Sensing her dilemma, Patrick whispered again, "It is fine."

Grae almost felt like she was in a suite, the room was so large. There were two beds and ample room for both her and

Esther to have some privacy. David offered to bring them some food from the tavern and after they had eaten their meal, it was time for Grae to enjoy her bath.

A very short, strong woman brought up several buckets of hot water to fill the cast iron tub. Grae sank thankfully into it and the warm water was like heaven even if the soap smelled otherwise. It was an amazing feeling in many ways, and Grae wondered if she would have an opportunity like this again. After drying off and slipping into her nightgown, she found Esther in the side room rocking the baby.

"Would you mind if I takes a bath?"

"Not at all, how do we get that woman to come back and change the water?"

Esther began to laugh, first it was soft, then it grew louder, then it shook her whole body.

"What did I say?"

"Lawd, have mercy on your heart, Miss James. This be da first time in my whole life that I be da second one in da bath water. Most times, I be at least the fifth or six. Don't yous worry your pretty head 'bout it, it be like my first day in heaven to sits in your water."

Grae took the baby out of Esther's arms and closed the door behind her. No matter how many things she learned about slavery and about the way of the world in another time, some things still amazed her and maybe that was good. Otherwise, being so far away from all she knew to be true would break her heart.

The next morning came earlier it seemed. Grae longed to stay in the warm bed. Patrick had a bag of country ham biscuits and a jug of fresh water waiting for them at the wagon.

"You both looked rested," he said as he helped Esther into

the wagon. As Grae handed the baby up to Esther, she turned to talk to Patrick.

"I am so grateful to you arranging for us to have that lovely room. It is the best night's rest that I have had since I have been in Virginia."

"You are in North Carolina now," David said, coming up behind her. Somehow the very sound of his voice was beginning to irritate her.

"I was speaking to Patrick," Grae said.

"Someone is a little grumpy; perhaps I should have let Alexander visit you while we were at the Peirce's."

"LET! Let him, you say," Grae spun around to confront David directly, only to find him lying on the ground. He had already been punched by Patrick.

The remaining days of their journey were much of the same. Long days riding rough roads, though the heat finally lifted after an afternoon spent crossing a waterway called Shallow Ford, and then camping at Chipley's Ford at the Yadkin River crossing. That night it rained so hard that by morning all of them were sleeping in the wagon.

As Grae got out of the wagon that morning, she was amazed at the change in the scenery. It was like the rain had washed all the dust away and the beautiful fall colors shined everywhere. "It's like one of those Technicolor movies Mom loves," Grae said out loud to herself.

"What you say?" Esther stretched and yawned as she got out behind her.

"Oh, what a beautiful morning!" Grae quickly replied, giggling to herself as she imagined the production of *Oklahoma!* that she and her mother had seen the previous spring at a local dinner theatre.

They left the Great Wagon Road on the ninth day and from there on, followed Sherrill's Path. Crossing the Catawba River at a shallow spot on the eleventh day, the last night under the stars was a quiet one. Esther had fallen asleep with the baby in the basket beside her as Grae sat with Patrick by the campfire.

"We will reach our destination by afternoon tomorrow," Patrick said. David had wandered off a few minutes earlier.

"How much further will it then be for you to your home?" Grae asked.

"Only a couple of hours, I shall stay at John's for a day or two to rest my horse, and then go home to prepare for a long winter."

Thinking that it might be her last time alone with him ever, Grae pondered what she could say that would ease his mind and heart.

"Patrick." It was the first time she had used his given name. The sound pleased him, he smiled.

"I want to thank you for all the kindnesses you have shown me. I am sorry that my resemblance to your lost one has brought you pain."

"You can stop pretending, Arabella. I know it is you." Patrick held up his hand as Grae started to speak.

"You are wasting your breath. I know it is you. At first, I thought you to be a witch, but you have no special powers. You only seem to do good deeds; there is no evil in your heart. After our encounter in my bedroom, when you found the bow, I remembered a man I met all those years ago while I searched for you. He was a man of science displaced in a small village. He thought thoughts no one dared dream about. He had theories that could only be whispered." Patrick took the red bow out of his pocket. The sight still stunned her.

"He took this ribbon in his hand and felt its softness, and then he looked me straight in the eyes." Patrick paused in deep remembering. "He said, 'She has left this time; she is no longer here.' It was grievous to my heart. It meant you were dead. I stopped looking after that."

Patrick rose and turned his back. "I only had to be in your presence an hour to realize what he had really meant. You had left my time. You had gone back to your time. You had journeyed home. I could not begrudge you what you most likely did not control. Now I have grown old and you are still young. I have spent a lifetime loving you after one tragically magnificent night."

"I do not know what you are talking about." Grae was sure blowing her cover would make her time in 1830 permanent.

"The night I killed Joseph Baker," Patrick said.

"It was not you, it was Sam." Grae gasped as she heard the words come out of her mouth. Patrick whirled around and she feared in that one misstep, she would never see her family again.

TWENTY EIGHT

David rode ahead on horseback that last morning to prepare the household of John Davidson Graham for their arrival. It was a silent journey. No more words than those necessary were exchanged between Patrick and Grae, and Esther, Jacob, and John followed the same behavior.

The sun was preparing to set when they finally reached the plantation. Its golden brilliance lit up the sky as it slid into a sea of red and purple. It was a stark contrast from the green which had plagued Grae's time in 1830. John Davidson Graham's mansion was massive and elegant. Upon her first view of its enormity, Grae wondered if it was the bar David had set for himself. This ambitious fortress of wealth and prosperity would be a lofty goal for even the most driven man.

As the wagon approached the front of the house, Grae saw a very old, but very proper looking, woman on the porch. She was wearing the most beautiful purple dress Grae had ever seen. She exuded an aura of royalty beyond measure. Breaking her silence, she asked Patrick, "Who is that woman?"

Patrick smiled. "That my dear, is Mittie Queen Graham. Major General Joseph Graham is her brother. He is John Davidson Graham's father. You won't hear anyone say John Davidson around these parts though. Around here he's known as Jackey". The Major General's wife, Isabella, died many years ago, and Mittie Queen has been the ruler of this house ever since."

A slave dressed in a suit coat offered his arm to assist Grae to get out of the wagon. She smoothed down her green dress and, for the first time, felt embarrassed at her appearance. The woman was barely five feet tall, but she might as well have stood seven feet for the commanding presence she radiated.

"You must be Miss Arabella James," the woman said. "We have been awaiting your arrival. Jackey, David! Where have you placed your manners? Put down that whiskey bottle and come out here. Our company has arrived." Her voice was as formidable as her command of attention and it took no time for the two men to appear like chastised school boys.

"I am Mittie Queen Graham, not Missus Graham, not Miss Graham, not Mittie. You shall call me Mittie Queen. I shall call you Bella as that was my dearest sister-in-law's name, and it warms my heart to say it again."

Grae nodded as Mittie Queen led her over the threshold of the house. She caught a gasp in her throat as she viewed the opulence of her new surroundings.

"Jackey's father, my brother built this home for our darling Bella. Sadly, she did not have many years here. But, it is full of life with Jackey's large family. There is always some mischief happening." The woman paused and looked directly at Grae.

"Before you try and ask someone, yes, I am very old, ninety-seven to be exact. I plan to live to be one hundred and one and not one day more."

Grae smiled at the woman's determination and exactness. She could not imagine that Death would dare come one day sooner or later than this woman dictated.

Grae and Esther were taken to a very spacious suite of rooms. A large room with a majestic bed of intricately carved cherry wood was given to Grae, and a smaller, but nice room for Esther, while the nursery sat between them. Grae was intrigued by the wallpaper in both rooms featuring tiny little tulips in pale pink and deep burgundy; it was an eye-catching contrast.

After Grae freshened up, she made her way down the long staircase to the foyer of the mansion. A crystal chandelier sparkled brightly in the center of the high ceiling. She could not imagine what an undertaking it was to light and extinguish each of the many candles that made possible such brilliance. She felt like a beggar in the dirty green dress she still wore, but she only had one clean one left, her dress from 1786.

In the dining room, Grae found the most elegant table she had ever seen, china and crystal sparkled, silver shined like a mirror, and she could not imagine where all the beautiful cut flowers had come from this late in the year. She would never know everyone's names of those who were there that night, but she did know how a princess must feel her first night in a castle.

Dinner chatter went on long after she had finished her meal. Despite her age, Mittie Queen did not seem to tire. From the head of the table, she commanded it; she had placed Grae near her, next to Patrick.

"David, have you told Bella of my proposition?" Mittie Queen's question silenced the table.

"No, but I cannot see how she could possibly turn down

such a generous offer." David looked Grae straight in the eyes as he took a drink from his wineglass.

Grae looked back at Mittie Queen questioningly.

"I understand that you are a governess. I think it would be a proper idea for you to stay here and raise this child that David has brought to us. He could be cared for by the slave woman and educated by you. No one would have to know his origin. We can raise him to be a proper Graham, an orphaned relative of a distant cousin."

Fear, deep fear, gripped every inch of Grae. She turned to Patrick, and he seemed to read her thoughts.

"But, David, I'm sure that Margaret and Joseph are counting on Miss James to return to their employment," Patrick said.

"No, they are not." Those four words sealed a deal that had been made behind her back. Margaret did not fear for her brother's mental state; she was helping him secure his son's future in this house.

"If you will please excuse me," Grae hastily left the table. She thought she might throw up. She wished beyond her wildest dreams that she could will herself back to the Mansion. To her bright blue room, to Clara's rolling balls, to this conniving man's slamming windows—she wanted to go home. She ran out the front door and into the night air. The sky was dark as coal, not a star was visible to wish on; her dreams would not come true. Patrick followed her outside.

"I had no idea that this was being planned. I do not know what to say." Patrick paced down the walkway beside of her. "Maybe this would be good for you."

"You do not understand." Grae raised her hands in the air. "I cannot get home to my time, my family, my real life, unless I am on the property of Graham Mansion."

"What?" Patrick looked confused.

"I cannot go home unless I am on David's land in Virginia. That is where I live in my own time."

Patrick allowed those words to sink in before he spoke. "And what century would that be?"

"Patrick, I have said too much already."

"What century?"

"The twenty-first century."

Patrick seemed to be doing math in his head. "Two hundred years from now?"

"Just about, it's a long trip."

"And you live with your family?"

"My mother, my brother, and my grandfather."

Patrick seemed to be carefully weighing his words. "And you have a love there?"

Grae took a deep breath. "His name is James Patrick McGavock, we call him Gav. He is the spitting image of you in 1786. You, no doubt, are a distant cousin or uncle or something."

A stern look crossed Patrick's face. "Go to bed."

"What?"

"Go to your room, change your clothes, tell Esther goodnight, and kiss the baby. Do everything you would normally do. Get as much rest as you can. Before the dawn breaks, I shall tap on your door. Take only the clothes on your back. Be as quiet as a church mouse and meet me downstairs."

"What are you going to do?"

Patrick turned and took hold of her hand. "The same thing I did the night we met. I am going to save you."

Grae did everything that Patrick told her and whispered a goodbye in the baby's ear before she closed the door to the nursery. She washed her face and changed into the dress that had brought her to this time. The dress that she had worn the night she met Patrick. She lay down in the beautiful bed and thought about how lovely she had thought this room was when she first entered. Now it seemed like a prison cell. There was no hope of dozing as her mind was racing too fast, her adrenalin in overdrive. Minutes seemed like hours, the house was silent. She longed for the whisper of a former occupant, but realized that the house was too young to have extra residents from another time, only her.

She heard a tap at the door and sprang into midair. She had not taken her shoes off. All she had to do was walk toward the door and carefully, carefully, get out of the house.

He was waiting for her as the dawn was breaking. He stood tall on his horse. His voice gasped as he saw her.

"My god, that dress, it's the same one…"

She shook her head and reached for his arm to pull her up behind him.

"It's the quickest way, but, unfortunately, not the most comfortable."

Grae nodded her head and put her arms around his middle and they were off into the darkness.

They rode from before dawn until after dark for nine long days, stopping only when their bodies begged them or when Patrick could no longer see to steer the horse. They travelled through deep forests and open fields, on marked paths and new ones they created. Torrential downpours soaked their clothes and muddied their travel, but then the sun would come out and dry all again. They slept little and spoke even less, and each day Patrick's color looked grayer. It worried Grae, but she knew that they must press on.

As they crossed the New River once again, Grae breathed a sigh of relief. She could almost see the Mansion, even if it wasn't built yet.

"How do you know when it is time for you to return?" Patrick asked, as they neared the road to the Mansion property.

"I do not know. It's only happened once."

"And how did it happen?"

Grae thought back to that fateful time, sitting in the cell with The General by her side. How she longed to see him!

"I was in the cell. They were about to move Bob, Sam, Aggie, and I. I knew it would be far away from the property. So, I took this key and opened the lock on the shackles," Grae pulled the chain hidden under her dress revealing the key. "It was then that I was transported back to my time."

"In that dress?"

"Yes."

"It travels well."

They arrived at the cabin on David Graham's property on the edge of sunset. Grae looked at the structure that just a few weeks before had seen such tragedy with the death of Ama. Over forty years earlier, it had been the home of Joseph Baker and his family and a different type of tragedy occurred just a few yards away. It made her think of Mary. She really needed to see her before she left; she needed to find a way to thank her for what she would yet do.

"What day is it?" Grae asked.

"I am not for certain, but I believe it is October 31."

"There will be another full moon tonight, a blue moon."

"How do you know it is a blue moon?"

"Ruth told me. Blue moon rare, shine like the sun, blue moon come when the crying done."

"Ruth is smart."

"Patrick, I thank you for all you have done. I'm sorry that I have caused you such pain." Grae looked at this strong man who had risked so much for her, then and now.

"It was not of your doing, it was not of your desire. I am so utterly thankful to have gotten to spend time with you again, to know that you did not leave me of your choosing, and to know that you love me in another time."

Grae smiled and hugged Patrick and gently kissed him. For a moment, she could feel those buttons, those brass buttons.

"I need to talk to Mary. I need to tell her something."

"I will send Ezekiel for her with some excuse. Joseph and Margaret cannot know of our return. I shall deal with them once you are gone."

"I wish there was something that I could do to heal the hurt all of this caused Evelyn. I feel like it was my fault that she did not get you." Grae looked up at Patrick and smiled.

"Pfaff, that would never have been, regardless of you. She is a crazy person, possessed she is. She even made a pact with a witch, I am told, and then burned the witch in her own small house when the spell failed to make me love her."

"Oh, Patrick, surely you don't think she killed someone."

"There is good and there is evil and that witch had powers, but no power can make you love or break the bonds when love is there. I have heard it told that when the witch died, she passed some of her powers to Eve through an object that she stole from the witch. She even told me once that she had gone somewhere far away and killed me. She's crazy I tell you and she's brought it upon herself. You go inside and rest; I will send Ezekiel and tend to the horse.

Grae's mind raced, something about this was familiar. Crazy, killed.

"Patrick, what did you call her?"

"Eve, it is the only name I have ever called her." Grae turned toward the cabin as Patrick walked away.

"There's a girl stalking Gav. Yes, the girl is crazy." Grae heard the words in her head. "It's like she cast a spell on him." "Mom says that maybe he knew her in a past life." Grae opened the door to the cabin and walked over the threshold. Carrie's voice inside Grae's head answered, "It's Eve." A burlap sack went over Grae's head. She felt something hit her from behind and everything went black.

TWENTY NINE

When Grae awoke, her hands and feet were bound behind her back around a support pole in the cabin. Less than two feet away, she saw a blurry figure also bound to the leg of the table where she had sat with Ama as she taught her about herbs. As her eyes regained focus, she realized it was Mary.

"Oh nooooo, Mary!" Grae cried out.

Mary nodded in the direction of the other side of the room. There sat Evelyn Newton, Eve, fingering that broach again and looking like the witch Grae now knew she most certainly was.

"What did you do to Gav?"

The woman began to rock in the chair, Ama's chair, back and forth, back and forth.

"He was much like Patrick. Handsome and strong and smart, but he just wasn't enough like him. All those new things in the future, it was terrifying. Fast wagons without horses, people shrunk down and trapped in little boxes on the wall, and those things that people talk into, as if someone can hear them, it was frightful. I hated it there. But, I loved being with Patrick. I loved watching him sleep."

"His name is Gav."

"What is she talking about, Miss James?" Mary yelled, terrified.

"HIS NAME IS PATRICK MCGAVOCK!" Eve stood up and shouted. "Then and now and in the future, he belongs to me! I made a deal that made it so!"

"But you broke the deal, you killed the witch. You destroyed her spell."

Eve slowly walked toward Grae. She paced back and forth in front of her, before kneeling down between her and Mary and gently stroking Grae's face.

"Such a pretty face, untouched by time, I can make it not so pretty."

Then, at that very moment, something quite extraordinary happened. Seemingly out of nowhere, The General jumped and hit a lit lantern that sat on the table. It fell on Eve's back, shattering the glass, and catching the woman on fire. She stood up, shrieking in pain, stumbling and falling into things. Everything in the room was either made of wood or cloth or straw, which only made the fire burn quicker and faster.

Grae pulled at the rope that bound her hands behind her back, but it wouldn't give. She looked over at Mary, who was doing the same, but Mary's hands were bound in front of her around the leg of the table. Her feet were bound and under the table. Grae inched her legs over to Mary. "Can you reach the hem of my dress?"

"My dress, you mean! I do not know how you got my special dress; I just finished it today. It was in my closet."

"There's no time to explain. Under the hem is a hidden pocket."

Mary's hands just barely reached it and took out the small knife, the small knife with the green handle.

"How did that get there?"

"Someday you will understand. Now, see if you can scoot over here and cut this rope."

Mary had just enough room to maneuver herself behind Grae. She slowly opened the knife and began working on the rope. It was sharper than Grae would have imagined. In a flash, the rope fell apart as the flames began to spread. Eve had collapsed on her back and seemed to be unconscious from the smoke and the pain. Grae quickly untied her feet and cut the ropes that bound Mary's hands leaving her the knife so that she could unbind her feet.

Out of the corner of Grae's eye, she saw The General standing next to Eve. Her hand was on the broach, the glimmering of the amethyst from the flames was almost blinding.

"Take the broach," The General whispered.

"What?"

"Take it! It's the seat of her power."

"I don't want her evil power."

"It's only evil if that is how you use it. In your hands, it might save someone."

Grae's thoughts immediately went to Gav. She reached down and ripped the broach from Eve's dress. Eve's hand fell away.

"Help me!" Mary yelled. Grae looked down at Mary's feet, they bound with a chain. The cabin was about to go up in flames. Grae dragged Mary out of the cabin as the ceiling began to cave in.

Coughing frantically, Mary began to speak.

"Patrick met me on the road and led me to the cabin.

Evelyn was waiting outside the barn and she hit him over the head, and then dragged me in there. You were lying on the floor."

"We've got to see about Patrick. Mary, I do not think there is time to explain to you all that has just happened. But you've got to promise me that you will not be afraid and you will embrace the life that is ahead of you. It will be a good life."

Grae looked at The General, and he nodded.

"I think I have something that will open those chains."

"Oh, here is your knife. Will that help?"

Grae smiled. "No, you keep it, you might need it later. Thank you, Mary. Thank you for being my friend."

Grae put the key in the lock of the chains around Mary's feet. As she turned, she looked beside her to see The General watching. The lock clicked, everything began to tilt, and Grae felt herself falling. The speed of the travel was pulling at her, from the outside, from the inside, like an unseen force gripping her soul. But this time it was different, a shrill sound was replaced by moaning and the rattle of chains. She saw Gav and Patrick as two separate people, and then as one. She saw the swirls of green and purple mist engulfing her, intertwining. She heard the slamming of the window as she landed back inside the closet. As her vision cleared, she saw her mother's face and it was filled with fear, but the only words that Grae could utter were...

"Help me."

Historical Timeline

1745: William Mack, Seventh Day Adventist and "Drunkard," Max Meadows, Virginia, namesake, is the first settler on Reed Creek, west of the New River.

1747: Joseph Baker is born to German immigrant parents in the Shenandoah Valley.

1756: Discovery of lead and iron ore by Colonel Chiswell; later known as Lead Mines; present day Austinville, Virginia.

1760: Fort Chiswell built; Town of Lead Mines established.

1767: Joseph Baker, Jr. born to Joseph and Nannie Baker; he is the first of six children. Baker serves in the Militia, which pays him through a Land Grant. Baker's home, farm, and distillery are located on present day Graham Mansion property.

1770: Botetourt County (western Virginia) formed from Augusta County.

1772: Fincastle County formed; Lead Mines is County Seat.

1774: Robert Graham, Squire David Graham's father, immigrates to America with his first wife, Mary Craig, from County Down, Ireland. They travel the Great Road from Pennsylvania through Virginia and settle in Mecklenburg

County, North Carolina, where he is a gimlet maker and land owner. Robert's sister, Ann, and brother, Samuel, also immigrate to Mecklenburg County, and the first five of Robert's fourteen children are born there.

January 20, 1775: Fincastle Resolutions, precursor to the Declaration of Independence, signed in Lead Mines; James McGavock was one of the signers.

May 20, 1775: Mecklenburg Declaration of Independence signed in Charlotte, North Carolina; Major John Davidson, and his future son-in-law, Joseph Graham, were two of the signers.

1775-1783: Revolutionary War. Joseph Baker, Robert Graham, James McGavock, John Davidson, and Joseph Graham serve in the Militia.

1775-1800: Over 300,000 immigrants and future settlers traveled the Great Wagon Road from Pennsylvania through Fort Chiswell en route to the Cumberland Gap and beyond.

1776: Montgomery County, Virginia, formed.

1782: Robert Graham moves his family from Mecklenburg County to the Boiling Springs tract in Montgomery County on the Great Wagon Road (present day Locust Hill area of Wythe County in Max Meadows, Virginia).

1786: Mary Craig Graham, wife of Robert Graham, dies leaving six children: Samuel (b. 1774), James (b. 1776), John (b. 1778), Robert (b. 1780), Nancy (b. 1781), and Margaret (b. 1784).

May 6, 1786: Joseph Baker is murdered by his slaves, Bob and Sam. The sheriff is paid with 200 pounds of tobacco for capturing Bob and Sam, who are thus tried, convicted, and hung. Widow Nannie Baker moves her family to "Baker Island" at nearby Foster Falls on the New River. Youngest son, John Baker, retains ownership of the original Baker tract where the future Graham Mansion will be built.

1790: Wythe County, Virginia, formed.

1790: Robert Graham marries second wife, Mary Cowan; they have eight children.

1791: Vesuvius Furnace is built by Major John Davidson in Lincoln County, North Carolina. Sons-in-law Captain Alexander Brevard (married to Rebecca Davidson) and Major Joseph Graham (married to Isabella Davidson) manage the iron-making and expand the business.

September 3, 1800: (Squire) David Graham is born to Robert and Mary Cowen Graham at Locust Hill.

February 2, 1806: Martha Bell Peirce is born to David and Mary Bell Peirce at Poplar Camp, Virginia.

March 13, 1811: Robert Graham's death.

1812: James McGavock's death.

1812: Joseph McGavock, son of James McGavock, marries Margaret Graham, (Squire) David Graham's half-sister. They live at the McGavock Mansion in Max Meadows where they have four daughters.

May 12, 1812: John Montgomery Graham is born, seventh of thirteen children born to Samuel and Rachel Montgomery Graham at Chatham Hill, in the Rich Valley area of Smyth County, Virginia. Samuel is the first born child of Robert Graham, a state legislator, volunteer Captain in the War of 1812, foundry owner, and other businesses.

1819: Mary Cowan Graham's death.

1826: (Squire) David Graham purchases 12 parcels of land totaling 2,000 acres from the Crockett heirs and John Baker for $10,000 with the mortgage to be paid in full by 1831. On the property were several buildings including cabins, barns, and a working iron furnace called Perry Mount (also "Paramount"). The future Graham Mansion will be built by Squire David on this property beside Cedar Run Creek.

1833: David Peirce's death. Joseph McGavock's death.

1835: Brigadier General Joseph Graham transfers ownership of Vesuvius Furnace to his sons, including John Davidson "Jackey" Graham.

December 15, 1835: (Squire) David Graham marries Martha Bell Peirce.

ABOUT THE AUTHORS

Rosa Lee Jude began creating her own imaginary worlds at an early age. While her career path has included stints in journalism, marketing, tourism, and local government, she is most at home at a keyboard spinning yarns of fiction and creative non-fiction. She lives in the beautiful mountains of Southwest Virginia with her patient husband and very spoiled rescue dog.

Mary Lin Brewer is a Carolina Tar Heel by birth, speech pathologist and school administrator by trade, and the mother of two miraculously stable offspring now in their twenties. A repressed history buff and late-bloomer to all things ghostly, Mary Lin is the official voice of the historical and haunted Major Graham Mansion. She resides in Dunedin, Florida, and Wythe County, Virginia.

To learn more about future books in this series, visit www.LegendsofGrahamMansion.com

Made in the USA
Lexington, KY
24 April 2013